DAMAGE CONTROL

CONTROL

Amber Dermont

ST. MARTIN'S PRESS ✹ NEW YORK

These short stories are works of fiction. All of the characters, organizations, and events portrayed in these stories are either products of the author's imagination or are used fictitiously.

www.stmartins.com

Design by Steven Seighman

Grateful acknowledgment is made to the following publications, in which these stories originally appeared: "The Order" in *Alaska Quarterly Review*, "Damage Control" in *American Short Fiction*, "Assembling the Troops" in *Crazyhorse*, "Camp" in *FiveChapters*, "A Splendid Wife" in *Georgia Review*, "Merchants" in *Gettysburg Review*, "Number One Tuna" in *Open City*, "Notes Toward an Anatomy of Pain" in *Seneca Review*, "Stella at the Winter Palace" in *Tin House*, "The Master of Novices" in *TriQuarterly*, and "Lyndon" in *Zoetrope: All-Story*. "Lyndon" also appears in the anthologies *Best New American Voices 2006*, edited by Jane Smiley; *Best American Nonrequired Reading 2005*, edited by Dave Eggers; and *The Worst Years of Your Life*, edited by Mark Jude Poirier. "Assembling the Troops" also appears in the anthology *Home of the Brave*, edited by Jeffrey Hess.

ISBN 978-0-312-64281-5 (hardcover)
ISBN 978-1-4299-8524-6 (e-book)

First Edition: March 2013

10 9 8 7 6 5 4 3 2 1

For my nephews: Joseph Heroux, Jasper Dermont, and Dashiel Dermont. You are my favorite stories.

CONTENTS

DAMAGE
CONTROL

LYNDON

My father died because our house was infested with ladybugs. Our French neighbors, the Heroux, had imported a hearty species of the insect to combat aphids in their garden. The ladybugs bred and migrated. Hundreds upon hundreds were living in our curtains, our cabinets, the ventilation system. At first, we thought it was hilarious and fitting for us to be plagued by something so cute and benign. But these weren't nursery rhyme ladybugs. Not the adorable, shiny red-and-black beetles. These ladybugs were orange. They had uneven brown splotches. When I squished their shells between my thumb and forefinger, they left a rust-colored stain on my skin and an acrid smell that wouldn't wash off. Dad used a vacuum hose to suck up the little arched creatures, but they quickly replaced themselves. The numbers never dwindled. Dad must have smoked a lot of pot before he climbed the ladder to our roof. My guess is that he wanted to cover the opening of the chimney. He'd suspected that the flue wasn't closed all the way. Our house was three stories high. When he fell, he landed on the Heroux' cement patio, his skull fractured, his neck broken.

For months after his death, I kept finding the ladybugs everywhere. When I stripped my bed, I'd find them in the sheets. When I did laundry, I'd find their dead carapaces in the dryer. When I woke up in the morning, I'd find a pair scuffling along my freshly laundered pillowcases. Then just like that, they were gone.

Long after the last ladybugs' departure, I pulled a pair of sunglasses from Mom's purse on the car seat, fogged the lenses with my breath, rubbed the plastic eyes against my chest, and said to her, "You missed the scenic overlook."

Mom swiped her sunglasses away from me. "There will be other stops, Elise," she said.

We were driving through the Texas Hill Country in an upgraded rental car, cruising a roadway called the Devil's Backbone. Our destination: LBJ. His ranch. His reconstructed birth site. The rental car guy had flashed a brilliant smile when he bumped us up from a white Taurus to a green monster SUV. Mom couldn't resist bullying the skinny clerk. "No one screws me on gas mileage. I'm not paying extra to fuel that obscenity. Knock ten dollars off the daily fee." As the car clerk hammered his keyboard and readjusted the price, Mom winked at me.

My mother the investment banker. Every morning, well before dawn, she would maneuver her own Ford Explorer across the George Washington Bridge into Manhattan, cellphoning her underlings while cutting off other commuters. Mom called her first-year analysts "Meat" and bragged that she, in turn, was known as "the Lion." Mom always wore her long, straightened red hair loose and down her back. She'd sport short skirts and sleeveless dresses, showing off her sculpted calves and biceps. Mom specialized in M&As, corporate restructuring, and bankruptcy. She traveled a lot. Dad had brainstormed our presidential sightseeing tours as a way for him to keep me entertained while Mom flew off to Chicago and Denver, dismantling pharmaceutical corporations along the way.

"I really think we were supposed to stop at that overlook." We coasted past juniper trees, live oaks, limestone cliffs. As far as I could tell, the whole point of driving the Devil's Backbone was to stop at that particular overlook and view the span of gently sloping hills from the highest vantage point. "Dad would have turned back," I said.

Mom just kept driving. I passed the time by reading snippets from the *Lonely Planet Guide to Texas* and rattling off the names of local towns: Wimberley, Comfort, and Boerne. I flipped down the sun visor, replaited my French braids in the vanity mirror. I'd worn my favorite outfit: red high-top sneakers, baggy khaki shorts, and a T-shirt I'd special-ordered at a mall in Teaneck. For twenty-eight dollars, a man from Weehawken had ironed black velvet letters onto the front of a tiny green jersey. The letters spelled out VICTIM. When my mother asked how I got off being so self-pitying, I told her it was the name of my favorite underground band.

The Devil's Backbone reminded me of the shingles sore tormenting my lower torso. The giant scab resembled a hard red shell. The family doctor had explained how sometimes the chicken pox virus remains dormant in a nerve ending, waiting for the immune system to weaken before reemerging. He was concerned because he'd never seen shingles in anyone my age. Usually he treated it in older patients, or in cases occurring with cancer or AIDS. People closing in on death. I told Mom the shingles were proof I was special. The agony wasn't limited to the blisters on my back. My whole body felt inflamed, as if a rabid wolf were hunting rabid squirrels inside my chest. The doctor recommended ibuprofen for the pain. He gave me pamphlets describing stress-reducing breathing exercises. The first few nights Mom slipped me half a Vicodin and a nip of Bénédictine. As I tried to sleep, I heard her roaming from living room to bedroom to family room. I listened. My mother the widow did not weep, did not cry out for her dead husband.

A year after my father died, my mother's breasts began to grow. She developed a deep, embarrassing plunge of cleavage, a pendulous swinging bosom that attacked my own flat body each time she hugged me good night. Mom's belly had pouted. Ballooned. I could detect the domed button of her navel pressing out against the soft silk of her blouses. Her ankles swelled and I became suspicious. Mom was maybe six months into her pregnancy. I did the math. Dad had been pushing dead too long to be the father. I was about to enter my sophomore year at the Academy of Holy Angels. Before school started, I wanted the shingles on my back to disappear, I wanted to tour the reconstructed birthplace of Lyndon Baines Johnson, and I wanted my mother to admit to me that she was pregnant.

With Dad gone, I'd insisted on upholding our family's tradition of visiting presidential landmarks. Dad and I had been doing them in chronological order. We'd sightseen the big ones:

Mount Vernon, Monticello, the Hermitage, Sagamore Hill. Weeks before Dad broke his neck, we'd spent a lively afternoon in the gift shop of the John Fitzgerald Kennedy Library, rubbing our faces in the soft velour of JFK commemorative golf towels. The less popular the sites, the more obscure the leader of our country, the more Dad got excited: "Elise, can you imagine? John Tyler actually sat in this breakfast nook and ate soft-boiled eggs from those eggcups." In Columbia, Tennessee, I tore white azalea petals from James K. Polk's ancestral garden while Dad rambled on about the Mexican War, the "dark horse," and "Fifty-four Forty or Fight." At the Albany Rural Cemetery, Dad and I knelt solemnly before the grave of Chester Alan Arthur. A giant marble angel with voluminous wings towered over us. We prayed to our favorite forgotten leader, the father of civil service reform. One year, we spent Christmas on Cape Cod at a beachside inn that had been a secret getaway for Grover Cleveland and his mistress. Mom couldn't make that trip, so Dad and I tramped by ourselves on the snow-covered sand dunes, plotting my own future run for the presidency. "You need a catchphrase. And a trademark hairdo so the cartoonists can immortalize you."

All day we'd been driving in various stages of silence and radio static. Mom asked whether I'd like to stop for sundaes. I considered patting her belly and making a joke about cravings for ice cream and pickles. I had expected Mom to nix my travel plans for us, but really, I just wanted her to be honest and say to me, "Elise, I can't fly. Not in my condition." Instead, when I said, "Johnson," Mom folded her arms against her burgeoning chest. She swung her hair over her shoulders and said, "Texas in August? Why can't it be Hawaii? I'm certain Lyndon Johnson loved the hula."

The day before, we'd visited the Sixth Floor Museum in Dallas. Mom and I took the elevator up to the top of the Texas Book Depository. We slowly worked our way through the permanent exhibit dedicated to the Kennedy assassination. Though a glass wall surrounded the actual Oswald window, Mom and I got close enough to size up the short distance between the building and the X on the street below. The X marked the spot where Kennedy was first hit. I'd always imagined Dealey Plaza as an enormous expanse of traffic and park, but here it was in front of me, tiny and green, more like a miniature replica made by a film crew. One SUV after another covered the X as the cars drove over the site in perpetual reenactment of Kennedy's last ride. This was the bona fide scene of the infamous crime. Mom whispered, "Even I could make that shot." She hugged me from behind and I felt the baby's heartbeat vibrate through her belly. In anticipation of our trip, I'd begun calling my secret sibling "Lyndon." I asked, "Is Lyndon kicking?" Mom ignored me. Weeks ago, when I'd asked her point-blank if she was pregnant and quizzed her on what she intended to do with the baby, instead of answering the question she told me that her new goal in life was to get me away from "the fucking Holy Angels."

Dad was the Catholic. Mom's family had come over on the *Mayflower*. "Elise, a lot of Yankees brag about tracing their roots back. Always be conscious of your place in history. Most of the people on that ship were poor. Your relatives were the lucky ones with money." Before her parents divorced and squandered everything, my mother grew up rich in Manhattan. Her childhood bedroom had a view of the Sheep Meadow and the Central Park Reservoir. Both of Mom's doormen were named Fritz. When she turned six, her folks hired Richard Avedon to take the snapshots at her birthday party. At sixteen, she'd curtsied before Princess Grace at a charity fund-raiser for retired racehorses. I often felt as though Dad and I were descended from one class of people, while Mom hailed from another class entirely.

My father sold pies for a living. Nominally, he was the vice president of the Pie Piper, his parents' international bakery corporation, but mostly what Dad chose to do was drive his pie truck around the Tri-State area. Checking and restocking Safeways and Star Markets. Shelving lemon cream, coconut dream, and chocolate meringue pies. Dad had a jacket with TEAMSTER embroidered on the back. He liked to brag that he knew the fastest routes in and out of Manhattan at any point during the day. He knew when best to take the Lincoln Tunnel.

Dad felt that my aristocratic heritage and working-class lineage would make me an ideal political candidate. He cast me as a liberal Democrat and cast himself as my campaign manager. Dad first ran me in third grade for homeroom line leader. I lost to Andorra Rose, whose mother, on election day, made two dozen chocolate cupcakes with pink rosebuds in the center. Dad viewed this loss as a tactical oversight. Our future campaigns always involved the Pie Piper, donating dozens of pies and pastries to Holy Angels. In fifth grade, I was class treasurer. In seventh grade, I was student representative to the advisory council on redesigning our school uniforms. Dad imagined I would win the governorship of New Jersey, and from there, if I could find the right Southern running mate, become the first woman president of the United States.

I was twelve the afternoon I caught Dad sprawled out on the Philadelphia Chippendale, one hand holding a silver lighter, the other hand cradling a short ceramic pipe. There'd been a bomb scare at Holy Angels and the nuns had grudgingly sent us home early. Dad was wearing his boxer shorts and watching a rerun of *The Joker's Wild*. He flung a cashmere blanket over his lap, swung his legs off my mother's two-hundred-year-old sofa, and said, "Honey, come meet James Buchanan." I sat beside my bare-chested father, his blond hair flattened on one side, and watched him twirl his pipe around. "Made this in college. Art class. The clay morphed in the kiln." He showed me the blunt end of the pipe. "Looks just like our bachelor president. His first lady was his niece. Handsome fellow." On the TV, Wink Martindale exclaimed, "Joker! Joker! Joker!" Dad smiled, "Don't worry. Your mom has seen me smoke."

My father confided to me that he'd had panic attacks as a kid. "I'd be paralyzed with fear. Knocked out with it. The only thing that helped was reading almanacs." Dad memorized historical facts, like the years each president served in office, and he'd repeat these dates in an effort to calm himself. "Zachary Taylor 1849–50, Rutherford Birchard Hayes 1877–81, Franklin Pierce 1853–57." At fifteen, Dad discovered pot.

I loved sitting in the living room while Dad toked up. Marijuana haze drifted around me, settling on the folds of my wool pleated skirt. I'd lean my neck down against my Peter Pan collar and catch the wonderful stink of weed lingering against my blouse. I was a nervous kid. I often threw up before big tests. No one at Holy Angels invited me to sleepovers anymore, on account of my loud, thrashing night terrors. Even my closest friend, Alana Clinton, often insisted I take a chill pill. I'd attempted hypnosis therapy to treat the warts on my hands, the muscle spasm in my left eye, the mysterious rashes that appeared across my stomach, my inner-ear imbalance, and my tooth-grinding problem. Only breathing in my father's pot smoke truly relaxed me. He never let me inhale directly from Buchanan, but he'd grant me a contact high. Afterward, the two of us would split one of my father's ancestral peach pies. This happened once or twice a week. Mom didn't know.

Mom and I pulled off the Devil's Backbone and stopped for soft-serve at a place called the Frozen Armadillo. She got a chocolate and vanilla twist with cherry-flavored dip, and I ordered a vanilla cone covered in something advertised as Twinkle-Kote. Outside in the August heat, the ice cream dripped down our arms. We decided to eat the cones in the air-conditioned rental car. I told Mom my theory about LBJ and the Kennedy assassination. I was convinced that Lyndon was the real culprit. Nothing that big could happen in Texas without Lyndon's approval.

"Motive is obvious," I said. "Who gains the most from Kennedy dying? LBJ gets to be president. Who's responsible for the investigation and subsequent cover-up? LBJ gets to appoint the Warren Commission. There's proof that LBJ actually knew Jack Ruby. All LBJ ever wanted was to be president. Not vice president. He was an old man. Time was running out." I told my mother that there had been talk of Kennedy dropping LBJ from the ticket in '64.

"How do you know so much?" she asked.

"It's Dad's fault," I said.

"You know, your father always wanted to be a high school history teacher."

"What stopped him?" I asked.

"Well, sweetie," Mom said, wiping ice cream off my nose, "convicted felons aren't allowed to teach children."

Mom balanced her own ice cream cone against the steering wheel and turned on the ignition. She headed out toward Johnson City. We drove past brown, sandy hills crowned by patches of cacti with round, thorned leaves.

"Take it back." I told her. "What you said. Take it back."

"You shouldn't idealize your father. You didn't know him as well as you'd like to think."

"From the looks of it"—I pointed to Mom's belly—"Dad didn't know you at all." I was deciding between calling my mother a "bitch" and calling her a "fucking bitch" when she chucked the rest of her ice cream cone at the side of my face. The ice cream splattered against my hair and cheek. The wafer cone landed on the side of my leg. I picked it up and threw it back at her. I pulled the top of my own ice cream off of its cone and aimed for Mom's chest. She shrieked, swerving the car and throwing back at me whatever clumps of ice cream she could pull from her cleavage. We each lost sense of our target, hurling any ice cream slop we could get hold of. The car's green cloth upholstery and side windows clouded over in a sticky, cherry-flavored film. Chocolate ice cream melted in streams down Mom's chest. The black velvet letters on my VICTIM T-shirt soaked up my dessert. Mom drove and swore. She called me ungrateful and threatened to leave me right there on the spine of the Devil's Backbone. Mom didn't notice the bend in the road. She screamed in confusion as our car lurched through a very real white picket fence, careening down a hill and into an orchard. She pumped and locked the brakes just in time for us to hit a patch of peach trees.

The air bags did not work. No explosion of white pillow. In that brief instant, as I watched the seat belt jerk Mom back and hold her safely in place, I thought of how the pressure and force of the air bag would have crushed Mom's belly, crippling Lyndon, killing the start of him. Mom saved me from the windshield by holding her right arm out straight against my chest. "Holy fuck," she said.

Mom surveyed me. "Are you all right?" she asked. We got out of the car together, the two of us still dripping with ice cream. We marveled at the damage. A peach tree appeared to be growing out of the hood of our rental car. Mom picked up a pink-and-yellow fruit, brushing the fuzz against her lips before taking a bite. "You and your presidents," she said. "That's it. I'm through. And you can be damned sure I'm not taking you to Yorba Linda. There's no fucking way I'm visiting Nixon."

I insisted on hiking the remaining mile and a half to the LBJ Ranch. The car was not my problem. I was a kid and this was my summer vacation. I stayed a hundred yards in front of my mother. She played with her cell phone the entire time, dialing and redialing numbers. From her loud cursing, I could tell that there was no service, no way to call a tow truck or taxi. No way to complain to her mystery lover about me. I imagined my mother had many young lovers. For all I knew, she didn't know who Lyndon's father was. I didn't want to think about the Lion having sex. I wanted to remember the Saturday mornings when I'd wake up early, sneak into my parents' room, and burrow a narrow tunnel between their sleeping bodies. I'd trace the beauty marks on Mom's back, naming the largest ones. With the tips of my fingers, I'd smooth out the worry lines on my father's forehead. Their bed was an enormous life raft. I would imagine that the three of us were the last family left in the world. I loved my parents best when they were asleep and I was standing guard.

On the LBJ tour bus, the man sitting closest to the door stood up to give my mother his seat. She smiled and said, "Not necessary." We'd taken turns washing up by ourselves in the ladies' room of the park's Visitor Center. While Mom pulled knots of peanut Twinkle-Kote from her hair, I watched a short film about the ranch, the birthplace, and the family cemetery. The birthplace wasn't really the birthplace. The original birthplace had been torn down. LBJ actually had a facsimile of the house rebuilt during his presidency. He decorated the house in period pieces, but none of the furnishings were original except for a rawhide cushioned chair. The film showed Lyndon in a cowboy hat and sports coat posing on the front porch of his make-believe home. Dad would have loved the film. He would have leaned over and repeated the story about LBJ and the goat fucker.

"Do you know about LBJ and the goat fucker?" I said to Mom. "When Johnson first ran for office, he told his campaign manager to spread a rumor that his opponent had sex with farm animals. When the manager pointed out that this wasn't true, Johnson said, 'So what. Force the bastard to admit, "I never fucked a goat." He'll be ruined.'"

"You curse like your father." Mom sighed.

The reconstructed birthplace was the first stop on the tour.

The park ranger/bus driver was a chatty older woman named Cynthia. She bounced around the bus taking our tickets, sporty and spry in her light green ranger's uniform. A row of bench seats ran along each side of the bus facing a wide center aisle. Another row of seats ran along the back. There were nine other people on the bus: the polite man closest to the door, a pair of elderly identical twin sisters who wore matching red windbreakers, a middle-aged German couple toting two large canvas backpacks, and a family of four. The mother and father of the family laughed as their young daughter hugged her baby brother and scooped him up onto her lap. The little blond boy had a crazy cowlick I wanted to flatten and fix. Mom and I sat in the very back row, several seats apart from each other.

As we drove past the banks of the Pedernales River, Cynthia described the Lawn Chair Staff Meetings Lyndon held at his ranch during Vietnam. She told us that Lady Bird had kindly donated all of the land and the ranch to the National Park Service but chose to live part time in the main ranch house. My shingles sore was rubbing against my T-shirt, the pain ratcheting up inside of me. I was still angry at Mom. I held my breath to calm myself and ran through dates: "Andrew Johnson 1865–69, Benjamin Harrison 1889–93, Warren Gamaliel Harding 1921–23." Mom leaned over and said, "Lady Bird is shrewd. Putting the ranch into a trust is an excellent way of avoiding taxes."

We drove past lazy orange-and-white Hereford cattle grazing by the river. An ibex shot out from behind a sycamore tree, and then another ibex followed, and another. The cows ignored the elegant brown-and-white horned antelopes. Cynthia said, "Lady Bird also runs an exotic-animal safari on the ranch.

As exotic animals are legal in Texas, hunters can pay the Johnson family to come and stalk rare creatures from the Dark Continent." My mother whispered, "Lady Bird's a genius."

I'd always thought that Dad liked Mom because her mother's maiden name was Van Buren. One afternoon, my father told me how he and Mom began dating. "You have to be careful with this information," he said. "Your mother doesn't know the whole story." My parents met their freshman year in college. The same day Dad met Mom, he also met another woman, a sculpture major named Lisel. She had wavy black hair, a German accent, and an apartment off-campus. Dad liked both women and was stuck deciding whether to pursue Mom or Lisel. He decided to go after Lisel. He was dressed up and on his way to meet the German sculptress for their first serious date when he bumped into Mom. "She'd been playing rugby and she was totally covered in mud and sweat. She asked me if I wanted to take a shower with her. I went back to her dorm." Dad smiled. "And that's the moment when my life began." He said something else about Mom being a sexy lady, but I clutched my hands to my ears and blocked him out.

The reconstructed birthplace was white with green shutters. It was small. Just two bedrooms, a kitchen, and a breeze-way. Cynthia showed us the bedroom where Johnson was birthed. A queen-size bed dominated the room. I noticed long, shiny black beetles crawling over the chenille bedspread. One of the beetles flew up and circled past me. Cynthia said, "His mother claimed that he had it wrong. She kept insisting that Lyndon was actually born in the smaller bed-room, but LBJ was adamant."

In the kitchen I saw the rawhide chair, the one authentic piece. I wanted to run my hand over the cow fur. Right by the kitchen table stood a baby's wooden high chair with LADY BIRD etched across the backrest. Cynthia said that the first lady had been kind enough to donate her own Roycrofter high chair for the replica. Mom mouthed "Lady Bird" to her-self and rested her hands on her belly. I pictured a plump, kicking baby fidgeting in the chair. "Mom, if you want," I said, "I could steal the high chair for you."

"What's a ladybird?" Mom asked Cynthia.

"A ladybird is what we in the South call ladybugs."

Mom looked at me. She shook her head. "Those little killers."

Sometimes when I hung out with my dad while he smoked Buchanan, I'd get paranoid. The nuns at school loved bully-ing girls, and though I understood in theory how women got pregnant, the Immaculate Conception confused and disturbed me. I imagined invisible sperm floating through the ether, landing on my leg and inching up my Holy Angels uniform. Once, I even imagined being pregnant with Dad's baby, but I couldn't imagine anything after that. In her grief Mom had fucked someone. Maybe the Lion had some Meat after all. She probably couldn't explain her own pain over losing Dad. At least not to me. I knew harboring a baby while I looked on could only make her feel alone. While he was alive, Mom was certain I loved Dad more than her. "The two of you have your own secret society," she'd say. Now that he was dead, Mom was convinced I'd love the memory of him more than I'd ever love her. I wanted to tell her she was dead wrong, but I wasn't sure that she was.

The Johnson family graveyard, nothing more than a small plot of land squared off by a stone wall, stood straight across from the birthplace. In the August heat, Mom and I wandered over to the cemetery. Cynthia and our bus mates were still loitering beside the house. Mom told me that Dad had been arrested before I was born. He'd been pulled over for speeding in his pie truck. The cop noticed a baggie of pot in the ashtray. A very big baggie of pot. Dad was arrested, tried, and found guilty of possession with intent to distribute. "Your grandfather could have made the whole thing go away, but instead he let your father do six months in prison. Minimum security, a life lesson. I was pregnant with you the whole time he was locked up."

Mom tucked a wisp of loose hair behind my left ear. "I figured you should know about your father's past, you know, for your political career."

I wanted to tell her that I was sorry. As much as I loved my father, I was mystified as to why Mom, who worked ninety hours a week, would stay married to a man who was happiest when lying down on a couch, a man who couldn't keep his balance on the roof of his own house. A man who could never find his wallet or remember to tie his shoes. A man who panicked every time the phone rang. I would never understand how she had come to love him.

"I'm sorry about the rental car," I said.

"Insurance will cover it."

Mom and I looked out at the family gravestones. The tallest one was Lyndon's.

"Honey, your dad was a wonderful, frustrating, lovely, ridiculous man."

When we reboarded the bus, our tour guide Cynthia smiled and informed us, "You're all very lucky. Lady Bird is in Bermuda this week. The Secret Service has okayed us for a drive-by of the ranch house."

Mom shouted down the length of the bus to Cynthia, "Can't we leave the bus and visit the inside of the house?"

"I'm afraid not, ma'am."

"But that's why we came here," the elderly twins said in unison.

"Sorry, ladies. Those are the rules." Cynthia turned the bus onto a red dirt road.

Without even the slightest look in my direction, Mom shouted, "My daughter has visited every other presidential home in the country. We came all the way from New Jersey."

"Security risk." Cynthia said. "Plus, the ranch house is Lady Bird's primary residence. None of us would want a bunch of strangers trudging through our homes while we were out of town."

"It's fine, Mom," I said.

"Besides, you've seen the birthplace," Cynthia said.

"The reconstructed birthplace," Mom retorted. "Elise, you came here to see the house, and I'm going to make sure you see it." My pregnant mother pushed herself up from her seat on the moving bus, clutched her leather purse, and waddled to the front. Cynthia continued to drive. Mom held on to a railing and leaned into the back of Cynthia's chair. Cynthia shook her head. And then she shook her head so violently that her mirrored sunglasses were flung off her face and skittered to the floor of the bus. Mom kept right on talking. She reached into her purse and pulled out her wallet. Everyone on the bus heard Cynthia say, "Ma'am, I am a ranger for the National Park Service. I cannot be bribed."

While my mother continued to buzz in her ear, Cynthia picked up the microphone on her CB and radioed headquarters. She spoke in a quick, clipped lingo that I did not understand. Then Mom swiped at the CB, grabbing at the spiral speaker cord. The entire bus and I witnessed their slap fight for control over the CB. Neither Mom nor Cynthia could hold on to the gadget, and the black cord snapped and struck against the dashboard console. Mom leaned in and appeared to snare Cynthia in a headlock. None of my fellow passengers moved. The polite man who had offered Mom his seat looked at me and said, "Can't you calm her down?" Mom let go of Cynthia and said in a hoarse voice, "You win." Cynthia announced that the bus would return to the Visitor Center, immediately. We would not be driving by the Johnson ranch house today. The German couple spoke German, in quick, violent snatches. The little boy with the cowlick put his hands over his ears and screamed in three sharp blasts before his sister covered his mouth with the back of her hand. I felt my shingles pain run down my neck and arms. Felt the ladybug shell on my back harden.

Mom strode down the length of the bus, past identical fierce glares from the twin sisters. She sat beside me. I shook

my head and said, "This is not Manhattan. We're in the Republic of Texas. Pushy doesn't work here."

Mom said, "Don't worry, kid. I got it covered."

Cynthia sped back to the Visitor Center. She tried to calm the
agitated passengers by turning on the bus's stereo system and
blasting Lyndon Johnson's favorite song, "Raindrops Keep
Fallin' on My Head." I stared out the window at the terraced
farmland and tried to remember why I ever cared about the
presidents. I loved them because my father loved them. Since
he'd died I'd been trying every day to reclaim his sense of history. All I'd managed to do was re-create his level of stress and
discomfort. The red sores on my back proved to me that I was
nothing more than the nervous daughter of a panicked man.
That was my place in the passage of time, my inheritance. I
could never be president. I was the would-be pothead child of
a convicted felon and a whore. I tried to picture my father relaxed, stoned, resigned to his shortcomings. His eyes blood-
shot, his smile goofy, a halo of ladybugs flying over his blond
head: that was the father I loved.

When Cynthia parked the bus, she pointed to Mom and
me and said, "You two stay seated. For the rest of you, I'm
sorry but this is the last stop." Mom clutched my arm. As Cynthia ushered our fellow travelers off the bus, I imagined the
Secret Service descending upon us. We were a family of felons. I figured the penalty for assaulting a park ranger included
a prison sentence. Maybe now, with the threat of incarceration pending, Mom would admit her pregnancy. I was furious with her. She'd ruined our vacation, stained my VICTIM
T-shirt, tarnished my father's reputation.

Through the bus window, Mom watched Cynthia confer with a fellow ranger in the Visitors Center. Mom said, "I told Ranger Cindy to wait ten minutes in case those Germans got curious."

The Johnson ranch house was smaller than I had imagined. The white paint on the outside needed a touch-up. The large bow windows sagged in their rotting casings. Before Cynthia dropped us off, she pointed out the security cameras and told us which ones were working. "I'll give you twenty minutes like we agreed. The house is locked, but you can view the grounds and Lyndon Baines Johnson's antique car collection."

A massive live oak stood on the front lawn. Lyndon, or some other hunter, had attached two plaques with enormous stuffed deer heads directly to the tree's trunk. Mom petted the buck's antlers. I'm not sure what Mom promised or paid Cynthia for our private tour of the Johnson Ranch. Mom believed in cash and always had at least a thousand dollars stashed on or near her person. She also believed in threats and bribes. With a phone call, Mom could place a lien on your ancestral home or buy you the ostrich farm you'd always dreamed of owning. Mom knew how to bargain. How to make a deal. She was fearless. She knew that she couldn't appreciate the presidents the way Dad and I had, but she could give me something Dad never could. Mom could provide access. She could make things happen. She had what it took to be president.

We walked into the open-air front of the airplane hangar that held Lyndon's cars: a red Ford Phaeton, a Fiat 500 Jolly Ghia, a vintage fire truck, and a little green wagon. The sun had tanned Mom's face. She looked beautiful, victorious. I put my arms around her, rubbed her tummy. "What is it?" I asked. She looked down at me and placed my hand flat on the crown of her belly. "It's a boy."

Inside the hangar, I recognized one of the automobiles, a small blue-and-white convertible. "This is one of those land-and-sea cars. An amphibious car. Johnson used to drive his friends around the ranch, take them down to the river, and scare everyone by plunging them into the water. The car turns into a boat."

Mom opened the driver's-side door. "Get in," she said.

We sat in the white leather seats, proud of our hard-earned view of the Texas hills. Mom took out a linen handkerchief from her purse and handed it to me. "Your father told me this thing helped you guys relax."

I knew by the weight and size of the gift that it was Buchanan. I unwrapped the pipe. The bowl was still packed with a small amount of pot. I'd never smoked Buchanan before.

"Your father died too young to have a will," Mom said. "Just think of this as your inheritance."

"I don't suppose you have a lighter." Mom handed me a silver Zippo with Dad's initials. She watched me light the pipe. I coughed. The smoke burned my throat. I offered Mom Buchanan, but she shook her head no and pointed to her belly.

"When the baby's older," she said, "I want you to tell him about his dad. I want him to know where he came from."

His dad.

We sat together in this magic convertible, me smoking, Mom breathing in the air at my side. We needed a new getaway car. One that could take us back home and beyond. Up the Hudson and along the Garden State Parkway. I gazed down the hill to the Pedernales. Mom pointed out a zebra. I laughed. It was just a gray spotted pony. Everything was clear. I would skip Nixon. Dad would understand. Instead, I'd take my little brother to Omaha, then to Michigan. Gerald Ford, 1974–77, born Leslie Lynch King Jr. He was renamed after his adoptive father. Ford didn't know who his real father was until he was practically an adult. I'd tell my brother about Ford and all the men fate brought to power, the chief executives, all the fearless men in charge. He'd know that Andrew Jackson was thirteen when he fought the British in the Battle of Hanging Rock. I'd explain the difference between John Adams and John Quincy Adams. I'd give him reasons to like Ike, to be grateful for the Monroe Doctrine, to appreciate the irony of William Henry Harrison dying of pneumonia one month into his term after staying out in the cold to deliver his endless inauguration address.

Mom said, "Now smoke in moderation. Don't get caught. Don't let your grades slip. Promise me."

I could hear the walkie-talkie static and chatter coming from the Secret Service agents. We'd been caught. Mom would certainly be arrested. Cynthia would lose her job. I'd be left to raise Lyndon alone. Dad's pot was strong but mellow. For the first time in our relationship Mom and I had a deal, an understanding. I began to hum "Hail to the Chief." As the agents approached in their dark, shiny suits, I promised Mom I would tell Lyndon, my running mate and my half brother, all the things I knew about my father, his father.

DAMAGE CONTROL

The twelve students in my Handshaking and Courteous Touching seminar are busy simulating an upscale charity gala when my cell phone chimes and interrupts their formal meet-and-greet. It's Landon Breedlove, my girlfriend, my bosses' daughter. By this point in their education, most of the students at the Sis and Hasty Breedlove School of Southern Etiquette have already mastered the fine art of telephone protocol. They've learned the discreet practice of dialing in public, the subtleties of call-waiting transfer, and the five easy steps for saying good-bye. They know never to interrupt a business meeting to receive a personal call. The single exception to this rule, of course, is the family emergency clause, an exception that works only if an apology has been extended to the client well in advance of the actual interruption. As a precaution, at the beginning of class, I warned the students of my potential family crisis. Landon and I might not be married, but I still have hopes for our future—despite her legal troubles. I need to take this call.

Donna Pearlman, our role-playing charity hostess, stops hello-shaking Bradford Melford's meaty hand and advises me, "Answer your phone already."

I politely remind her of the power of *please*.

She says, "Mr. Foster, we know it's your lover. I saw her last night on Court TV. Find out if she's going to the slammer."

My phone stops ringing.

Molly Caine, the young lady I typecast as our pretend gala's celebrity entertainment, strikes the metal barbell impaled through her tongue against the back of her invisible polymer braces. When I cluck my own tongue, signaling for Molly to stop joysticking her piercing, she says, "Prison's not so bad. The time my pops did for embezzlement was the best summer of my mom's life. She went to Cabo, got lipo, and met my stepdad."

Nick Flower laughs, forgetting to cover his mouth. With his snowboarder swagger and country club good looks, he's the only boy confident enough to play one of the charity cases. I remind the entire class not to stray from our list of appropriate conversation topics, the Five *C*'s of Climate, Clothing, Cuisine, Culture, and Colorful Current Events. Donna makes the letter *C* with her hand and insists it's my fault for dating a "Criminal."

I explain that Landon has not been accused of any lawlessness, that the grand jury has yet to report on its findings, that Blustre Wind Resources was only minimally engaged in creative accounting practices, and that the woman I love is, at worst, a victim of the cash nexus, a minor figure in what may amount to be nothing more than a complex mishandling of corporate finances. I need to excuse myself from my current responsibilities. Politeness demands that I call Landon back.

I lead all twelve students down to the Jacaranda Room, where my boss, mentor, and would-be mother-in-law, Sis Breedlove, waits in a pink wool suit, a string of cultured pearls clasped around her neck, white kid gloves shielding her sunspotted hands. Sis also sports a raggedy pair of lawn green terry cloth house slippers. Ever since her husband, Hasty, died quickly last year from pancreatic cancer, Sis has struggled to maintain both her physical appearance and a level of investment in her work. When the grand jury's investigation into her estranged daughter's business activities began, Sis invited me to move in with her at the school, a Greek Revival mansion in more-or-less-old-money River Oaks, to trade my nondescript apartment complex for a marble colonnade, lush canopies of magnolia, live oak, and old-growth palm trees, and a bronze statue of Narcissus lovestruck in the water garden. The school is now my home, and Sis, my wealthy widowed companion. Some afternoons, she barely makes it downstairs for tea. She stopped teaching her favorite course, the Mysteries of Silverware, the day she caught herself confusing a pickle fork with an oyster lance. I tried to convince her that this was a common mistake, an ultimately insignificant blunder, but when a grieving Sis accused the eager divorcées in How to Be a Better Wife of "flabbiness" and "marital atrocities," we both decided that it was time to limit her duties. These days, I handle admissions, hire faculty, and teach the core courses. I also cook and eat dinner every night with Sis and sometimes stay on to watch her watch a repeat of *Are You Being Served?* on PBS. As Sis laughs at the sexual innuendo between Captain Peacock and Mr. Humphries, I often pause to remember how much Hasty adored his wife. How he loved to hold her in his arms and dance the Texas two-step. How he called her, no matter how she aged, his radiant and eternal bride.

The students practice their double-handed soft/slow shake for the elderly on Sis, lightly resting their palms around her supple gloves. She nods her bonnet of silver hair and addresses each child by his or her full name. "Good afternoon, Bradford Alfred Melford. Welcome to tea, Peter Calvin Castle. Lovely to see you again, Corwin Winifred Crownover. And what a lovely shade of blue you're wearing, Donna Esther Pearlman. No more charity ball role-playing," she says. "For the next thirty minutes, we'll all just pretend to be ourselves."

The tables are set with sterling kettles of Darjeeling and carousel trays filled with powdery Mexican wedding cookies and pale yellow petits fours. While the students find their place cards and sit in their assigned seats, I announce, "Though we've had the pleasure of one another's company for seven weeks, I've noticed that shyness has precluded many of you from interacting. Teatime is a great occasion for the girls to develop and fine-tune their personal confidence through establishing new male acquaintances."

Molly Caine tugs on the bottom point of my thick silk tie, "If I have to spend the next half hour stuck with all these geeks, could you at least fetch me a Diet Coke?"

I duck into my office overlooking the azalea courtyard and phone Landon three times before reaching her.

"Well, it's official," she says. "I've been indicted."

"How do you feel?" I ask.

"I have this volcanic cyst on my chin and my hair's falling out. The lawyers are terrified I'm going to lose my good looks. Beauty, I'm told, is the one thing I have going for me."

"You're also innocent," I say.

Landon breathes and sighs, and I know she's smoking again. Telephone etiquette demands that a caller never smoke without first receiving permission. Landon huffs and coughs, blowing static into the phone. She whispers, "Martin, we shouldn't discuss this over an unsecured line."

The azaleas outside my window are beginning to bloom in vibrant jewel tones of purple and magenta, satiny and fine like Landon's lingerie. I'd imagined we'd exchange our wedding vows right here under these trumpeting flowers. I want to invite Landon to stop by the school, to visit with her mother, whom she hasn't seen since Hasty's funeral, to marvel at the obscene beauty of this garden, and to remember all the promises she made to me.

"On the bright side," I say, "I haven't been subpoenaed."

Landon takes a long drag on her cigarette and exhales. "One of the reporters for the *Chronicle* is calling me Lady MacTheft. The anchorgirl for *Live at Five* dubbed me Scarlett O'Stealer on Tuesday, then, yesterday, Little Red Robbinghood. Which do you think will stick?"

When she sleeps, Landon's red curls cascade over her pale chest in a kind of Pre-Raphaelite madness. I hate to think of her hair falling out all on account of a few overvalued stocks and inflated quarterly earnings statements. I hate to think of these journalists making light of a dire situation. "You're innocent," I once again remind her.

"I'm also broke," she says. "I had to use what's left of my trust fund to post bond."

The company Landon works for, Blustre Wind Resources, is the ecofuel and proenvironment subsidiary of RIGG, the same energy conglomerate her grandfather, Kit Breedlove, helped found when he and a couple of wildcatting friends broke through the shale at Humble Field and tapped the biggest gusher in Texas since the 1901 discovery of oil at Spindletop. Because so many of our students are heirs to oil fortunes, Hasty loved to lecture them on the history of Texas and the significance of the liquid fuel age. As the former CEO of RIGG, Hasty, were he in my situation, would know what friend to call, what favor to cash in. He would gallantly, covertly protect Sis and Landon from harm.

Before our lives were overrun with scandal, Landon wanted me to quit my job, abandon the family businesses, and leave the Republic of Texas forever. She thinks teaching teenage girls how to maintain their posture in strapless evening gowns, how to freshen their breath with radishes, how to alternate between demure indifference and coquettish flirtation in dealing with prospective teenage suitors, is an unacceptable profession for a twenty-eight-year-old man. Landon thinks I'm limiting myself. She doesn't understand how much this institution has given to me.

Sis and Hasty Breedlove began their School of Southern Etiquette as an attempt to garner friendships for their shy, ornery daughter. Sis coaxed the neighborhood youngsters to their home by throwing elaborate, ritualistic tea parties.

Though Landon would often hide under the canopy of her four-poster bed, her mother loved training the rude, messy children. Hasty, the successful energy executive, recognized the earnings potential of their generosity. The opportunity to diversify his business holdings—from oil to manners. Why not charge the parents to teach their kids the proper way to hold a teacup, use a napkin, and sit still in a chair? The couple focused on educating children before moving on to businessmen. When the Asian stock markets first surged and flourished, Hasty hired a Japanese-American economics professor from Texas A&M to teach a class on Eastern business etiquette. The year Landon left for her New England boarding school, Hasty converted her playroom into a kitchen and brought in a French chef to run a course on continental dining. He hired the chef's Italian wife to provide advice on couture shopping. During the savings and loan scandals, Hasty invited a prominent defense lawyer to design a program instructing businesspeople on the fine points of delivering depositions and courtroom testimony. The famous legal stratagem "Deny, deny, deny" was first popularized at the Breedloves' school. Though Sis longed for a return to the days of parasols and polo matches with Hasty, the business was less about manners and more about money. At its height, the school offered a rotating catalog of more than two hundred afternoon seminars, mini-courses, and semester-long programs including Princess Lessons, Competitive Floral Arrangement, Divorce Decorum, How to Behave at the White House, Planning Your Born-Again Baptism or Conversion Circumcision, Rules for Bereavement, Living Through a Public Scandal, Husband Hunting, and Rising Above Your Social Station.

—————

When I return to the Jacaranda Room, uncertain of how best to tell Sis about her daughter's indictment, Donna Pearlman is busy chasing Bradford Melford around the tea table chanting, "Molly Caine was in a porno, Molly Caine has no bush." Sis is noticeably absent. I ask everyone to quiet down and return to their assigned seats. Donna whips her long brown hair at Bradford and says, "Mr. Foster, don't you think Molly's hot?"

Though Molly has natural strawberry blond hair and deep dimples in both cheeks, I know from her medical file that she suffers from borderline personality disorder, eczema, and chronic night sweats.

Donna continues, "Molly showed us her bikini wax. Want to see it?"

I turn to Molly, who is sitting with her coltish legs outstretched over Nick Flower's lap. Molly flutters her mascaraed eyes and says, "I barely flashed them. Donna maybe saw thong."

Donna Pearlman is fifteen, the lanky, unloved daughter of a pair of corporate lawyers. She and her family moved from Manhattan to Houston a few months ago to take advantage of the recent rash of bankruptcies, foreclosures, and indictments. In order to aid her daughter's transition, her mother determined that charm school would be the best place for Donna to "gain some self-respect and find a decent boyfriend already." Seven weeks into the twelve-week Dining and Decorum program, Donna is my least accomplished student. She lies during Getting to Know You and forgets to listen during Getting to Know Others. She fumbled with her corncob throughout the Difficult-to-Eat Food tutorial and flunked the ABCs of Formal Dining when she clamped down on Peter Castle's crotch with biscuit tongs. Donna is my special case, my Eliza Doo-little, my Kiss Me Kate, my shrew to tame.

Sis scuttles back into the Jacaranda Room, her emerald slip-pers flapping against the marble floor. She's embracing an oversized photo album and, before I have a chance to stop her, says, "My wedding gown is packed away for my daughter, but these are the pictures from my reception. The pages are brittle, so you'll have to gather around while I turn them."

When Donna mockingly skips toward Sis, my impulse is to grab this child by the elbow and swiftly lead her to my of-fice. I hesitate. To my surprise, Donna uses my instruction from Courteous Touching to tenderly drape her own arm around Sis's shoulder, guiding the nostalgic widow to a cush-ioned chair. Donna orders the other students to fall in and tells Sis to start from the beginning. Molly comments on Sis's "sick dress" and her "teeny waist." Nick Flower tells Sis that she's "tricked out like a healthy Olsen twin." I'm suspicious, but I watch as the children appear to show genuine interest in the postwar wedding crazes of Houston high society.

Donna winks at me and says, "Mr. Foster, we should to-tally do a wedding role-play. A shotgun wedding. I can be the husband and Miss Molly Caine can be my knocked-up bride."

The dirty secret behind the Sis and Hasty Breedlove School of Southern Etiquette is that the boys not only go for free, they're paid to attend. It's my job to recruit them. While I'd prefer to find my quarry on the ninth hole of the River Oaks Country Club, I often lure willing prospects away from skate parks, the graphic novel sections of bookstores, fish taco stands, discount music shops. I'm discriminating, but only up to a point.

Hasty found me at sixteen, serving pizzas in a giant mouse costume. "There must be something better you could be doing with your life," he said. I explained to this tiny man with his meringue of white hair that if he wanted to talk to me he had to speak directly into the mesh screens that ventilated my mouse head and stood in for my eyes. When I got off work that afternoon, I was surprised to find Hasty leaning against his Jaguar, reading the pink pages of the *Financial Times,* and waiting for me. "I was certain you were tall, but it's a good thing you're handsome," he said. "I couldn't quite tell from that costume." Hasty promised me cute girls, ten bucks an hour, and free etiquette lessons for life. At the time, I drove a 1978 Pontiac Phoenix and was living with my aunt in a bungalow in Sharpstown while my night nurse mother worked out her daytime addiction to yellow jacket Nembutal. My pharmacist father had already failed to work out his own addiction to seducing drugstore trainees while Mom slept. I'd always longed for order, wealth, and dignity. Hasty wore cuff links made from whalebone and his wife knew how to say thank you in forty-two languages. They were better than parents— they were saviors.

When Landon enters a plea bargain in federal court, I'm busy driving the school van, escorting my class on their week-eight field trip. Corwin Crownover, the most accomplished student in Dining and Decorum, sits in the front passenger seat and reads a news headline off of Donna Pearlman's BlackBerry.

"Lady MacTheft Cops Plea." Corwin butterfly-pats my shoulder and says, "Mr. Foster, I'd like to extend my deepest sympathies and my resounding support." While other students echo her condolences, only Corwin has mastered the art of sincerity, and as I briefly glance into her watery eyes, I am struck by her effortless gift for compassion. Corwin begins to cry. I lift one hand from the steering wheel, reach into my front suit pocket, and pass her my handkerchief. I watch my favorite student sweep the linen under each wet eye and think to myself, *This is real, Landon may go to prison.* Though I have my suspicions, I've never fully considered the possibility or extent of her guilt.

As I pull into the parking lot of the Menil Collection, Donna and Molly slide open the van's door and threaten to toss Peter Castle out onto the asphalt. Today we're mixing Art Small Talk and Behaving in Public Spaces with Dating and Courtship. Donna grabs Peter's arms and torso as Molly clutches his legs. The girls wear matching wife beaters with TWEEDLE DIVA rhinestoned across their budding chests. Together, they carry Peter over to the grassy park in front of the sleek metal and cement building. I pause inside the van and watch as my ladies-in-training straddle and bed down a boy I had hired to be their gentleman caller.

Bradford Melford knocks on the van window and opens my driver's-side door. "Sorry to interrupt, Mr. Foster, but the rude twins are about to make Peter their man slave."

All I have to do is get out of the van for the girls to stop their horseplay and for the rest of my students to assemble in a halo around me. I brief the class on the museum and our mission. Sis, who considered the art collector Dominique de Menil to be a good friend and a terrible hostess, taught me everything I know about art history. When I speak, I hear her words. Before we enter the museum, I demonstrate how to impress a companion with an impromptu anecdote. I tell my students about Mrs. de Menil's art naps. How she ordered her curators to set up a cot on the second-story storage floor. Whenever she was in the mood, Mrs. de Menil would visit her museum and ask that a favorite painting—one of Max Ernst's fantasy birds or De Chirico's lonely train stations—be placed at the foot of her bed. She thought the paintings helped her dream, and when she woke up, that particular palette of colors and light—the primary reds of Joan Miró, the slate grays of Jasper Johns—would be the first thing she saw.

Donna pulls at the rhinestones on her chest and says, "Mr. Foster, we should all sleep with a picture of you at the foot of our beds. If your face was the first thing we saw every morning, our manners would like totally improve."

For today's lesson, I've paired the boys and girls into couples. Corwin and Bradford. Mollie and Peter. As a special treat, I had planned on matching Donna up with Nick Flower, but Nick left a cryptic voice mail warning me he'd either be late or a no-show. By default I must play the role of Donna Pearlman's escort. As the class disperses throughout the galleries, I remind the students to spontaneously share their own prepared anecdotes with their dates.

Plea bargain, I keep thinking. What does that mean?

On our art stroll, Donna points to a Magritte painting of a sky raining down with hundreds of miniature men in swank suits and bowler hats. She says, "This stuff is okay, but I've been to Italy. In Florence, at the Uffizi Gallery, I saw Tori Spelling posing beside a Botticelli. She was on her honeymoon. Her new hubby tried to take her picture with *The Birth of Venus,* but the guards freaked out."

Lowering my voice to demonstrate, I say, "In a museum you must always speak in a stage whisper." I ask Donna what she notices about the Magritte painting.

"The way the figures repeat reminds me of the wallpaper pattern in my gynecologist's office."

"That's very astute," I say. "Before Magritte became a painter, he actually designed wallpaper."

"I'm pretty smart, you know. In New York I had real wattage, but Texas has reduced me to a wiseass." Donna stares at the painting and balances her weight on one foot. She lifts up her shirt just enough to expose her navel and begins to rub her pale belly. "These paintings are too happy, like this guy wasn't tortured enough as an artist, like nothing bad ever happened to him."

"Actually," I say, "his mother died when he was a little boy. She drowned herself in the River Sambre and had to be fished out by sailors."

"My mom knows how to swim. She thinks I'm a lesbian. Is that a Picasso?" Donna reaches out to stroke one of Warhol's electric chairs.

Molly Caine sidles up behind us and lightly slaps Donna's hand away from the painting. "Don't fondle the art," she says.

Donna sticks out her stomach and rubs her distended tummy. "Molly, I'm a mommy."

"No, you're not." Molly lifts up her shirt and begins to rub her own tanned belly. "I'm a mommy."

"Baby catfight!" Donna smiles. The two girls lock arms

and face off, pushing and pulling, tussling right there in the Surrealism gallery. Donna winks at me. "Mr. Foster, you know you want some courteous touching."

I'm not supposed to ever come into contact with a student. Sis has all types of insurance policies, but nothing protects school owners against claims of physical or sexual assault. I could break the fight up, only to have the girls manufacture a story with the refrain, "Mr. Foster touched me." My line of work is more dangerous than most people suspect. The best strategy is to simply say, "Stop it," and then back off and walk into the Special Exhibits gallery. I remind myself that Landon has enough legal troubles for both of us. Landon once asked if I ever got turned on working with all of these young, under-dressed debutantes. I assured her that sixteen-year-old girls are too needy, too selfish, too whiny. "At close range, they are the least attractive creatures on the planet. About as sexy as their shopping bags." Landon didn't believe me. She left the school and came back that evening decked out in a plaid miniskirt and a white button-down two sizes too small. As Landon climbed onto my lap, unbuckling my belt, she said, "Like my uniform? I played defensive sweep for St. Sebastian's field hockey team. It was my job to prevent the offense from pen-etrating." The only thing Landon proved to me that evening was that a full-grown adult woman impersonating a sixteen-year-old girl is undeniably hot.

The museum catfight escalates as Donna reaches for Molly's Tweedle Diva rhinestones, pinching the cotton of the shirt and twisting Molly's right nipple.

Bradford Melford applauds. "Direct hit!"

Molly grabs hold of her breast, crying in long sharp swaths of sound. She says to Donna, "You know how sore my tits are," just as a guard with a walkie-talkie calls for backup.

When we return from the museum, Nick Flower is sitting in the tearoom smoking menthol cigarettes with Sis and Landon. I want to rush over to my guilty girlfriend, carry her upstairs to my office, and brush and brush Lady MacTheft's red hair until it catches fire. Decorum prevents me from doing this.

"Your young man was keeping us entertained." Landon stands, extinguishes her cigarette, and kisses me on both cheeks. "I'm screwed," she whispers in my ear.

"We have to talk, boss," Nick interrupts, pulling me away from the woman I love.

I found Nick at the Houston Rodeo. He wasn't riding Brahmas or roping calves. Handsome Nick was busy serving funnel cakes to senior citizens and future farmers. The way he chatted up his elderly customers and dolloped extra whipped cream on the cowgirls' strawberries convinced me that this kid was special. I recognized something of myself in Nick. He wasn't poor—Nick was the heir to his parents' concession stand fortune—but his money, like my own parents' money, was working-class money, the kind of money you feel guilty spending. Nick had aspirations, and when I told him about the school, he had one question, "These girls—they're top shelf, right?" I explained to him that we catered to the best Houston society had to offer. "I'll be honest," I told him, "they aren't all pretty, but they're all worthy." Nick motioned over to the 4-H rabbit exhibit and said, "Purebred bunnies. What could be better?"

Nick paces inside my office, lowering and raising the bill of his John Deere gimme cap, flashing his yellow-green eyes. Men often claim that it's impossible to tell whether or not another man is attractive. That's basically a lie. Sometimes men choose not to have the language to describe what they see. When I first noticed Nick, I was struck by his unblemished olive skin, his broad, well-defined body. His evenness. Nick had this smoldering glow like his face was perpetually being lit by firelight. I knew the girls would benefit from having him in their classes. We hire the teenage boys so that the teenage girls will have someone to practice on. Someone who will feign interest when a girl rambles on about organic diet supplements, the Moroccan theme at her bat mitzvah, her fear of failing driver's ed, her father's affair with a flight attendant. Someone who will disagree when a girl insists that her arms are chubby, that her ankles are thick, that her nose is either crooked or bulbous. Someone who will flirt back when the girl dares to be funny. When I first make contact with a prospective employee, I am careful that the boy understands the business proposal—that he doesn't mistake me for a pervert, that he knows what's expected of him. Nick trusted me from the start and excelled at his role, listening to the girls, complimenting their attire, laughing at their jokes.

"Mr. Foster," Nick says, removing the cap from his head, "I'm not going to drag this out. I believe I've let you down. A few of the girls are in a delicate condition, and I guess you could say it's my fault."

I'm impressed that Nick remembered his euphemism vocabulary. *The Glossary of Euphemisms* was something I put together one slow summer. Hasty loved it, found a publisher for it, and now it's used at etiquette schools across the nation. I haven't seen much profit from the book, but in the past Sis and Hasty had both dropped hints that, one day, the school and all that it entails would be mine. They have groomed me to be their successor.

Nick slaps his cap against his right thigh and says, "I could handle one girl, but with three, I think I'm going to need your help."

That night, Landon stays over for the first time in months. "You need to understand," she says after I've taken her upstairs and stripped her naked, "I've been a terrible executive." Here in my bedroom at the Sis and Hasty Breedlove School of Southern Etiquette, we smash our bodies together in crude, unflattering ways, grinding and gasping. Landon rolls her slenderness on top of me, her red hair loose and riotous. I cradle her small breasts, excited as much by the sight of my hands on her skin as by the breasts themselves. This is what I've been missing. There is no please or thank you when we take what we want, just a chorus of *more, more.*

The first time I met Landon she was rude to me. We were seventeen and she was home on break from prep school. I was simulating small talk with a debutante from Upper Kirby when a tipsy Landon wandered into the Jacaranda Room, knocked over my teacup, and asked, "Are you the hired help?" Landon has always looked down on my profession. "Etiquette," she likes to say, "makes people feel like outsiders." In my defense, I often explain that manners are neither commonsensical nor elitist, but rather an inclusive, complex methodology for making people feel comfortable. I detail the lengthy history of etiquette from the ancient Egyptian instruction of Vizier Ptah-hotep, who advised his fellow citizens to offer their opinions sparingly and to treat women with compassion, to God's own Ten Commandments and their prohibitions against murder and theft, to the conniving court of Louis XIV, the exhaustive compiling of Emily Post, and onward, critiquing the advice columns of Amy Vanderbilt, Letitia Baldrige, and my favorite, Judith "Miss Manners" Martin. Over the years, I've assured and reassured Landon that etiquette is nothing less than the grammar of living, the rules for civilization, the means by which humanity ascended to and reached its true potential. When Landon was first charged with five counts of securities fraud and one count of conspiracy to defraud the U.S. government, she asked me to defend good manners. "What, my kind sir, would be the proper etiquette for dealing with this sordid affair?"

Landon shatters through the quiet, coming in loud, whistling breaths, and in deference to her pleasure, I pull out and watch her as she writhes against the mattress. I worry that the sound will carry through this cavernous mansion. I place my hand lightly over Landon's mouth to silence her. She kisses my palm and says, "I can't defend myself." The bed is a disaster of sheets and sweat. Landon feels around in the dark, sliding behind me, propping pillows to support herself, slipping her naked arms and muscular legs around my chest like a beetle on its back, holding its prey. "This used to be my bedroom," she whispers. "Remember the first time you ravished me here? I've always wondered whether my dad paid you to date me."

There will never be a good time for me to ask this, so I simply ask it. "Landon, why did you enter a plea?"

"You really love Sis and I know you worshipped Hasty."

Landon squeezes me, and in her arms, I feel small and unsafe.

"Funny thing," she says. "I never bought into the etiquette or the oil or their Texas romance. Even as a little kid, I was always suspicious of Mommy and Daddy. Sometimes, I think I went to work for Dad just to have those suspicions confirmed."

Landon details the mechanics of how her father controlled the Blustre division of RIGG through a separate company— a shell company, she calls it. Blustre, in turn, paid millions of dollars in management fees to the decoy. "Hasty diverted all of Blustre's profits and buried the whole scheme in bond prospectuses and fraudulent accounting. The school, your etiquette school, was our shell company.

"I'm not a whistle-blower," she says. "There's a paper trail. All of this would come out eventually. Look, the judge still has to approve the plea bargain. The prosecutor will recommend I receive a suspended sentence. Cutting the deal destroys the school, but we can still be together."

As my girlfriend presses her breasts against my back, I understand that what she needs from me is my approval. I'm not ready to grant it. I'm not ready to choose between the façade of the past and the reality of the future. "Hasty couldn't have possibly been involved. He was retired from RIGG," I say. "He taught classes on writing thank-you notes."

Landon pushes me off to the side and jumps up onto the mattress, bouncing her lithe body in the dark. "Martin, we live in rude times. Houston, with all its Southern charms and pretense, is really just a breeding ground for disingenuous businessmen. The city began as nothing more than a swampland real estate scheme put together by a couple of slick New Yorkers. The oil business is built on speculation and hype. Our company was called Blustre, for God's sake. I'm not sure we even owned any wind turbines."

"Quiet now, or you'll wake Sis." I bury my face in a brocade pillow.

Landon stops bouncing, kneels on my chest, and says, "Everyone you love is corrupt."

I was seventeen when my mother was arrested for stealing barbiturates from an elderly epileptic. She went into rehab just as my father was taken into custody for insurance fraud. Sis and Hasty briefly gave me a home above their four-car garage but never attempted to replace my parents. On Sundays, Hasty drove me to Huntsville to visit Dad in the state penitentiary. "Cigars make a nice gift," Sis would remark as she packed picnic lunches for the drive. "Your father can strengthen friendships by trading Cohibas for protection." Even prison has its own protocol.

"Please," I tell Landon as she rolls over on what should have been our marriage bed, "all I want tonight is for us to go to sleep and for me to wake up in the morning and have you be the first thing I see."

When I come downstairs for breakfast the following day, Sis is waiting for me outside in the azalea courtyard, reclining on a chaise longue facing her bronze Narcissus. An ozone warning is in effect, and the air is dense and cottony. I struggle to breathe. Defying the heat, Sis wears a plush velour tracksuit, her silver hair held back in two short pigtails. In the bright Houston light, she looks like a girl ready for a game of hopscotch. Sis hands me a warm blueberry muffin from a straw basket and says, "Texas just passed parental notification laws, so you'll have to take the girls to Oklahoma. We'll say it's an overnight trip—pretend you're headed to Dallas to visit the Mary Kay Museum. I'll make up permission slips so the whole thing looks legitimate."

Sis picks up a cordless phone and begins flipping through a tattered address book. She hums "Deep in the Heart of Texas" and taps her fingers in time to the music. I haven't seen her this invigorated since she planned Hasty's funeral. "I knew that Nick kid would be trouble. You've got to stop recruiting the pretty ones."

I pull the top off the blueberry muffin and stuff half of it in my mouth. Chewing and talking at the same time, I tell Sis about Landon's allegations and apologize for spreading gossip. I pace, dropping muffin crumbs all over the brick courtyard. A grackle pecks at my mess, then boldly hops and lands on the muffin basket, thrusting its beak into a blueberry. I tell the bird to go away, but it just stares at me in defiance. I am disheveled, a wreck. I notice that my shoes don't match my belt.

"Well," says Sis, "my daughter has always had an active imagination." Her posture is ramrod perfect and her Texas accent, usually muted, drips out like syrup on a hot spoon. "I myself knew nothing of my late husband's business." Sis smiles with her thin, defiant lips. "Now sit here with me, Martin, and help me find a good abortionist."

While Corwin and Molly sleep in the back rows of the van, Donna adjusts the radio and tries to teach me the words to a song about milk shakes. I indulge her, and when we cross over the state line, I lead her through the opening musical numbers of *Oklahoma!* We are harmonizing "Surrey with the Fringe on Top" in full-pitch, garbling the lyrics, when I realize that we might wake the other girls. I am polite to a fault. Donna can stay quiet for only a few moments before asking me, "Who's paying for this?"

I remind Donna that it is never appropriate to discuss financial matters in mixed company.

"The great money no-no." Donna looks out the window at the flat endless plains. "Nick told us you paid all the boys."

It would be wrong of me to play dumb, to pretend I didn't understand. I tell Donna that while it's true that we compensate the boys for their time and services, our arrangement is a simple matter of supply and demand.

"My threesome with Molly and Nick was also a matter of supply and demand. He wanted her, she wanted him, and I furnished the water bed."

Although I don't know the details or specifics, I have a general sense of how we all wound up on this field trip. "Donna," I say, "I respect your privacy, but if there's anything you want to tell me, I'll listen."

Donna smiles a big bright grin and says, "Molly thinks I'm polymorphously perverse. But on the porno tape we made, I can't watch the part where it's just me and Nick. The footage is grainy and humiliating. I fast-forward through Molly and Nick too. There's only one scene worth watching."

Polymorphously perverse. Porno tape. I think, *What are these girls doing with words like that? How have they come to know such things?* Since I offered to listen, I can't cut Donna off as she describes how it felt to finally press her body against Molly's. To kiss her friend's long neck. "I know it's crazy," Donna says, "but Molly tastes like the nectar you sip from a honeysuckle."

I don't tell Donna that the honeysuckle in Houston has soured from acid rain. In the rearview mirror, I can see that Molly is awake and eavesdropping. I should signal to Donna, but I don't. These girls are a mystery to me. Their rituals and desires terrify me, and I feel myself getting lost among them.

Donna bites her fingers and giggles. "I have no clue how Corwin ended up on this field trip, but I love that she's here. When she cried at the art museum, I knew something was wrong."

I think back on how moved I was by Corwin's tears, how clueless I was about the cause.

Donna says, "Corwin will make a great mom someday. Molly and I are too selfish." She leans over and kisses me on the cheek, something she should know not to do from our week-three lesson Refined Rules of the Road. "You're my hero," she says.

We drive past a rural cemetery overgrown with wheatgrass and thin tilting gravestones. I imagine God straightening the rows of skeletal limestone and blessing his dead. Before we left, I described the reproductive services offered to the girls. I was careful to use the term "vacuum aspiration," and I explained that the IV sedation would lull the girls into a twilight sleep. "Donna, you understand what we're doing. How final it is?"

Donna brings her arms up and squeezes her breasts together, exaggerating her cleavage. "It's totally the right thing. My mom likes to joke that a mother should always have the right to kill her children—whether they're a fetus or a thirty-year-old."

From the backseat of the van, Molly laughs and says, "Donna, you're hysterical."

"That's what you love about me, isn't it?" Donna asks Molly, climbing over the gearbox to join her friend in the backseat. "Mr. Foster, can you give Molly lessons on laughter?"

"What do you mean?" I say.

"How does one do it? How does one laugh appropriately and politely? What's the secret?"

I tell her that she has asked an excellent series of questions and that I answered them in the second week of the course. "It is best to laugh quietly, but with enthusiasm. Cup your right hand to your mouth to hide your teeth and to prevent the spread of spittle."

Molly says, "But isn't it rude not to laugh full on? I mean if something is really funny, shouldn't you give it its due?"

Donna says, "Yeah. Shouldn't you laugh like you're about to piss yourself to let the other person know how funny she is? Isn't it selfish not to?"

I can't withhold my love for these children. I tell them that they are both right, and then I lead them in a round of enormous laughter. Deafening howls of joy. We smile and squeal and let loose all of the happiness we've been afraid of sharing. Our racket wakes Corwin from her slumber. She doesn't know why we're laughing, but true to her manners, she joins in. As we pass a field of waving windmills, their steel blades slicing the dry hot air, I watch my students with their smiles and glee.

When I visit Landon in federal prison, I will try to describe the look on these young faces. When I explain to Sis how much she will enjoy her retirement, we will reminisce and chuckle over how far I've come—from the fast-food boy in the mouse suit to the owner of the Martin Foster School of Southern Etiquette.

Soon we will be in Tulsa, and the girls will be counseled and prepped for their procedures. They will wear white gowns decorated with blue snowflakes, and though they will hurt when they wake, I will be the first one there to comfort them, to buy them ice cream, sparklers, movie tickets, painkillers, anything they want. Everything will go as planned, as ordered and conceived by me. These girls are my future and my family, my destiny, my choice.

THE ORDER

When the baby fell out of the car, she bounced twice.

This happens later in the story, almost at the end, but I need to describe it to you first so you can forget. And you will forget. When the blue car door swings open and she drops belly up onto the asphalt and her pink legs rise together in a perfect O, you will say with agitation and fear, "Why didn't you warn me?" But I did warn you. There are orange hazard cones around these words and yellow police tape to hold you back, but you run to the baby just as I did, mistaking yourself for a savior.

On the road to the Carmelite nuns, I miss our turnoff. Grandma blot-blots the side of her face with the all-occasion napkin she keeps tucked into her watchband. She is angry and certain that the makeup I applied over her black eye will weep into her corneas and cloud her vision. I'm too busy scanning for bowling alleys to argue. Sister Michael told me to take a left after the Empire Lanes but all I've seen are miniature-golf courses and Chinese buffets. *It's not my fault you fell,* I think. My grandmother is ninety-one and in a nursing home. I put her there. Two nights ago she escaped from the Brook Farm Rehabilitation Center by pulling the fire alarm and scampering barefooted in her floral pajamas past the security doors and out onto the shoulder of the Veterans of Foreign Wars Parkway. She rambled for almost a mile before the police and fire trucks arrived to capture her. Two rookie officers and a fire marshall brought Mary McCarthy down onto the soft evening grass as she beat at their blue chests and called them demons. Kicking out from underneath these men, she crawled, rising to a crouch, scrambling away on unslippered feet. The men gave chase. My grandmother's only mistake: a look backward. She tripped over her toes and landed sideways, her ass bumped up against a World War II monument dedicated to the men and women who fought and died in sandy Tunis and Bizerte.

When Grandma demanded from her hospital bed that I file assault charges, I asked her where she'd been headed. "Home," she said, "and I would have made it, too."

I sleep in my grandmother's bed now. I am twenty-four years old and my grandmother's legal caretaker. Too young to rent the car I'm driving but old enough to raise Grandma's levels of Haldol and Ativan. She is mine. I think of her some days as the doll I carried at my side as a child. The ugly doll I stripped naked. Her hair a blond snarl, her harlot face rouged with mom's lipsticks. I'm learning to be a better doll keeper now. I pluck the coarse white hairs that grow on Grandma's chin and trim the mustache of darker whiskers above her lip. I shake out and comb the pearlescent wig that hides her small bald head. I rub her calloused feet with lotion that smells like Christmas candy. I care for her house that is rotting on Ruskin Street. On work nights, when I return from tour guiding at the Museum of Fine Arts, I scout the yard for fallen archaeology: window moldings and lintels, railings from the widow's walk. I bring the pieces that belong on the outside of the house inside and make lists of what to fix. The gutters need to be flushed of leaves, the roof needs another layer of tar shingles, and the kitchen walls need plaster from the hammer hits Grandma planted. I need to remember to fuck the boy next door so he remembers to mow the lawn in the spring and to shovel my sidewalks this winter. When the time is right, I will let Grandma come home to die. I am preparing all of the time. I am hers.

But Grandma couldn't live with me in the house any longer. Not with Martha McCloughlin and the Little Boy, those furies inside her head.

"I can't find the convent," I say to Grandma.

"You got us lost."

"Not on purpose."

"Lost is lost." Grandma glares at my hands on the steering wheel.

On the shoulder of the road ahead, a man in a baseball cap walks a brindled mastiff.

"Ask him," Grandma says.

I pull up beside this man and lower the passenger-side automatic window. Before I have a chance to question him, Grandma takes over.

"Do you have any children?"

"No." He smiles. "Just pets."

Like a good guard dog, the mastiff jumps up onto the car door. His giant paws grip the seam of the open window as strings of slobber drool down his jowls. The man pulls once hard on the leash and the dog obeys.

Grandma sings, "Bad doggie, bad doggie." She beams at the man, who removes his hat. "This is my granddaughter. She runs the museum. She lives in my house now but I live in a home."

"I'm a tour guide. I don't run the museum." I lean over Grandma and say out the window, "We're looking for the convent."

The man ducks his body down and directs me up the hill. He smiles at Grandma. "What beautiful hair you have. Did you just have it done?"

"Yes," she says.

"It's a wig," I chime.

"What a nice man." Grandma turns to me as we drive away. "You shouldn't be so picky."

Grandma is convinced I'll never marry. She doesn't know about the boy next door or the electricians and carpenters I suck and sex to keep the house from rubble. I'm ruining myself for her but she doesn't know.

Sister Michael woke me early one Saturday morning calling to find out what had happened to my grandmother and why she'd stopped writing to her best friend, Mother Francis. The two women had been girls together. They were tennis partners during the Harding administration. They wore matching white lace-and-organza gowns for their first communion and memorized the Stations of the Cross. I'd never met Mother Francis but I sensed that she was one of Grandma's first loves. Mother Francis was about to turn ninety. I was in bed that morning in Grandma's old room and the call reminded me that I needed to remove the golden crucifix and the palm reeds that slouched over the mantel. I explained to Sister Michael about the nursing home and Grandma's illness, and when she said, "I see. I see," I knew that what she really meant was, "How could you? How could you?" She asked about my mother, who had been a nun of the Cenacle. I told her Mom lived in Flagstaff, Arizona, with her boyfriend who was also named Michael and wasn't it funny that Michael meant "Who is like unto God" but could also mean "Who is what God is," and wasn't there a difference between the two. Sister Michael laughed. I offered to bring Grandma out to the convent for the birthday celebration but Sister Michael explained that the party would be private, just the other sisters in attendance. Since the two best friends hadn't seen each other in years, and since ninety is too old for long-term plans, I insisted on driving out to the convent that week.

Unlike the nuns of the Cenacle, the Carmelites are a cloistered order. They don't go out in the world to work or save souls. Their work is prayer. My mother was semicloistered. She was among the first of her sect to go to graduate school and to teach. My mother has told me ridiculous stories about the convent, like the time she was punished for laughing. She and a young nun from England were supposed to be singing a psalm about the Lord scattering deceitful lips when they both became hysterical. "We started and we couldn't stop. The laughter got worse before we gained any control of ourselves." Mom explained to me that as a result of her hysteria, she and the English girl had to eat all of their meals kneeling on a stone floor, in front of a low slate table, while the other sisters ate together. For a whole week, after breakfast, lunch, and dinner, as the sisters left the dining room, my mother and her friend kneeled with their backs bent and their faces to the floor and pressed their lips against every pair of feet that filed by. "Were they barefooted?" I asked. "No. We kissed their shoes." She smiled. "I don't know if that's better or worse."

Every Catholic family loves to sacrifice a lamb of their own, and when my mother left the convent, Grandma put her hopes on her grandchildren. For several months in college, while I was living on green grapes and black tea and learning to sleep in class with my eyes open, I wanted to join the Cistercians of Mount St. Mary's, the strictest of the Benedictines. As I studied Michelangelo and Caravaggio in my art history courses, I imagined the day when I might take a vow of silence and speak only to sing the Divine Office. I wanted to be anorexic like Jesus. I dreamed of hallucinating visions, the way Saint Thérèse of Lisieux promised upon her death to send a shower of roses down from heaven. What Thérèse didn't know was that the roses were her own blood coughed up from lungs wet and thick with tuberculosis.

Another thing I know about nuns is that the Catholic church doesn't take care of them in their old age. No nursing homes or health insurance. The nuns rely on charity.

I park on the hill in front of the convent and take a moment to reapply Grandma's makeup. I dot a yellow-tinted base around her eye to hide the purple blotches and a green cream makeup to contrast the red bruises. I'm a failed artist but I know what colors cancel each other out.

"Fix my shoes," Grandma says.

I run around to the passenger side and open the door. "You sure are bossy."

"I have bossy feet."

I notice that Grandma's hands are shaking. One of the side effects of her meds is a type of palsy that often leads to a loss of equilibrium. The drugs are supposed to keep Grandma from hearing Martha McCloughlin and the Little Boy. Why the Little Boy doesn't have a name is unclear to me, but not having one makes him real in a way that Martha is clear fiction. Martha came first. Grandma claimed that Martha hosted a television series called *The Mary McCarthy Show*. I thought she was kidding. We'd been living together then for over two years and we'd always managed to stay out of each other's way. Grandma liked that I cooked her roast beef and baked scrod. She mostly overlooked the fact that I went to mass with her only when she couldn't find a ride and had to take the bus. Then one day, she complained that Martha had announced during the homily that she, Mary, had peed on the kneeler. The next Sunday, Martha declared that Grandpa wasn't a Catholic. "That's why Mary's had so many miscarriages," Martha claimed.

The women on my mother's side of the family outlast their husbands and live long healthy lives until their nineties, when everything turns dark. My own father died a few months after I graduated from college. Mom swiftly replaced Dad with sad-eyed widowers and military bachelors. She is fighting her legacy. My great-grandmother Marguerite spent her final years suspended in a white sling inside the wooden bars of a giant cradle. She was crazy in a state hospital, and I imagine the folly of her hanging above that bed cocooned in sheets and shame was meant to prepare me for my own inevitable fate. For months, I didn't want to see that Grandma was leaving me. I told my mother about the ranting and the babies living in the walls and Grandma's attempts to free them only when part of the kitchen ceiling threatened to collapse. Even now, on her meds, Grandma is at times lucid and witty. She sleeps more, true, but when she's awake, she's mean and demanding, the way I remember her.

The Carmelites hide behind something called "the barrel." The barrel is a short round door built into the wall. The door is set on a lazy Susan and one side opens so that a person might put things inside the door like a loaf of bread or a baby and spin it around to the other side where one of the nuns stands to retrieve it. Any nun working the barrel can speak to visitors through an intercom. For a moment, I consider putting Grandma in the barrel and swiveling her to the other side. The convent could raise her. They'd have to take her in. A new story for the Bible.

Edith Stein looks out at me from across the entryway, ravishing like Lillian Gish in *Birth of a Nation*. She is all soft curls and pouting lips with tiny fingers. This photograph must have been taken when Edith was a young girl and still a practicing Jew. Now she is a saint for the Catholics. But being martyred at Auschwitz wasn't enough. The pope needed a miracle and so poor Edith, who had better things to do, pulled some small child who ate too many aspirins out of a coma. I believe that the beatification and canonization ceremonies would have embarrassed Edith and her sister, Rose, who died breathing in the gas, at her side.

From the barrel, a voice instructs us to walk to the room at the end of the hallway. The lights are dim and I hold on to Grandma and the bouquet of Gerber daisies for Mother Francis and the tomato juice and cracker snacks I packed for Grandma in lieu of lunch. Banners hang on the walls with slogans like JESUS WE WILL COME and YOU ARE THE ALMIGHTY, THE MOST HIGHEST, ONLY SAY THE WORD, and THE WORD IS THE LORD. There is desire in these words. I'd worn a skirt for the nuns. Out of respect and to show off a little leg.

The room at the end of the hallway is bisected by a metal grating that I can only compare to what I've seen in movies when family members visit relatives in minimum-security prisons. I stick my arm sideways through the metal bars and think, *They won't be able to hug.* Our half of the room has a dozen or more folding chairs and I pull a pair up to the grate. Grandma sits with her ankles crossed and for a moment I see her as she must have been at the Ritz-Carlton that night up on the rooftop, overlooking the swan boats and the Public Garden, waiting for my grandfather the young law student to ask her to dance to Lester Lanin's orchestra. Even before they dated, Grandpa always called her Queen.

Two sisters, one tall and nimble, the other short and dimpled, clutch a shrunken ancient who must be Mother Francis. The women are probably in their fifties, but they swing their bodies in girlish skirmishes around their Superior, coaxing her along.

Grandma sits up from her chair and says, "Tiny! You grew into your nickname."

Mother Francis lifts her head, and as the nuns settle her into a chair, I hear the old woman swear, "Shit, shit, fucker."

The tall nun says, "Mother Francis has learned some new words."

I introduce myself and learn that the tall one is Sister Michael and the dimpled one is Sister Grace. They both exude such happiness and charm that I forget how rare it is for them to speak to outsiders. Everyone shakes and blesses Grandma's hands through the bars. The two sisters tell her how good she looks. Grandma has held up better than Mother Francis, ravaged by arthritis and unable to open her own hands.

Her glasses are taped to her ears.

I hold out the flowers and Sister Grace tells me to put them in another barrel along the wall. She retrieves them and shakes the blossoms in front of Mother Francis. Grace says, "See, what lovely flowers."

"Don't yell at me." This is the first coherent thing Mother Francis has said.

I laugh. I can't help it. This little woman reminds me of King Lear naked on the heath, unwilling to give up the power of her kingdom.

"Mary," Sister Michael says, "you have been such a loyal correspondent over the years. After vespers, Mother Francis often asks one of us to reread an old letter of yours for her. You've told us so much about your granddaughter and she truly is lovely."

"Yes," Sister Grace agrees, "so lovely."

Mother Francis motions for me to move closer to the metal grating. I lean in nose to nose, the cold steel shadowing our faces. The crook of her gnarled thumb brushes my forehead through the bars like she's anointing me with holy oil. She stares at me, then holds a finger up to her lips as though she's about to shush us all. Finally, she peers over the tops of her glasses. She says to me, "Your eyes are green."

I blink.

"Can you create hope?" Mother Francis asks me.

I don't know what to say. I'm saved when a younger woman enters holding a fancy camera.

"Mary," Sister Michael says, "this is our postulant Ruth. She's about to become a novice."

Ruth bows and says nothing. She is a middle-aged woman with bad teeth and short red hair that the nuns will soon shave and crop. The first time a nun cuts her hair is a ritual. The other nuns do it for her, shaving the neck and trimming the top so that her cap fits just so and tight. I picture this redhead wearing only a thin white slip against her freckled skin, standing on a square of brocade cloth, her hair dry and the sisters circling around her. As the teeth of the electric shaver shiver against her pale neck, the air glints with skeins of red. The sisters plow the sides, then scissor the top short and feathery. There is no flourish of mirror. No approval of the job done. Rather, the nuns dress the new novice, crowning her head and hiding their work. After the initiation, the novice takes care of the cut herself, but that first time must feel wonderful with everyone watching you go from girl to nothing.

I stand up.

"Will you be staying?" Sister Michael smiles.

I didn't know until this moment that I hadn't planned to stay. "No," I say. With every word I back out a little more. "I have to run some errands. I'll be back in an hour or so. These two need to catch up. Grandma has snacks in her bag. I won't be long."

I find the Empire Bowling Lanes by accident and pull into the parking lot. It's 11 A.M. I'm not sure if people bowl before noon, but there are three other cars parked and the red collar around the giant bowling pin sign is alight with neon. I tell myself that Grandma will be happy that I've left her the center of attention.

The black-haired boy behind the counter looks like he's skipping school, missing third period. He has a scar clear across his neck, the skin of it flock-dotted orange and pink like some botched repair job. Maybe something kids are doing now instead of tattoos and piercings. I know some kids cut themselves for the pain. He is skinny and wears a tight purple T-shirt, through which the bump of a nipple ring protrudes. I imagine my tongue curled around the loop. I ask for a lane and a pair of size-six shoes. The boy judges my hands.

"You need a child's ball," he says.

"No, I'll be fine."

"This is a five-pound ball. Take it."

"All right. Then bring me a pitcher of beer."

I go to my lane and put on my shoes. The wooden floors of the alley are dull and rough and the alley leading down to my pins looks splintered and chapped. The boy brings me a single short glass and a plastic pitcher spilling over with foam.

"We hardly ever get ladies in here alone." His hands shake as he pours me my first beer. "You must be killing time."

"I dropped my grandmother off to visit with a friend."

"I don't have grannies anymore." He takes out a pack of cigarettes and opens the lid. The pack is empty. He rubs it flat along his jeans but we're both disappointed that he has nothing to offer me.

I drink a beer straight down, refill the glass, and lift it to the boy, as if to say, "Here's how it's done." I rock my fingers and thumb into the holes and heave the ball down for a strike. As I wait for my ball to return, I drink another beer and point to my neck.

"What happened?"

"Magic trick." He smiles. "Tried to saw off my own head."

I hold my hands over the blowers and dry the sweat from my palms. When my ball comes back, I take it, and I pretend like I'm serious about the game, marching my three-step approach and readying my slide. But this time, I pull the ball back and toss it several lanes over where it bounces and then lands in the gutter.

"What the fuck," the boy says as he stalks away.

I finish the frames with three strikes and a spare and drink enough beer to spill the rest. I leave to go to the bathroom and the beer hits me. The boy points around the corner to the LADIES sign. As I walk away, I toss my hair and wink at him.

These shoes squeak on the linoleum as I crouch over the toilet and pee. Once, when my mother was still a nun, she had to help a girl who chose to lose a child. The girl was visiting a relative in the convent. My mother found her in the bathroom bleeding, the cord broken and a giant krill, swollen and clotted, floating in the porcelain bowl. I imagine the girl was grateful for the splash of the birth hitting the water. Her guilt assuaged somewhat by ending the child in a convent. My mother gathered the fetus from the bowl. She needed both hands to hold what remained. At bedtime, I would always beg my mother for this story.

I go to the sink to lather and wash. I gulp a handful of

water, and, when the boy opens the door, my chin drips as I turn to look at him.

"I cleaned the bathroom this morning," he says.

"It smells clean."

The walk from the sink to the door is a short one. I lean against his skinny body and I'm surprised when he lifts me off the ground and pulls me between him and the door. I want him to know that I'm not doing this because of the scar. That I'm not a girl who falls for injury. He holds one hand against my breast so long that I think it might stick. His nipple ring is gold. The metal warms in my mouth. His hair is cut close on the sides, and as my fingers play with it, I think of the nuns and their postulant. "I can create hope anywhere," I say.

He bites my chin.

I ask him between breaths and thrusts, "Do the nuns come here?"

"What?"

"From the convent up the hill?"

"Sure," he says and pulls his face into my neck. "All the time."

The nuns bowl. Each one in her own lane. Sister Michael, the most athletic of the bunch, instructs the others how to pivot off of their front foot. Sister Grace keeps score, masking her frustration over her own seven-and-ten splits. Ruth, the novice, is the most nervous of them all. Her balls skirt the gutter. She is grateful for a single spare. Finally, Mother Francis takes her turn. She's been bowling the longest, even carries her own ball in a monogrammed leather case. The sisters lead her up to the line. She stands with her legs apart, knees bent, and takes the ball, cocks it between her legs and dead-aims it for the one-pin, thundering the bones down. A prayer before release. I see all of them in their magpie dance as the balls crash against the pins. Their wool serge robes and brown scapulars flap-flap behind them. Their heavy silver crosses fan against their chests, and the plumage of white silk that runs down their backs and over their heads bobs in celebration. I am drunk and fucking a throat-slashed boy to the sights and sounds of virgins playing.

I still haven't told you about the Little Boy. The reason I suspect he might be real is that I heard him or at least I heard Grandma running up and down the attic stairs on his command. I believe that he lived in that house with us and that he controlled the tenor of our lives. Because she never named him, I assumed that he was one of the children she delivered stillborn, buried now at the foot of my grandfather's grave. The Little Boy liked to abuse himself. He rubbed and whacked his groin all night as Grandma would beg him to stop. "Please, please," I heard her plead. The Little Boy told Grandma that there were babies living in the walls and so she listened for them, swung the hammer for them and struck a blow against my chest for them. I imagined them, small and clinging, dressed in pink and blue with crocheted jackets and bare heads. Their skin like orange plastic. If I let Grandma wield her hammer, it's only because I saw the babies the way she did.

When I called the police and told the operator that I was hiding in the butler's pantry while my grandmother attacked our house, the dispatcher asked only if two squad cars and an ambulance would be enough.

––––––

Back in the car, the thought occurs to me to leave Grandma
at the convent. To drive home, sell the house, and keep on
driving. This is the same impulse that hits me each time she
asks to be aired out from her nursing home and wheeled in a
chair along the parkway. I know there's a dip in the sidewalk,
where, if my hands loosened their grip, and if the chair lurched
with a life of its own, Grandma would become part of traffic.
She would die from this. I am uncertain that she will ever die,
and as she overwhelms my daily life, my daily bread, I long
for her exit.

All of the convent's nuns are sitting, enjoying Grandma
when I return. An exhausted Mother Francis has nodded off,
but Grandma is at the center of things and full of new vigor.
A clever vampire who has drained her friend and gained from
her suck. As Sister Michael photographs her through metal
bars, my grandmother flirts with the Filipino nuns she knows
are from wealthy families. I want so much for this visit to end
with buoyancy and goodwill and I'm glad that my makeup
job has held up and that Grandma's black eye is known only
to me. And I take pride in her skill and labor to let the medicine take hold, to put Crazy behind her. Then Sister Michael
spoils it all.

"I told you how much we love Mary's letters, and you
know, sometimes, when we open an old one, we find a check."

In the car, Grandma won't stop talking. She tells me the story
of how Mother Francis lost her real blood sisters, Gertrude and
Alma, when one of them had a heart attack in her son's pool
while house-sitting. The other sister drowned trying to save
her. Grandma told me how the two women floated together

for days before a grandchild found them. I can imagine this water waltz all too clearly, only I see Mary in her blue-skirted bathing suit and Francis, her waterlogged robes pulling them both down, suspended in the aqua. Peaceful and devastating. I write deaths for others.

Grandma says, "Before, I was sorry we couldn't go for her birthday, but I think this worked better. This way, the visit was about me."

She takes energy from others. That's how she stays strong and alive. She took the strength of those police officers wrestling her down and used it against them. She took my mother's faith and religion and made it her own sacrifice. She's used my sex and youth to recover from dementia.

"We didn't see the chapel," she protests. "It's lovely. The windows are Tiffany glass. Cardinal Cushing drove out here himself to dedicate the building." Grandma looks out the window. "Oh, well," she says. "Next time."

I stop myself from saying, "There won't be a next time."

We aren't on the highway yet, and I am far enough back from the blue Chevy that when we follow it around a sharp turn and its passenger door swings open, I am able to stop myself, put on the brakes, and keep my head. The bundle that falls from the car loses a blanket. I see small feet kicking. The baby bounces twice as she lands on the pavement in front of us. With a lean forward, Grandma summons her palsied arm out stiff and points to the lolling child in the road, commanding me. The baby's mother stays in her car. I catch her looking back at us through her rearview mirror. Grandma unbuckles her seat belt. I warn Grandma to stay where she is. This is for me to take care of.

The baby wears a cloth diaper. A yellow shirt almost covers her belly. She cries on the asphalt without shaking or wriggling her little body, and I am afraid to move her. Slowly, the mother gets out of her car. "Where did she go?" she asks. The mother is younger than me. She spreads her fingers out as though her nails are wet.

"Is this your daughter?" I ask.

The woman kneels beside the child, cups her hands to her own eyes, her ears, and then her mouth.

"Your baby needs care. There's a fire station two blocks away." I remember this from the nun's directions. "I can take her. You follow me."

I worry about moving the child, but the baby claps her hands and feet demanding to be held. The child relaxes as I ease my arms around the warm engine of her tiny body and lift her to my chest. The mother murmurs, "Baby seat, baby chair." I race to my car, open the side door, and give the baby to Grandma. She clutches the bundle in her lap, supporting the child's neck in the sink of her elbow. Grandma kisses the baby and the child wails, a piercing warning that cuts through me. My grandmother sings, "Sweet, sweet, hush," while the baby blinks at her wrinkled face, her little fingers grabbing for my grandmother's nose. "You," the baby says, pointing at Grandma, indicting her in this accident. Grandma's skin turns ashen, her black eye visible through the melting makeup. The baby stops crying and begins to laugh and grin. "Something is wrong," Grandma says.

I know that it was right for me to give her this child just as I can feel the child pull all of that newfound life from Grandma. This child will save me. I turn to the young, breathless mother and I say, "I've just come from the convent. Everything will be all right."

A SPLENDID WIFE

The second wife vanished five days after the first wife, late on a Sunday morning. Dr. Reginald Diamond, a board-certified plastic surgeon, reported dropping his wife off at the north entrance to the Darling Vista Park and Reservoir, a hundred paces from the Japanese Rose Garden. When he swung by in his Dodge Viper to pick her up three hours later, no one from the Portsmouth chapter of the Rhode Island Botanical Society recalled seeing the wife at that afternoon's luncheon. Her name tag had gone unclaimed at the registration table. Her gift bag, which included a pair of purple gardening gloves, a miniature bottle of lavender hand lotion, an envelope of wildflower seeds, and a chocolate trowel wrapped in pink foil, was hand-delivered on the following day to the doctor's home. Dr. Diamond's cell phone records revealed that he had called his wife's best friend, her manicurist, four times that Sunday. Three of the calls occurred before he drove back to the park. He placed the fourth just after dialing 911. The calls, lasting a total of forty-seven minutes, were covered under the Unlimited Free Weekends clause in Dr. Diamond's payment plan.

The first wife disappeared on a Tuesday at dusk. The husband, Dr. Charlie Grouse, a gynecologist, claimed he'd left his wife with their border collie, Pal, near the south exit of Darling Vista. Dr. Grouse had gone back to his Viper to retrieve Pal's Frisbee. "We were rehabbing my wife's knee. I didn't think she'd get very far." When Charlie returned to the path, he was annoyed to find Pal leashed to a honeysuckle branch and his wife of thirty years, the gray-haired mother of his two sons, nowhere in sight. He didn't suspect foul play, not at first. "My wife enjoyed her solitude. She was always wandering off. To the perfume counters, the public restrooms." Charlie offered Pal the Frisbee and the two best friends tore up the gravel pathway, playing fetch with their plastic toy, breathing in the crisp evening air. Together, they manned a bench on the hill overlooking the sparkling reservoir, waiting for the wife to crest the peak. Charlie watched the sun descend, watched the sky turn from blush red to indigo. There was no moon to speak of. The park emptied before Charlie panicked, before he called out his wife's name to the trees and the pitch-black surrounding him.

After searching the park for a period he estimated at twenty minutes, Charlie drove the two miles back to his family's three-bedroom colonial. He dialed 911 from the kitchen phone and reported his wife missing. Then he poured Pal a fresh bowl of water, peeled a banana for himself, and waited for the cops.

According to Detective Mitchell Landry, Charlie was immediately referring to his wife in the past tense: "She meant the world to me. I loved her dearly. She was a splendid wife.

The happiest wife ever." Landry made note of this strange choice of grammar in his report. The initial search of the house was cursory, a hide-and-go-seek run-through of linen closets, shower stalls, and cobwebbed, millipede-infested crawl spaces. Dr. Grouse was not a suspect yet. He was the one to contact the police. There was no probable cause.

Darling Vista Park encompassed not only a reservoir and walking trails but also a zoo, botanical gardens, a nine-hole golf course, a baseball diamond, playing fields. A three-story Ferris wheel, a butterfly sanctuary, an outdoor amphitheater where, a week before, the Grouses had enjoyed a performance of *Henry VIII*. In addition, the park boasted a red-and-gold pagoda, three snack bar centers—one in the park proper and two in the zoo—and a marble statue of the Puritan heretic Anne Marbury Hutchinson, who was killed by Indians during the massacre of the Antinomians in 1643. The preliminary search of Darling Vista began at the "last-seen" site. A dozen officers patrolled the woods, the beams of their flashlights flickering like aimless fireflies. One lucky lieutenant equipped himself with night-vision goggles. For well over a mile, he stalked a deer.

Dr. Grouse's missing wife became the second story on the eleven o'clock news. All three local affiliates decided to lead with a piece about the Patriots' first day of summer training camp up in Foxboro.

Detective Landry spent the next few days on background checks. Both husbands had attended Portsmouth Abbey, the town's elite prep school. However, Reggie Diamond graduated a decade after Charlie Grouse. Both men—Landry made note of this—attended colleges in Worcester, Massachusetts. However, Reggie Diamond went to Holy Cross while Charlie Grouse earned his BS from Clark University. Both men received their medical degrees from Brown, where each was near the bottom of his class. Landry could find no evidence the men had ever met. On the other hand, both happened to have played the tactical position of face-off man on Portsmouth Abbey's varsity lacrosse team. Ancient yearbook photos of the doctors as boys, trim and decked out in their lacrosse gear, appeared on page four of the *Providence Daily Journal* with a caption that transposed their names, ages, and the years the photos were taken. In each picture, both men wear their helmets, the smiles on their teen faces obscured by the protective metal cages.

The adult Charlie was bald. He had a round, fleshy face. He wasn't the handsomest gynecologist. His patients described him as having a calming presence and kind, confident hands. The adult Reggie wore a blond Dutch boy haircut that his stylist admitted to tinting and highlighting with a product called Miss Clairol's Dazzling Gold. Neither man smoked. Both drank, but only socially, and then only single-malt scotch. Their exercise regimens consisted of biweekly visits to the park for after-dinner power walks around the reservoir with their wives. During the winter months, each couple browsed and strolled through the Ocean State Mall.

The police did not want to spread hysteria and fear. Nothing indicated a serial killer or a kidnapper. At this point the story was still local, and the police reminded the public that wives often left their husbands, that coincidence was part of life, and that there were no signs of a struggle, no bodies, no weapons, no proof.

True, the blood splatters on the interior passenger-side door of Charlie's Viper were his wife's, but she had just had knee surgery two months before. Her stitches had bled. Transference of her blood to the car was ruled completely reasonable. It proved nothing. Similarly, the raw cuts and jagged scratches that the police noted on Reggie's left and right forearms were consistent with the markings of a recent squirrel attack: "I'd been gardening when the damn thing flew onto my chest." The scars did not necessarily constitute signs of a violent struggle with his wife. Yet even at this early stage, Detective Landry had grave doubts about the husbands' innocence. His fellow cops politely listened to his theories but privately agreed that Landry should not have been assigned to this investigation. Six months had passed since Landry had himself become a widower. The man was still in mourning.

Undeterred, Landry recommended draining the reservoir and closing down the entire park. The parks commissioner refused, countering that Darling Vista was not only a community resource but also a site for healing: "We have a moral obligation to keep the gates of Darling Vista open." Instead, he let a team of police divers swim the reservoir, searching the bottom for anything resembling a wife. A rookie cop in scuba gear plunged to the center of the waters and pulled up the remains of a five-year-old girl who had drowned at Darling Vista the previous summer. Her parents were "relieved yet saddened" to finally put their child to rest.

The third wife was a fiancée. She disappeared exactly two weeks after the first wife. Toby Kipling was in the final year of his medical residency. He'd met the future almost Mrs. Toby Kipling at a Halloween party. They'd both come dressed as Marie Antoinette and proceeded to date for six months before Toby proposed. Their engagement had lasted for two years. His fiancée, a redhead with long coltish legs, often jogged at Darling Vista during her lunch break. She was in charge of endangered species at the Portsmouth Zoo. A minor zoo celebrity, she'd recently negotiated with Spain to bring one of the world's rarest animals, the Iberian short-tailed lynx, to Darling Vista. No one could say for certain whether or not Toby Kipling's Almost Wife had gone running on the day she vanished. Toby Kipling told the police that he hadn't seen her in more than two days. He'd been on duty and awake for forty-six hours straight when a zoo security guard paged him at 3 A.M. to report that his bride's gold Dodge Viper was still parked at the zoo's staff lot.

When the third wife disappeared, the story went national.

Unlike the Almost Wife, the other wives didn't work. Little was known about the Grouse wife, whose two sons, Barton and Kenneth, were unsure of how their mother filled her days. "She had a domestic who did most of the cleaning," Barton recalled. "I know that Mother liked to cook, or at least she cooked us dinner most nights. I once saw her stuff forty cloves of garlic under the skin of a roasting chicken. She liked doing that sort of thing." When Detective Landry went to visit Kenneth, the younger son, at a drug treatment center in the Berkshires, he was struck by how much the son resembled the pictures Landry had seen of the Grouse wife in her youth. Both had heavy eyelids, thick curly lashes, and naturally tan complexions. "Once, when Mom came here to see me, she brought a box of clementines. We talked about the weather and cocaine. Every couple of minutes, she'd peel off the orange skin and hand me a segment." Charlie Grouse who, hours after his wife's disappearance, had begun a whisper campaign against his son's Pawtucket dealers, told Detective Landry that he and his wife had received late-night calls from gruff, threatening voices.

The Diamond wife was childless. Glamour shots of her in a black velour bikini posing beside a life-sized ceramic panther appeared on CNN. The news media speculated that her husband, the plastic surgeon, had worked on her nose, enlarged her breasts, and injected collagen into her lips. Dr. Reggie Diamond denied operating on his wife, but he did admit to shooting Botox once every five months into her crow's feet. "It helped with her migraine headaches," he said on *Good Morning America*. The Diamond wife held a master's degree in social work. Before getting married, she'd spent five years removing abused children from their troubled homes and placing them in foster care. Dr. Reggie called the work "thankless" and assured Detective Landry that his wife "had many enemies in the foster child community."

Detective Landry looked for anything that might connect the two wives and the Almost Wife. Each woman belonged to a monthly book club, but not the same monthly book club. Each had recently purchased the hardcover version of a biography of Sunny von Bülow. Dozens of copies of the book had been remaindered at a local discount chain. They'd been stacked on a table directly in front of the cash registers. The dust jacket featured a photograph of the flaxen heiress posed in an emerald evening gown, her head tilted downward and her eyes staring demurely into her own cleavage. All three of the couples were known to spend weekends in Newport, where, in the bathroom of a waterfront mansion, a maid first discovered Sunny von Bülow's comatose body.

Another week passed without any new missing wives.

Then five wives disappeared from the park on a single day. One by the polar bear exhibit, one while on her way to purchase a snow cone for her son, one while training for the bicycle portion of an Ironwoman competition, one after promising to return from a trip to the bathroom, one while watching her son's soccer team lose. Detective Landry familiarized himself with the details of each woman's life. He referred to these new missing women as "the Darling Five." The Polar Bear Wife's husband was a phlebotomist. He had no alibi. The Snow Cone Wife's husband, an EMT, was infuriated to find out that his wife had left their son alone on a cement bench while she went off to purchase the kid a snack. "Our son could have been kidnapped," the EMT told *Nightline*. The Ironwoman Wife was separated from her husband, a chiropractor, who advertised on classic rock radio and was known by the slogan, "I can snap your back, back into shape." The Bathroom Wife had been married to a male nurse for thirty-seven years. His alibi was a streetlamp, beneath which a Quaker church group saw him standing. The Soccer Wife had represented Bristol in the 1978 Miss Rhode Island competition. Her husband, a veterinarian, was the team's official sponsor. He said about his missing wife, "I was on the sidelines, yelling at my son. He'd missed an easy penalty kick. I mean we're talking a straight shot, the little sissy. Then I looked up and noticed she was gone."

Although many residents of Portsmouth stayed away, for some, the park became more popular than ever. When another wife vanished while waiting in line for the Ferris wheel, the lines for the Ferris wheel started to snake all the way to the antique pagoda. Some wives claimed that a trip to the park was the ultimate test of a relationship. The park vendors started selling T-shirts emblazoned with the slogan I LEFT MY WIFE IN DARLING VISTA. Husbands photographed their wives posing seductively in front of the notorious "last seen" sights. Parking, which had always been free at Darling Vista, now cost two dollars an hour.

Means, motive, opportunity. The three magic requirements for establishing guilt. Two days after reporting his wife missing, Dr. Charlie Grouse played nine holes of golf at Darling Vista. Three days after reporting his wife missing, Dr. Reggie Diamond sold his Viper and replaced it with a Hummer SUV. A week after his Almost Wife was reported missing, Dr. Toby Kipling flew to Bermuda with his friends. "Nothing will take your mind off things," he said, "like parasailing over the Atlantic. My one regret is that I couldn't take her with us."

Detective Landry had grieved for his own dead wife by refusing to bury her. The funeral parlor held his wife's body for three weeks before laying her to rest without any ceremony. The afternoon her body was found, Detective Landry purchased a brand-new green silk tunic for her. The zipperless dress had to be slit down the back in order to be fitted over her body.

When a wife goes missing, her family and friends may hope and pray for her return, but in every case that Detective Landry had worked on the police department operated with the presumption that the missing wife was dead. When his own wife disappeared, Detective Landry kept insisting she was safe, insisted she would soon return to him. He still tried to imagine her alive. There she was fresh from the shower, drying her long auburn hair. His wife was a small woman with a memory for time lines. She'd been a history professor at Roger Williams University. He loved to sneak up behind her, slide his arms around her chest, and press his palms against her nipples, which were always slightly firm and pointy. He recalled the rich, canorous sounds of her voice as she sang to him in the mornings, "Wake up, sleepyhead." He tried to dream about her at night, tried to wake himself to the sound of her voice. The droves of missing wives had taken over his dream life. He began to believe that all of these wives had been sent to him. That he was meant to discover their where-abouts.

What if the wives were all still alive? Detective Landry imagined them hiding out together in the park: sneaking cotton candy from the concession stands, putting on late-night performances of *Joan of Arc* in the amphitheater, swimming naked in the reservoir under a three-quarter moon. Detective Landry started to believe in a conspiracy of wives. What if these women had somehow banded together and plotted to disappear, to make their husbands care about them and miss them for the first time in years? What if the wives knew that it was only through their absence that they could ever be appreciated or understood? At first, Detective Landry sympathized with the wives, but slowly he grew angry at the thought of these wives abandoning their husbands and families. He tried to imagine the Grouse wife deserting her son Kenneth just to play a midnight croquet tournament with a bunch of middle-aged women. Dr. Charlie Grouse had called his wife "splendid," and Detective Landry began to wonder how many of the other wives could be described as splendid. Had the Snow Cone Wife been splendid when she left her eight-year-old son alone? Had the Ferris Wheel Wife been splendid when she argued with her husband about the likelihood of throwing up on a Ferris wheel? Had the Almost Wife been splendid when she negotiated to bring an endangered Iberian lynx to the understaffed and underfunded zoo? Surely Landry's own wife had been, at various times, splendid.

Detective Landry was inclined to believe that all of the husbands were culprits, that every case after the Grouse case was a copycat. He was desperate to account for the similarities: the Dodge Vipers, the medical profession. Over three hundred Vipers were registered in Rhode Island. Of those, eighty-seven were registered to doctors. Dr. Grouse and Dr. Diamond both had vanity license plates. Dr. Grouse's was GYNO12. Dr. Diamond's was PLASTC. Dr. Toby Kipling's Almost Wife did not have a vanity plate, but she did have a World Wildlife Fund sticker of a giant panda on her bumper. No matter how hard Landry tried to force a connection between the victims and the Vipers, the cars were not a clue. The cars were happenstance, a part of life. Not evidence. Sales of Dodge Vipers among medical professionals surged throughout New England in the months following the first disappearances. The car was sexy, expensive, and fast. Dodge unveiled its new line of Vipers under the slogan, "The perfect ride for a man on call." The Rhode Island chapter of NOW responded with a letter campaign encouraging housewives to boycott the automotive giant.

The medical connection was harder to explain away. Had each woman secretly aspired to be a doctor's wife? A doctor was an authority, a safe harbor. A doctor would know how best to treat a Valium overdose, to set a broken neck, to operate on a gunshot wound. Detective Landry began to realize that doctors had the expertise and training to understand the nuances of murder in ways that a policeman never could. A doctor would know the weakest spot on a skull, one that might be fractured with a ceramic panther. A phlebotomist could locate the jugular—neatly, efficiently—with a knife blade. A male nurse would know how to disguise the bitter taste of narcotics in a dish of applesauce. But where were the bodies? Certainly, the doctors were not also magicians. How had these husbands made their wives disappear?

In light of the inexplicable lack of physical evidence, Landry tried to build psychological cases against each husband. Detective Landry studied articles on Intimate Femicide. He came to understand that women are most often killed by men they've been intimately involved with. Men who either oppress their wives and kill them when the women try to free themselves, or men who feel oppressed by their wives and kill them as a way of freeing themselves. Detective Landry learned the five stages of Intimate Femicide: Stage I, Pre-Murder; Stage II, Precipitating Event; Stage III, Lethal Act; Stage IV, Post-Murder; and Stage V, Adjustment to Incarceration. He translated the stages to the following: he wants to kill her, she does something to annoy him, he kills her, he has no memory of killing her, he tells the prison guards he didn't kill her.

The television was a constant reminder of the missing wives. CNN Headline News maintained a wife count. The official number was eight and included the first two wives, the Darling Five, and the Ferris Wheel Wife. Dr. Toby Kipling's Almost Wife was officially "not a wife" and therefore could not be counted. Before the disappearances began, one of the local cable stations had scheduled a film called *100 Ways to Murder Your Wife* on heavy late-night rotation. The film starred Chow Yun-Fat. The television guide had awarded the movie four stars and provided this plot summary: "Two married men get drunk and plan to murder their wives, living with the hilarious consequences the next day." The film was unrated. There were attempts to pull it from the lineup, but it aired. After the disappearances began, Biography ran a segment on "the Fugitive," Dr. Sam Sheppard, who was wrongly convicted of murdering his wife, Marilyn. Detective Landry watched the special and was surprised to discover that Dr. Sam Sheppard had turned to professional wrestling after being released from prison. He wrestled under his own name and became famous for a suppression hold that involved pressing down on the nerves underneath his opponent's tongue. This hold causes immediate paralysis in its victims. It is still used today.

Detective Landry proposed a temporary moratorium on marriages in the state of Rhode Island. It wasn't safe to get married or to be engaged. He wondered what it meant exactly to be a wife. Why would any woman, knowing that she could go missing, choose to become one? At least, he knew that he hadn't killed his own wife. She jumped off a bridge in the middle of winter. His wife walked off the Mt. Hope Bridge wearing a flannel nightgown embroidered with bluebottle butterflies. And where was the detective at the time? Asleep. There wasn't anything he could have done to stop her. There was no way for him to understand why she had killed herself.

Landry and his wife had often visited Darling Vista. His wife loved the butterfly sanctuary. She'd wear a pink floral blouse and make him wear a Hawaiian shirt. Together they'd enter the glass atrium, and the swallowtails, the vibrant commanders, the Malayan Jezebels would alight on their flowered clothing. The exotic butterflies would applaud the couple, clapping their thin wings. His wife would say, "That butterfly mistook me for an orchid." This was the happiest he ever saw her. Landry had wanted his wife to see a doctor. She'd taken a sabbatical from Roger Williams in order to revise a book on the history of revisionist history in America. In the months before her suicide, she wouldn't stop sleeping. He'd return from work only to find his wife slumbering in the bathtub, the water cold, her skin shriveled. His wife claimed that she was tired. This was her sabbatical, after all, and she deserved to rest. The history book could wait. Detective Landry thought his wife might have a thyroid problem or an iron deficiency. A seasonal disorder or a mild case of depression. Landry wasn't sure what was wrong. He wasn't a doctor. His wife slept through the two doctor's appointments he made for her. Sometimes, he was unable to find her. She'd disappear for hours only to reemerge from beneath a pile of comforters and pillows.

During the investigation, Landry found himself returning to the marble statue of Anne Marbury Hutchinson. The statue had become a makeshift memorial for the wives. Mourners left bouquets of stargazer lilies and plush stuffed animals on the statue's pedestal. Landry tried to recollect the stories his wife, the historian, had told him about Anne. She was a heretic who'd moved to Portsmouth only after standing trial alone against a panel of forty-nine men, after being found guilty of blasphemy and sedition, after being banished from the Massachusetts Bay Colony by Governor John Winthrop. He remembered how his wife, whose lips were often chapped during the winter, had told him that Anne believed anyone could communicate with God directly without a Bible or a husband to tell her how to worship. Anne was certain that you could do anything you wanted to in this life because your future was predestined by a higher power, who knew, before your birth, where you were headed. Hell or heaven. To Darling Vista or a bridge on Narragansett Bay. He remembered his wife's rough, wet lips against his mouth. He imagined the wives coming out at night, abandoning their secret hiding places to kneel and worship at Anne's feet.

The last wife left Portsmouth on a Wednesday at dawn, three months after the first. Her name was Sylvia Liseaux. She was seventy-five years old, a retired naval officer, former electrical engineer, and the mother of three children. Her daughter Ruth reported her missing, after Sylvia had gone for a walk alone and never returned from it. She was carrying an expandable titanium walking stick that her son had given to her to use for support and as a weapon against unleashed dogs or other attackers. She fell along the Reservoir Walk after suffering a heart attack. Her body rolled off the pathway and under a chokecherry tree. Several of the tree's white blossoms landed in clusters on her chest and in her hair. When Detective Landry found her body eight hours into the search, he knelt beside this old Ophelia, lowering his face against her nose and mouth to check for breathing. He wanted to close her eyes— they were violet—but he knew better than to touch the body. He wanted to lie down next to her just to be close again to someone. He stretched himself out, his back flat against the grass and leaves, and looked up past the canopy of branches to the sky. "This is what it feels like to be a wife," he told himself. He did not know then how she'd died. He did not know that she was a widow.

The Liseaux husband had been a toy designer for Hasbro.

He suffered an aneurysm while driving his Ford Taurus from a toy trade show in Boston six years prior.

All the missing wife cases stayed open. They are still open. They will never close. It was discovered that Dr. Charlie Grouse liked to wear women's clothing and frequent male prostitutes. This was not evidence. Dr. Reggie Diamond waited eight months before having his wife legally declared dead. He waited two more months before marrying his wife's best friend and manicurist who had been a tremendous support to him during his time of need. This was not evidence. Two years into their marriage, the manicurist stabbed Dr. Diamond to death with her cuticle scissors. She'd caught him in bed with her hair stylist. Dr. Kipling acknowledged that his Almost Wife was three months pregnant. Detective Landry explained to Dr. Kipling that the most common cause of death for pregnant women was homicide. Dr. Kipling said he'd already known that from an episode of *Law and Order*.

Landry tried focusing on the first three wives, as if they were a code to crack, a code that would reveal a formula that could explain the others. This helped him to forget his own wife, as he hoped and suspected it would. She'd been sad for a long time before she killed herself. She hadn't been "the happiest wife ever." Her sadness was one of the things he loved about her. She had been crying when they first met. Had he been wrong to love her sadness? He was certain that these other husbands did not know their wives well enough to appreciate their sadness, their longing, their sense of how little the world knew or cared about them. He suspected that the Grouse wife hated cooking chicken, that the Diamond wife missed social work and was embarrassed about the Botox, that the future Mrs. Kipling had made a mistake when she told her fiancé about the results of the pregnancy test.

Wives continued to disappear, but husbands found it more difficult to blame the disappearances on Darling Vista. Landry was almost certain that none of the wives had died there. The park had become a scapegoat for some deeper inexplicable epidemic. Like all epidemics, the Spanish flu, the bubonic plague, the sickness had run its course. Detective Landry continued to study the cases, continued to search for clues. He wasn't satisfied. For him, this was no way to end a story.

Detective Landry did his best to imagine that all of the wives were still alive. The night he discovered Sylvia Liseaux, he drove to and parked on the Mt. Hope Bridge as he had done many nights after his wife committed suicide. For Detective Landry, the wives were no longer hiding out at Darling Vista. They were playing on the cables and girders of this suspension bridge. The wives were perfecting their own act and getting ready to take it out on the road: the Missing Wives Traveling Circus. There was Lilith Grouse, her knee in perfect shape, teaching Carol Diamond how to strut on the high wire. There was Holly Wannamaker, the Almost Wife, training imaginary lions. Isabel Winter, the Polar Bear Wife, paired up with Mary Jo Fernandez, the Snow Cone Wife, in a death-defying trapeze suite. His own wife, Kelly Landry, dazzling as the ringmistress, dressed in a satin top hat and a sexy red leotard, drew the crowd's attention to the "Fearless" Cherika Johnson, the Ironwoman Wife. She juggled knives, ate fire. Detective Landry knew that the Bathroom Wife, Samantha Amis, had studied ballet, and so he placed her on top of an agreeable elephant and danced her gingerly over the bridge. The Soccer Wife, Cecilia Kang, taught yoga. Suspended thirty feet above the bridge's deck, she contorted her legs over her head, did midair splits. The Ferris Wheel Wife, Alison Reese, was an old-fashioned red-nosed clown. Detective Landry knew that the circus was scheduled to leave soon on its tour, but every night for a week, Landry watched his favorite ladies get stronger and stronger. He delighted in their synchronized arabesques. He was so proud of what they'd managed to accomplish.

STELLA AT THE
WINTER PALACE

The little girl beside me pulls on the orange safety whistle tethered to her life jacket. I wink at her, and she hands me a single white ballet slipper, still warm from her small foot. She is a confection of blond, disheveled pigtails, pink satin, lace ruffles, and tulle. Two jagged seams on the back of her gown mark a place where, recently, wings have been removed. A naughty child. I know that what she wants most in the world is to blow wild and hard on her plastic instrument, to breathe loud, sweet music into my ear. Leaning over to return her shoe, I whisper, "Our ship is sinking." The child does not budge.

Across from us, her sequined mother drinks a complimentary Hurricane and scans a long sheet of bingo cards. We, the passengers of the cruise ship *Valkyrie,* are assembled here in the Valhalla Lounge, awaiting further instruction from the voice on the loudspeaker that comes to us in blasts of English, Spanish, French, German, Norwegian, and Japanese. We play bingo in American. Randy, our sunny cruise director, who just last night had a hard-on for me, distracts us from the rumors of flood and engine fire by feeding our hopes of winning the snowball jackpot. He calls out B10. "Nancy Kerrigan went to the Olympics and she got B-Ten."

It is past midnight. We are adrift in the North Sea, our giant ship lit up and dazzling in the black water like some lady's lost jeweled purse. When we set sail from Barcelona nine and a half days ago, this ship was obscene, a marvel, twelve white decks topped off by a fifty-foot rock-climbing wall. Twenty-four-hour room service, a seven-story lobby of glass and marble. Dueling Steinways in every lounge. Now, we're forbidden to flush a toilet or venture below Deck Seven. The waiters, who still wait on us even though their lives are as endangered as our own, ceaselessly patrol Valhalla, spinning round trays with frozen drinks. They hand out free bags of cinnamon peanuts and wag their fingers at anyone who dares remove the orange life vest from around his or her neck.

I haven't seen Stella since Oslo.

The little girl in pink touches her toe to my knee and says, "At home, I have a swimming pool."

I say, "All of this is my fault."

Stella loves the slots. When we first embarked on the *Valkyrie* in Barcelona, our beds were pushed together and made as one. I tried to explain to Anton, our house steward, that Stella and I needed separate beds, but Stella kept interrupting with, "What about the casino? How loose are your slots?" Our cabin—a deluxe upgrade with balcony, sunken bathtub, and executive minibar privileges—is the size of a monk's cell. A mirror running along the length of the wall facing our beds doubles the size of the room and keeps Stella in constant view. The toilet doesn't flush so much as suck, loudly and violently.

Stella, my fake grandmother, my Waterloo. Stella is all bad wig and loose skin. She looks old the way a young actress looks old after a makeup artist ages her face with epoxy and latex. Her neck and chin are one. She wears a rotating lineup of matching skirts and blouses in optimistic shades of fuchsia. Stella has no lips, but she has many lipsticks. She draws thin broken lines where her mouth should be. For an eighty-six-year-old—I peeked at her passport—Stella has great legs. Thin, muscular calves with delicate knees. Having been a professional dancer, I know a nice leg when I see one. In Barcelona, I asked Stella what she thought of me. She shook her head and said, "Too skinny."

Nowadays, I'm a professional granddaughter. Women pay me to vacation with them. Part escort, part tour guide. Once, in Lisbon, I grabbed a client from behind and Heimliched her waist until a clump of paella dislodged itself from her windpipe. A bit of a nursemaid as well. My clients are older loners, widows mostly. Women who have outlasted their husbands, second husbands, and retirement community boyfriends. It's a beautiful thing to watch a woman who has struggled and sacrificed under the weight of a marriage suddenly turn dynamic and wonderful after she buries a husband. To cheer her on as she flirts with a gondolier under the Bridge of Sighs, haggles with a rug salesman in Istanbul, and gets hammered with Parisians at a zinc bar. When this transformation happens, I'm a happy witness to it. But mostly, there's a lot of fetching— forgotten sweaters, extra desserts, false teeth—and kvetching. I fetch, they kvetch. Because I'm paid to listen, I don't tire of the old stories.

The first thing I tell my clients is that I'm a widow. They enjoy this. When I first met him, my husband, Rainer Mc-Cloud, had been dying since he was fifteen. One of the early symptoms of Hodgkin's disease is itchy skin. For a brief period, when he was a teenager, my husband's secret pleasure was hiding in his mother's closet and scratching his underarms and neck with the sharp heels of her snakeskin Ferragamos. Rain used to say that of all the cancers to have, he had the best. The recovery rate was high, and the survival rate was getting better all the time. "I can be healthy for a few years, work real hard, then get sick and take a break from it all."

Rain's parents were wealthy enough that Rain could afford to be a public defender. He loved setting the guilty free. The guiltier the better: the john with the lapful of prostitute, the ex-con with the stolen police scanners in the trunk of the stolen car, the girlfriend with the dead boyfriend's blood under her fingernails. I once asked him, "Don't you feel bad setting those people free?"

"Why should I feel guilty?" he asked. "It's my job." He explained, "I'm not there for the innocent people. If an innocent person is charged with a crime, it means the system isn't working. The duty of a real defense attorney is to defend those who deserve to be behind bars. I'm there to defend the recidivist flasher, the teenage arsonist, the statutory rapist."

I met Rain at Chumley's, an old speakeasy in the West Village. I tell most people that I'm five foot ten; I'm actually over six feet tall, a Nordic Amazon with pale gray eyes. Rain was the only man in the bar taller than me. He had thick black hair, yellowish-green eyes, and a cleft in his chin. We kept talking over other people's heads. I ridiculed his name and refused to tell him my own when he asked me. Slut that I was,

I slept with him. In the morning, he informed me that he had cancer, that he dated a lot, and that I owed him twenty dollars. I called him an asshole and wished him a lovely case of stomach cancer. I wanted to say ass cancer, but I'd already called him an asshole, and I like to avoid unnecessary repetition.

It never occurred to me that I'd see him again, but there we were a few weeks later, outside the Guggenheim Museum in bad weather, staring at the CLOSED ON THURSDAY sign. We'd each come to see an exhibit on the history and art of motorcycles. "Harleys or Indians?" he asked me. "Triumphs," I said. "My dad had one." Rain had a beautiful umbrella. Slut that I was, I slept with him again.

We were together for six weeks before his illness reappeared. The chemo made his mouth sore, made him stop wanting to be kissed. The follow-up radiotherapy on his upper body made his chest hair fall out and his skin prickly. When he returned to work after several weeks, he wore layers of T-shirts under his button-downs to hide his thinness, and sunglasses to hide the black circles under his eyes. A crack whore he was representing nicknamed Rain "the Undertaker." Later, after the steroids made him swollen and puffy, a car thief would greet him as "Jake and the Fat Man." Rain got better, and because I was there to wash his coffee mugs, pick up his lawyer suits from the dry cleaner, and taxi with him to and from the hospital, I thought I had something to do with his recovery. I moved into his apartment in Chelsea. We had four more years together.

Stella's dead husband was named Stanley. When she told me this over the phone, I laughed. "Right out of Tennessee Williams."

"Never been there," she said.

"I mean the playwright."

"My Stanley was a baker."

"No. *Streetcar Named Desire.*"

"We had a Cadillac. Each year, my husband traded in for the new model."

Stella first called my office in February to book a Taste of Europe cruise for July. I explained to her that I would need either my own accommodations, or a room share with an upgrade. We discussed my fee—fifteen hundred dollars a week plus any additional expenses paid—and I promised to make the necessary arrangements. I asked her if she'd seen my ad in *Modern Maturity,* or if she'd visited my Web site (www.granny friend.com), and she said, "No. I'm a friend of Carol McGuffin. She told me all about you."

Carol McGuffin was never a client. I met her nearly five years ago on a honeymoon cruise to Egypt that Rain booked for us a few weeks before he died. How we came to marry was simple: Rain got sick again, the doctors chose a more aggressive treatment, the stronger poisons weakened his immune system, and the cancer came back full throttle. Rain decided that the one thing he wanted to do before he died was marry me. We pooled our money, rented out the Guggenheim for two hours on a Thursday evening, and, arm in arm, we walked down that sloping nautilus shell and into the cavernous lobby. Our vows echoed loudly off our friends and relatives, the Pollocks and Picassos. Rain looked like a sad-eyed Modigliani, gaunt cheekbones, rail-thin hands. I wore a red silk gown and carried a bouquet of snapdragons. Rain, who would never dance with me—frightened of dancing with someone who danced for a living—he danced with me—carefully, slowly, while someone we paid sang "Just One of Those Things." In two weeks' time, I went from girlfriend to fiancée to bride and then newlywed. The following week, I went from wife to grieving wife to widow.

I had nowhere else to go, so I went on my honeymoon. Whenever anyone on the ship asked me how I was doing, I'd say, "I'm doing great. I'm on my honeymoon." They'd ask me where my husband was. "He's dead," I told them. I liked scaring people away. It brought me pleasure and solace. There was something wrong with me, the same wrong thing that made me a good dancer, extending and contorting the lines of my body, and made me terrible to be around offstage. I'd been a member of a fairly prominent modern dance company. The women in our group were famous for tossing and catching the men. I'd given up touring to take care of Rain the second time he got sick on me. From then on, while I watched him die, I did fund-raising and administrative work for the dance company, and even though I stayed in shape, I didn't have it in me anymore to lift men in the air and catch them.

Carol McGuffin was seventy. She had lustrous white hair, perfect posture. She taught me how to play bridge. How to master canasta. The cruise ship company paid her a lot of money to teach passengers how to play cards. Because I needed someone to take care of, I brought Carol seedless grapes, Bloody Marys, and caviar from the midnight buffet. After a week, I started helping all the old women. The service on the ship was good, but the stewards didn't always know when to move a deck chair into the sun, when to pour more water on the lava rocks in the sauna, when to ask questions about favorite grandchildren. Carol told me that I'd make a great traveling companion. When I returned to New York, I needed something to keep me occupied, so I used my business contacts, placed ads with AARP, and billed myself as an attentive and engaging friend for elderly women. No sex. Minimal health care. The response was amazing.

Stella wasn't much for seeing the sights. She liked leaving the ship, but it was often enough for her to check out the duty-free gift shops in the port terminals. In Gibraltar, Stella worried the Barbary apes would steal the wig right off her head. When we arrived in Le Havre, I tried to convince her to take the train into Paris, but she claimed that she'd "seen all that French stuff before." She had no interest in Hamburg—"What is that? Germans?"—and all she wanted to visit in Copenhagen was the statue of the Little Mermaid. Unfortunately, some angry youths had recently hacksawed the mermaid's bronze head and made off with it. As we set sail for Norway, I was beginning to get antsy.

In my experience, the seven-day/six-night cruises are no problem. It's just enough time to relax without getting restless. The longer cruises are another story. By day eight, a client will begin to complain about the quality of the cold fruit soups. She'll notice that the rugs on the elevator that brightly announce the day of the week—*Today is Friday*—could use a nice shampoo and vacuum job. By day eight, my skills for fetching will start to be put to the test: "I asked for an éclair. This is a cream horn." Day eight is almost always claustrophobic, a full day at sea with no ports of call. This is the day the motion sickness pills start wearing off.

On the morning of day eight, Stella and I fought over sugar. We had decided to go to the main dining room for a full breakfast. Usually, we ate in the self-service cafeteria on the Old Norse Deck. Stella preferred the cafeteria because she liked to keep our cabin stocked with bananas, crackers, and small boxes of cereals. Froot Loops. Stella would hide her loot from Anton, constructing an elaborate wigwam of napkins over the food. I'd tried explaining to Stella that we were allowed to have whatever food we wanted, that she'd already paid for it, that Anton wasn't in the Cereal Gestapo. "Oh, you don't know," she assured me.

Stella didn't like dining with other people. "I don't want to hear about no one's troubles. I got my own." We had a private table at dinner, but breakfast and lunch were open seating. I asked the head waiter if we could have a table for two. He seated us at a table for four, promising that no one would join us. The expansive dining room windows showed off a panoramic view of the North Sea: dark cobalt waters and a cloudless sky. We passed the flaming stations of offshore oil rigs. I'd been hoping for some sign of sea life, but the engines and the ship's propellers frightened away any potential displays of flying fish or porpoises.

Stella's wig was down too low on her forehead. I pointed to my own forehead and motioned for her to pull the wig up a notch. "Thank you," she said. "I don't want any eggs this morning. Only a cup of tea and a doughnut."

"I'm sure they can arrange that."

"Do you like eggs?"

"I like them okay." I scanned the menu.

"Do you like them with cheese?"

"Everything tastes better with cheese." I smiled.

"Do you like potatoes?"

"Depends. I like mashed potatoes and au gratin potatoes. French fries."

"I like a baked potato, but not too hard. The ones they've been giving me are too hard."

"I can mention something to the waiter."

"I don't want to get you into trouble."

The waiters served me coffee and brought a cedar box filled with different teas for Stella to select from.

"Got any Lipton? I don't like this fancy stuff."

A busboy was commissioned to bring Stella her bag of orange pekoe. I ordered the waffles with strawberries.

"I thought you wanted eggs." Stella began overbuttering a small croissant.

"I said I liked eggs, but this morning I prefer waffles."

"So you don't like pancakes?"

"I like pancakes."

"But you didn't get any. You like maple syrup?"

At this point in the conversation, I realized that I had no idea where I was or who this person across from me might be. I was fairly certain that this woman, this Stella, was not my own grandmother. My own two grandmothers were safely interred in the ground. I remembered sitting in the back of a courtroom listening to Rain argue with a judge over a deadbeat's ability to pay child support: "But your honor, tell me how he's going to pay off the ten grand he owes if he's in the clink." I knew that I wasn't in jail, not exactly, a luxury cruise ship hardly constituted the layman's definition of a prison.

Stella's tea bag had arrived, and I watched her plunge it in and out of the hot water. She shook four packets of sugar to-gether, ripped open the corners, and poured the contents of all four packets into her tea.

"That's a lot of sugar," I said.

"Their sugar isn't as sweet as ours." Stella drank her tea.

"Sugar is sugar."

"No, it isn't. Stanley was a baker, and I know that some sugars are sweeter than others."

"Well, aren't you the brain trust."

"You think you're bigger than me."

The couple involuntarily seated at our table, Art and Judy Groebecker from Dayton, heard only the tail end of our heated exchange. They murmured weakly. Like most of my clients, Stella insisted that I always introduce myself as her grand-daughter. Stella didn't have a granddaughter. She had two bachelor sons, both of whom had fatal heart attacks in their fif-ties. While I politely chatted up the Groebeckers, Stella refused to look up from her tea. I commented on the smoothness of the seas and asked Art and Judy if the odd-looking cloth bracelets around their wrists were for motion sickness. Art was explain-ing the significance of pressure points and acupuncture when Stella interrupted.

"All he wanted was to see Atlantic City one last time. He didn't know. Sugar isn't just sugar." That said, Stella stood up, wrapped her doughnut in a paper napkin, and left.

The Groebeckers invited me to join them for a game of horseshoes. I left the dining room and wandered around the ship. I found a library with overstuffed leather chairs, a signed framed photograph of Robert Ludlum, and a complete collec-tion of Patrick O'Brian's maritime novels. I paged through a children's picture book of Norse gods. The illustrations were strangely sexy, lots of pouting lips, round breasts, and micro-waists. I learned that the Valkyries were demigoddesses of death, an Old Norse word for "choosers of the slain." It was the job of these warrior goddesses to scout battlefields on chariots drawn by fire cats or golden-bristled boars. Blond vixens in their scarlet corsets, gathering the bravest souls of the slain for a much-deserved afterlife in Valhalla.

I knew that I needed to apologize. My behavior had been unprofessional. It occurred to me that when I used those brown Sugar in the Raw packets, I did often need more than one. I began to think about brown sugar, powdered sugar, simple syrup, NutraSweet. Even though they all tasted the same to me, I was certain that a professional might be able to detect a difference. When I entered our cabin, Stella was nowhere to be found. Anton had once again made our two beds into one. Day eight. Everything turns to shit on day eight. I decided to go for a swim.

Someone had found a tampon applicator floating in the outdoor pool. As a result, an undulating mass of humanity had packed into the indoor one. A family of Japanese women had taken over the dry sauna, but the wet sauna was empty. I changed out of my clothes, wrapped a towel around my naked body, and sat in the blue-tiled steam room. I thought about Rain. Whenever I wanted a rise out of him, I'd bring my arms up to my face and kiss my biceps. He'd pout at me, "How dare you. I thought I was the only one allowed to kiss you." Later, when he was sick, I'd kiss myself for comfort. Having sex with a dying person is not an easy thing. Even when I could still get Rain erect, I'd feel guilty for fucking him, for making him tired, for stealing what little strength he had left. Sometimes, he'd ask me just to let him reach between my legs. Other times, I'd dance for him, pulling off my leotard and teasing him with my breasts. He'd tell me that I'd missed my true calling as a stripper. I hadn't slept with anyone since Rain died. I needed time to get around to it.

The wet sauna relaxed me. I was alone. The clouds of steam made my skin feel soft and lush, and I began touching myself under my towel. It felt good, and I was just about to come when the family of Japanese ladies walked in on me. I was more annoyed than embarrassed. I couldn't tell if they'd seen anything. As I sat up to leave, the oldest woman removed her towel. Pretty soon, they were all naked. Together they looked like a chart of the stages of life: the prepubescent child, the buxom teenager, the flabby mother, the desiccated octogenarian. I couldn't determine what stage I was in at the moment. During arguments with Rain, he'd make fun of me by saying that I was always guilty of "estrogen logic." My side of things rarely made sense to him. I smiled at the Japanese women, and the youngest girl pointed at me and said, "Giant lady."

I tried making nice with Stella that evening by watching her play the slots. She was good, to the extent that one can be called good at playing something that is random and rigged by a computer. Stella methodically patrolled the labyrinth of one-armed bandits. She sought out the machines along the aisles, the ones most frequently used, stuffed with tokens, especially likely to jackpot. She also preferred the old-fashioned-looking machines with cherries and lemons over the more high-tech diamond and star motifs. Every gambler in the ship casino knew Stella by name. They asked her which machines she recommended, what number of tokens to wager. She'd smile and tell them, "I don't give nothing away." Stella gave me a hundred-dollar bill and asked me to turn it into tokens for us. "Half for you, half for me," she said. I lost fifty dollars in seven minutes. The lights kept blinking and the buzzers kept beeping for Stella, as she guarded several plastic cups filled with tokens. I couldn't help but be impressed.

She was deep in her casino zone. I almost never went off duty during a job, but I wanted to head upstairs and watch the ballroom dancing. In the Valhalla Lounge, I drank four whiskey sours, tying the stems of maraschino cherries with my tongue. My bartender wasn't impressed. The ballroom dancers were a sad lot. Mostly married women dancing with other married women. The orchestra was tight and upbeat. "Just One of Those Things" once again in my life. As I listened to the lyrics, it occurred to me that my husband was a real asshole for choosing that song, as if our life together was some kind of fluke. *Just one of those things.* "How dare you leave me with that," I said aloud to myself.

Odin's Den was throbbing with bass and synthesizers. In my black evening gown, I played the part of drunken spectacle. Dangerous long arms waving, my cleavage bouncing. I danced to Prince's "Sexy MF" and when the chorus repeated, "Shakin' that ass/Shakin' that ass/Shakin' that ass," a ring of men and women seemed to form itself around me. I did just as the song instructed me to do. The DJ switched over to "When Doves Cry," and a man in a tuxedo handed me a drink. It was Randy, our cruise director. He asked me where I'd been hiding. He was shuffling and spinning in front of me. Randy had moves. He was taller than me, and his hair was perfect. True, something about Randy reminded me of the men's leisure-wear section of the 1979 Sears, Roebuck catalog, but I hadn't danced with anyone in a very long time. Randy asked me if I'd heard him sing. Everyone on the ship had heard Randy sing. He performed nightly in the Scandinavian Legends Theater, and copies of *Randy Live!* were on sale in all the ship's gift shops. I told him no, that I had no idea he could sing. He offered to play me his rendition of Supertramp's "The Logical Song," the fifth track from his CD. He asked me again, "Where have you been hiding?"

This was a good question. Since Rain's death, I've taken forty-six cruises, mostly Caribbean. Mostly for senior citizens. I've seen the white windmills of Mykonos, the heads on Easter Island, the cemeteries at Normandy, the Great Barrier Reef, the Alhambra. I've heard the same comedian crack exactly the same jokes on two different cruise ships two summers apart. I've eaten poi. I've taken snapshots of my oldest trick, a feisty ninety-four-year-old who claimed she was President Taft's illegitimate daughter, in front of the Mendenhall Glacier. I've gotten altitude sickness at the citadel of Machu Picchu. I've escorted twin sisters around the volcanic maze of Pompeii. I've paid five dollars for a piece of scratchy toilet paper at Ephesus. Of the sixty-two clients I've serviced, nineteen have died. I've been to every continent except Antarctica. They all looked the same. I have been out in the world, and I have hidden myself from the world. It all felt the same. My travels are not liberating for me. Unlike the women I work for, I never had a chance to grow sick and tired of my husband.

Randy our cruise director grabbed my ass and pressed his body against mine. I hesitated, briefly, then pressed back.

Randy's cabin was on Deck Three. He didn't have to bunk with the waiters and the crew, but I could tell he was hoping to shack up in my room. The disco had been dark, too dark. The lighting in the hallway was too bright. I noticed a beige streak of makeup along Randy's jaw and what looked like rouge on the upper half of his cheeks. He asked me to wait outside while he fixed his room. He shouldn't have done that. Once his door closed, I headed for the elevator. I raced back to Stella.

Stella was in bed asleep when I barged into the room. She'd left a night-light on for me. I whispered, "Stella," and she sat up in bed. Her wig retired for the evening, her long, silver hair was loose and wild around her neck. I wanted to tell her that she looked beautiful. Instead, I said, "Randy. Randy our cruise director just hit on me."

"Handsome, and what a voice."

"I was up in the disco, dancing."

"Why are you here, then?" Stella asked.

"Well, it's not like I could do anything." I took off my shoes. Our beds were still pushed together.

"So he didn't want you?"

"No. He wanted me. Right now, he's probably searching the hallway outside his room. He's probably very confused, somewhat desperate."

Stella rubbed her face. "You left a handsome fellow in the lurch just so you could tell me this story."

"I didn't think it would be appropriate."

"I think there's something very foolish about you. Every man is an opportunity. I've had half a dozen boyfriends since my Stanley died, and each one made a difference. It's how you recover." Stella smoothed the blankets around her.

"My husband, my Rain, was my first great love."

"A first love?" Stella laughed and rolled over. "That's the one you can never keep."

I went into the bathroom to change. I slipped my evening gown over my head and put on a pair of silk pajamas. As I brushed my teeth, I noticed Stella's wig perched on the bathroom counter. I picked it up. The wig smelled like violets and Aqua Net. I spun it around on my finger. It was lighter than I'd imagined. I pulled it on, tucking my hair up underneath. While I didn't exactly look like Stella, I resembled some subspecies of Stella. Some distant ancestor. Rain told me that when he first got sick as a teenager, his mother sent away for a free wig from some cancer support group. The wig he received was orange, and yet the label on the inside lining claimed that it was made from "100% natural human hair." Rain wanted to send the kind soul who'd donated his hair a skullcap. He hid the wig inside his closet and hid his stash of weed inside it.

Stella's wig made my skin look sallow, made my face look emaciated. I was mad at Stella for calling me foolish. For pointing out what I already knew: that I was afraid of losing Rain, of moving beyond my memories of him. As I tore off the wig, the hairpiece slipped from my fingers and landed in the toilet. Floating in the water, the wig resembled a timid muskrat. I picked up a stray clothes hanger with the intention of hooking the wig and rescuing it. I didn't fish it out. Stella didn't need the wig. She looked more beautiful without it. I used the hanger to plunge the wig down deeper into the toilet bowl's water. Then I flushed the handle. I never expected the mighty plumbing to respond with such suction and force. The wet tail of the wig fluttered once, then disappeared. I left the bathroom and climbed into bed with Stella. She was warm. The steady sound of her breathing helped soothe me into sleep.

Oslo was our last official stop before sailing to Harwich, England. I woke up early. Stella must have woken up even earlier. I hadn't heard her in the bathroom or rustling around in our closets. I showered, dressed, and waited for Stella to return. When Anton knocked on the door to make up the room, I decided to go for a walk.

The air in Norway was clean and crisp. My lungs felt revitalized instantly. Unlike most of the industrialized ports we'd docked at, Oslo's harbor was picturesque: square-sailed brigantines, topsail schooners, and fake Viking ships. Fishermen sold fresh pink shrimp right from their wooden catboats. The houses in the city were painted in closely orchestrated shades of soft yellow, light coral, and white. The city was a model of order and beauty.

The National Gallery opened at 10 A.M. I was the only one waiting when the guard opened the door. I wandered the well-lit galleries, my sneakers squeaking on the cold polished floor. I didn't expect to come upon Edvard Munch's *The Scream*. Almost everyone in the world knows that painting, but for six minutes that morning, it was exclusively mine. This little white-faced figure, his mouth an elliptical horror, his body a black cloak, floating terrified on a pier. The sky a red sailor's delight. Most people think the screamer is alone, but two top-hatted figures brushed in blue lines loom in the background, either walking away from or toward the desperate face. I noticed a repaired rip in the upper third of the painting. Some visitor must have attacked the canvas. Munch himself used to leave his canvases out in the Norwegian winters. He'd torture them with a rifle or gut them with a bayonet, half the time destroying his own art. That was his modus operandi. How he painted. Standing in front of the one thing he's known for, I suddenly wished I'd brought Stella. I knew that she'd probably put her hands to her cheeks and say, "Didn't they use this in a movie? The one about the little boy whose parents leave him home alone?" I knew she would say this, but I didn't mind, because this was Stella's vacation.

I returned to our cabin. Anton had made the beds right this time. Stella was still missing. Since we were in port, the casino was closed, so I checked the cafeteria, the atrium, the gift shop promenade. I thought that Stella might have ventured out on her own, on a mission to buy a wig. I wandered around the port terminal, browsing the alley of makeshift stores all selling the same snowflake sweaters, hairy trolls, and reindeer figurines. With my own money, I bought Stella a crystal Christmas ornament in the shape of a star.

There were two other cruise ships in port with us. I started to worry that Stella might board the wrong ship. For most, it's not easy to get on a cruise ship, since guards check IDs on the gangway, but I could imagine a guard questioning Stella and then letting her on anyway out of frustration. I panicked. I raced along the peaceful harbor, shouting up to the ships in my most passionate Stanley Kowalski: "STELLA. STELLA. STELLA." I'd never lost a client before.

The *Valkyrie* sailed at 6 P.M., on schedule. I explained to the lady at guest services that Stella was missing. She reminded me that the ship was enormous and asked if I'd done a thorough search of our cabin. "Well, I stood in the middle of the room and spun my head around. Unless she's hiding in a drawer, I don't know where she could be." The guest services lady explained that clients often missed the ship's departure from port. "She can contact a cruise line representative and make arrangements to meet us at our next destination." I didn't want to argue and explain that Stella probably didn't know the name of the cruise line, never mind our next port of call. I convinced the guest services lady to page Stella every half hour for three hours.

I watched the other cruise ships leave the harbor before the *Valkyrie*. I imagined their journeys. From Oslo, many of the ships sailed south around the horn of Sweden, through the Baltic Sea, and up to the Gulf of Finland. By now, Stella is in Helsinki. Purchasing a sable coat for the trip eastward. Her ship is docking in St. Petersburg. Peter the Great, or else a man resembling him, is waiting in an army coat at customs. A handsome fellow. "Do you like borscht?" he says. "Do you like blini?" The two of them meander arm in arm along the Neva River, toward the Winter Palace. They're stalking the dark galleries of the Hermitage, in search of the Malachite Room. He takes the sable off her shoulders and tells her something funny about Ivan the Terrible. "Do you like radishes?" she says. They're dancing. She flaunts her taut calf through the slit of her skirt. Her head is wigless, silver hair shimmering. The two of them are lost together among the royal plunder, on display, the lovesick czar and his czarina.

The little girl in pink is asleep on my lap. Stella's whereabouts are still a mystery. I feel responsible. I feel terrified. I feel indifferent. A man from Milwaukee won the snowball jackpot on B12, "the vitamin shot." When I first heard about the water and sewage flowing freely through the corridors of Deck Three, I thought of Randy. The ship is not just sinking but stinking. It didn't immediately occur to me that Stella's wig might be responsible. People flush a lot of stuff down toilets. I picture the rodent wig clogged in some far recess of the ship's plumbing.

For the last hour, the loudspeaker has not said anything in any language. In Norse legend, if a soldier saw a Valkyrie before heading into battle, he knew that meant he would die. It was an honor to be selected for defeat. The Valkyries chose the most honorable for the afterlife, leaving behind the unworthy. I lift the little girl up off my legs and place her gently in my chair. I stroll the length of Valhalla and back again. No one notices me. I have lost my power. No longer a Valkyrie. I am pitiful. Someone will save this ship.

When my husband died at home in our bed, I was in the living room looking out the window, watching a graceful fat man dance. He wasn't dancing exactly. He was sweeping his floor, but the fat man had his back to me, and I couldn't see his broom until he twirled around. I was holding a cup of chai for Rain, waiting for the tea to cool. I wasn't always patient with my husband. Sometimes, if I had a dinner tray ready to serve him, I'd get angry if he took too long to sit up in bed. I'd often let an extra day pass before washing his shrunken body and changing his clothes. Rain had bedsores. As I stood at the window, I thought I heard Rain defending me to a judge: "Yes, your honor, she didn't always wipe my ass as well as she should have, and yes, she once called me an angry corpse, but look at her now. Let her off with community service."

THE LANGUAGE OF MARTYRS

My sexy, nicotine-addicted mother forever insisted I follow one piece of advice. I was eight the first time I heard it. Dad had convinced us to suffer through a halfhearted Thanksgiving at his parents' minor mansion on the Gold Coast. We ate chicken instead of turkey, instant mashed potatoes weeping in thin, watery gravy. No stuffing. For dessert: a convenience store pumpkin pie. Mom knew her in-laws could do better. That the plastic tablecloth was their way of saying, "You aren't worth the trouble." After dinner the sky over Lake Michigan began to half rain, half snow and Mom, eager to leave, took me by the hand, whispered, "Five minutes," to Dad, and together we retreated to the safety of our Firebird. Mom, who modeled eveningwear for Spiegel and I. Magnin catalogs, who had been both Miss Champaign-Urbana and a National Merit Scholar, crouched in the driver's seat with the window rolled down, hiding the brilliant burning cherry of her Lucky Strike. As mom feathered her bangs in the side-view mirror, I watched

Dad kiss and embrace his mother. She held on, pulling her only son down to her bosom, stroking the back of his neck with the barbed tips of her fingernails.

Extinguishing her cigarette, Mom turned to me and said, "Lucy, my light, whatever you do, marry an orphan."

When I agreed to meet Katya Kalinnikova for lunch a week before Thanksgiving, I did not anticipate that my boyfriend's mother would bring along a mail-order bride. While Katya introduced me to this high-cheek-boned czarina, this silent émigré, this Zinaida Petrova, I couldn't help but imagine Katya purchasing this skittish beauty from a Web site. Pointing and clicking her way to an arranged marriage. Pimping for my boyfriend, her scientist son. Zinaida and I shook hands hello. I wanted to warn Zinaida about Katya's brutality, about her love of the put-down, her need always to be right. Instead, I smiled a dimpled grin and nodded as Katya proclaimed in her glorious splintered English, "Russian women make best wives."

The three of us slid our silver trays down the steel railing of Paradime Inc.'s corporate cafeteria. Katya in cold war paisley and wool. Zinaida in perestroika leather and angora. Listening as they joked in Russian, I thought of the Crimean War, the Great Purge, the Battle of Stalingrad, of all the brave soldiers and civilians who'd given their lives for their country. I bit the inside of my cheeks to keep from saying, "Widows. I thought Russian women made the best widows."

At Katya's request, I'd taken a sick day from teaching eighth graders in order to visit her at work and plan our holiday dinner menu. In my classroom in Cambridge, some unlucky substitute was being called "Puta" by Bobby Parrilla while Damien Beauvais punched Eliot Glazer in the throat and Whitney Barbosa sneaked off to the supply closet to hand out hand jobs. Missing even a day of work would compromise what little order and respect I'd built up in my classroom at MLK Middle. Matvei, my boyfriend of over five years, had warned me against this lunch. "My mother is setting you up for failure. For her, Thanksgiving will be a success only if the turkey you cook poisons one of us."

Pushing my empty tray, I grabbed a banana, a plate of egg noodles, and a carton of orange juice, and followed Katya to a table beside floor-to-ceiling vinyl drapes. As we sat down, I pulled back the curtains hoping to reveal the sunlight, the foliage. I wound up staring into a beige concrete wall.

"Only executives have windows." Katya pointed to a private dining room. "When I get promotion, Zinaida and I will eat there."

Ever since fleeing the former USSR, Katya had supported her husband and their three children as a computer programmer. Upon their arrival in Boston, Matvei's father, Ilya, a Russian checkers champion, declared the need to write a book about his life. "I must capture pain while it is raw. Not my memoirs, memoirs of Soviet Union." After twenty-five years, he was still laboring over the first draft. He accepted jobs as a freelance translator, but mostly he mourned. When I visited the Kalinnikovs, I was stunned to see Ilya forever lounging shirtless, his hairy belly slung over the elastic waistband of cotton pajama bottoms. An amusing, depressed bear of a man still reeling from the loss of his country.

Though Paradime Inc.—a computer and software conglomerate—was known for its indiscriminate layoffs,

Katya, with her specialized source code expertise, had survived every corporate restructuring. She was pink-slip-proof. Part of me admired her strength and resilience. Another part of me believed that Katya relished her power as the family's sole support. Pushing the egg noodles around my plate, I looked down into this tiny mother's deep-set chocolate eyes. Katya was short. A pocket-sized martyr, a redheaded action figure whose superhero skill set included the badger, the guilt grip, the supreme glare of disappointment. I fended off Katya's powers the only way I knew how—with politeness. When Matvei first introduced us, Katya pinched my arm, snapping her plump fingers, bruising my biceps with a radiant violet welt. Katya grinned and warned, "I did not bring son to United States for you to harm."

After broaching the subject of Thanksgiving, Katya insisted the meal take place at her home. "Your apartment is too small. Zinaida and I will cook what you can't. Matvei will love her stuffed cabbage."

I'd just purchased a dining room table that expanded to seat twelve and a Capital Precision Pro-Style gas range that could handle two sixteen-pound turkeys. "I'm very happy to host the dinner. We have plenty of room."

"The way you eat"—Katya pointed to the plain egg noodles on my plate—"is best if we give Thanksgiving."

I was stunned. I turned to Zinaida and said, "Do you like to cook?"

"Little," she said. "Forgive English."

At that moment, I wanted to reach out and pet the fluffy angora that sprouted from Zinaida's shoulders. Instead I clutched the sleeves of my own black cashmere turtleneck, a present from Matvei. My boyfriend developed artificial intelligence at MIT. He was part of a team that engineered wearable technology. Surgical computer gloves that enabled a doctor in Palo Alto to operate on a cancer patient in Seward, Alaska. GPS socks that navigated rescue workers through the maze of a collapsed copper mine. From the time we'd started dating, Matvei had been fine-tuning a clip-on earring/universal communicator that would allow an individual to speak in and understand foreign languages without any practical knowledge. Sound would travel from the earring through the central auditory system down something called the vestibulo-cochlear nerve to the brain stem, the thalamus, the temporal lobe, and back again. "Project Polyglot," the wealthy geeks at MIT called it. Matvei wanted the world to speak in tongues.

"What do you do here, Zinaida?" I asked.

"She works in Human Resources." Katya leaned forward and whispered, "Her story, such a story you would not believe."

"Is there a man involved?" I asked.

Katya nodded. "Isn't there always."

I had little trouble conjuring Zinaida's journey from Moscow to Boston. So many of my students were new arrivals: immigrating from Haiti and Puerto Rico, fleeing refugee camps all over the Sudan. Knowing their poverty, their ambition, I did what I could to fill them with hope. Along with my eighth-grade class, I ran an after-school program that focused on pop culture trivia and conversational American. Matvei referred to my efforts as Assimilation 101. "I'm not mocking," he'd claim. "I wish I'd had a teacher like you when I was being pummeled with dirty snowballs and taunted by a chorus of, 'Do you believe in miracles?' "

Zinaida, with her long eyelashes, her overprocessed hair, her pabulum-colored sweater reminded me of my own needy students. "I could give Zinaida language lessons."

"Ilya gives me lessons." Zinaida smiled. "Is good man."

"But." Katya pushed back her chair. "I require favor. Since you have room, you bring Zinaida home."

"To live?"

Katya picked up her tray. "Only temporary. She needs hiding place. I know my Matvei would agree."

A recipe for corn pudding, expired Butterball coupons, a broken electric carving knife—these were all gifts I was prepared to accept and later discard on the commuter rail home from Lowell to Cambridge. A spouse for my boyfriend was not a trifle I could politely receive and then abandon on an empty train seat. Ilya Kalinnikov might have been a two-time Russian checkers champion but Katya was a stone-cold chess master.

"How long am I supposed to hide her?" I asked.

"Thanksgiving." Katya lifted her tray. "Bring her with you when you come to our house."

My parents died during a trip to Israel. Terrorists bombed their hotel in Haifa the day before they checked in. The following afternoon a cargo van filled with six-inch nails, carpet tacks, and explosives blasted in front of a restaurant twenty minutes before their scheduled arrival. My parents called from the Holy Land to let their only child know that they were okay, that it was a miracle, really; if they'd booked the trip for the day before, if their taxi hadn't been stuck in traffic, they would have died so violently, so horribly. I begged them to come back, and when they refused, when my mother said, "Lightning can't possibly strike three times," I said good-bye and insisted on picking them up at the airport even though it was a thousand miles from Cambridge to Chicago.

Perhaps it was the disappointment of seeing the Dead Sea that killed them. "The salt waters are evaporating," my father sighed over the phone. "Our resort used to be right on the banks. Now it's a mile away from the shore." On their way home, my parents changed planes in England and within moments of liftoff, both seemed to fall asleep so soundly that they wanted no dinner, no beverages, not even a blanket. It was impossible to judge which one had died first, but each had suffered a mortal tear in the heart muscle.

All of this happened years before the other fatal flights, the two wars, the insurgency. But when asked about my parents, I described the hotel and restaurant bombings first. Recounted the terrorism, the shrapnel, the anonymous loss of life before acknowledging my parents' near misses. This helped me cope. At the memorial services my ninety-eight-year-old grandmother complained to the other mourners that her son had been too old to travel, that his wife, my mother, had pushed him into the trip. "You're wrong," I told her. "Dad always wanted to make a pilgrimage. Mom indulged his every happiness."

The day I met Matvei at a Russian-themed coffee shop in Harvard Square, I was nine months into my life as an orphan.

———

Matvei had his mother's eyes—velvety brown and searching. When I arrived home that night with Zinaida, he was sitting with his laptop perched over his legs, the computer humming like a warm, loyal pet. From the intent way he stared at the screen, I knew that he was playing one of the many video games he'd invented. His favorite game enabled him to run almost any major or incidental historical figure for president of the United States. He'd pit Barbra Streisand against Henry Kissinger. George Washington against King George III. Martin Luther King Jr. against Strom Thurmond. George W. Bush against Al Gore.

I kissed the crown of Matvei's curly hair. "You should race your mom against Joseph Stalin."

"Stalin wouldn't stand a chance." In one motion, Matvei paused his game, moved his computer, and gestured to pull me onto his lap. When he saw Zinaida, he stopped himself and said hello to this stranger and to the plastic suitcase that stood guard at her side.

I made tea and heated up leftover curried chicken. All afternoon I'd tried to reach Matvei at the lab while waiting for Zinaida to finish inputting employee benefits records. When I saw Zinaida's suitcase, I'd cursed Katya and the knowledge that I'd been set up. At the train station, I bought *Glamour* magazine. Paging through the fashion mishaps, the slick makeovers, Zinaida and I nodded our approval and scorn. For years I'd struggled to learn the Cyrillic alphabet, to master the most basic phrases. The only thing I absolutely knew how to say in Russian was not "I love you" or "Where's the bathroom?" but "Leave me alone." I knew about Mat—the Russian system of swearwords based largely on variations of mother abuse—but I also knew from Matvei that these terms were verboten. It would have been wrong of me to tell Katya to fuck off or, as the phrase translated from Russian, "go to the penis."

After dinner I listened from the kitchen as our houseguest entertained Matvei in rapid, excited Russian. Matvei spoke English in calm, accentless tones. In Russian, Matvei sounded happy, sounded high. Waving his arms in exuberant flourishes, breathlessly coaxing the Slavic music from his chest, pouting his lips and sucking in his cheeks as though smoking the best cigarette of his life. In English, he often asked me to repeat myself, often paused endlessly before answering, but in Russian each question received an immediate response. Though I knew better than to tease Matvei, I needlessly teased my boyfriend, taunting him that he heard better in Russian, that despite his English fluency, we'd never really be able to communicate. In turn, Matvei called me his sweet xenophobe.

That night Matvei and I suffered on the pullout sofa while Zinaida snored in our king-size bed. By the confident way he pressed his skinny body against mine, I could tell that Matvei wanted sex, and though I wanted sex too, I feared that we were both shamelessly turned on by the presence of a stranger in our home. Zinaida had ignored me all night, preferring to entertain Matvei. She'd even shown him photos of herself in a crocheted bikini at a lakeside resort in the Ural Mountains. *Let Zinaida catch us,* I thought as I guided my boyfriend's hands to my breasts. The two of us liked to talk as we touched. Liked to hold a normal conversation while we grabbed and molested each other. We'd discovered this one night when we were snowbound and forced to sleep across the hallway from Katya and Ilya. Our chatter—a mock argument over the usage of windchill factor versus windshield factor—obscured the sound of the sex. "Fucking and Talking" we called it. We both got off on the irony of screwing around and dialoguing as though nothing intimate was happening.

Matvei slid his warm hands over my breasts and explained how he'd gently quizzed Zinaida on her journey to the States, discovering that she'd come over on a K-1 "fiancée visa."

"My father the checkers champion is to blame for all of this. He mistranslated the correspondence between Zinaida and her husband. The guy wanted a baby-machine housekeeper and instead he wound up with a barren economist."

"What her husband really wanted was a human souvenir." I bit Matvei's neck and whispered, "Your mother hates me."

Matvei rolled on top of me. "No. She's trying to fix my dad's mistake. Zinaida's like the Russian daughter my mother always wanted."

"Your mom has two daughters."

"You're forgetting." Matvei smiled in the dark. "My sisters were born in America."

Bobby Parrilla laughed every time I said "Squanto." I led our class through the Massachusetts State-Sanctioned Social Studies Skill Set Packet on the Ethnographic Implications of the First Thanksgiving, trying to explain the significance of Squanto, the Native American who was twice stolen by Europeans and enslaved only to return to the New World to find that his entire tribe had died from smallpox. "Squanto spoke nearly perfect English. He taught the Pilgrims how to insulate their homes, how to fish for eel, how to fertilize their gardens."

Damien Beauvais raised his hand. He had long, tapered fingers that pounded out Bach concertos and pounded down b-boys who dared call him pussy. Damien asked, "What did Squanto get for helping white people?"

"What do you mean?" I leaned against my desk.

"Did he get paid?" Damien high-fived with Bobby Parrilla.

Bobby did the Cupid Shuffle around his desk, singing, "I got to get paid." He opened a black plastic wallet and flashed a wad of neat ten-dollar bills.

I let Bobby finish his dance.

"Squanto wasn't specifically employed by the Pilgrims, but he benefited from living with them—it was a sort of give and take," I said.

"Sounds like a whole lot of taking to me." Damien shook his head.

"Teacher's like Squanto." Whitney Barbosa turned around and addressed the class. "She helps you fools."

"Who you calling Squanto, Squanto?" Bobby threw one of his ten-dollar bills at Whitney. "That's for last night."

I'd long given up on sending students down to the office for cruel or insensitive comments. Whitney would be less embarrassed if I allowed the prostitution implication to slide, if I spoke to Bobby at the end of the day, if I let Whitney know in private that I appreciated her defense of my character. For the rest of the year "Squanto" would become a universal term for anything bad or worthless. My students even managed to turn it into a verb: "You Squantoed that shit up." I had failed my Native American hero.

"You're right to wonder why Squanto would help a group of people who had previously enslaved him, who were responsible for spreading a disease that killed his family, a group of people who would eventually betray Squanto, kick him out of their plantation, and possibly even poison him." No one else in the class seemed to care, but Damien looked right at me. "Squanto," I said, "didn't want to see anyone freeze or starve to death."

"But they killed him," Damien said.

"Sometimes," I said, "you have to believe in something enough to want to suffer. You have to be a willing martyr."

Bobby snatched his ten-dollar bill back from Whitney. "Martyrs go hungry. Pilgrims get to eat."

For an entire week Matvei and I woke up early, flipped pancakes, grilled sausages, and carved pink grapefruit for our guest. When we escorted Zinaida across the ice and snow to her train, she often linked arms with Matvei, leaning on him for balance. I tried not to feel threatened. Preferring to think of Zinaida, this buxom economist, as my own practice daughter. Despite our lengthy relationship, Matvei and I rarely spoke of marriage or children. I had my students to worry about and my mother's orphan warning to heed. Matvei liked to joke about the vast number of Nobel prize–winning scientists who married Las Vegas showgirls as their second wives. Then he'd promise to never leave me. I wasn't afraid of Matvei abandoning me but I did fear being driven away by Katya.

The day before Thanksgiving, Zinaida and I both came home early from work. She asked me to take her shopping. "I need present," she said.

It occurred to me that Zinaida wanted to buy Matvei and me a thank-you gift. "There's no need to get us anything," I said. "We're happy to have you as a guest."

"No." Zinaida shook her head. "I need special for man."

Zinaida had revealed to Matvei that there was a secret lover, a married man she wanted to leave her mail-order husband for. The situation was complicated—Zinaida had to stay with her husband for six more months before they could legally divorce and she could legitimately stay in the country. The married lover would then need to be divorced enough to marry Zinaida. When her husband found out about the other man, about Zinaida's plans to divorce and remarry, he became abusive, hurling insults and porcelain figurines, kicking her out of their three-bedroom colonial, making INS threats. Zinaida had fled to Katya, who promised to find her friend a temporary and then a permanent safe haven.

Though I had a deep-dish apple pie left to bake, I decided to take Zinaida to every great boutique in Harvard Square, to treat her for drinks at the Charles Hotel, to be her Squanto. At the bar that afternoon, we drank pumpkin-flavored martinis and cheered on the hearty rowers who sliced their sculls through the cold gray river. By the third round of cocktails, Zinaida confessed that all of her coworkers at Paradime impersonated Katya. "We sit on knees to be midget, make eyes huge, point arm and say, 'Let me tell you why you are wrong.'" Zinaida bugged out her eyes, giggled, and spilled her drink. I laughed, grateful for this gossip. Shopping together, a little tipsy from the Grey Goose, Zinaida and I took turns smiling and telling each other, "You are wrong." For her lover, Zinaida bought an antique meerschaum pipe carved with the face of a beautiful gypsy. She also purchased an expensive clove tobacco. "He loves to smoke," she said, "but his wife won't let him."

"Zinaida," I heard myself say, "you need to do everything you can to claim the man you love. Even if it means bringing him back to Russia—steal him away."

At home I cuddled with Matvei on our couch-bed and repeated the story of the Paradime workers mocking his mother. I said, "I feel so much better. I'm not alone." I reached my lips out to his. "No one can stand your mother."

"That's not very nice." Matvei tossed my legs off his lap, retreating to the kitchen.

When he didn't return, I followed him. Before I could apologize or decide if I wanted to apologize, Matvei said, "My mother always speaks very highly of you. She thinks you're much smarter than I am."

I coughed. "She just loves that I went to Harvard."

"Why?" Matvei asked. "Because she's a status-conscious immigrant? At least my mother never took her clothes off for money."

"My mother modeled evening gowns."

"What about that other thing?"

My mother had briefly waitressed at the Playboy Club in Chicago. This was where my parents met. Dad, a young smitten ad executive, convinced Mom to give him her phone number and her fluffy cottontail. To honor their origin myth, a framed black and white photo of Mom wearing the infamous bunny suit was prominently displayed over my parents' bed. As a flat-chested teenager, I often lured boys home after school, leading them to my parents' room, using my mother's cleavage to seduce them. I'd never told Matvei about the photo, but I'd once hinted that my mother had a connection to *Playboy*. I'd mentioned this early on in the flirting stage of our relationship. Later, when I attempted to find this relic, when I searched through the crates of belongings I'd hauled off into storage, I realized that the picture was lost. My mother—so sexy in satin, so loved by her husband, so maligned by her in-laws, so brutally honest with her daughter—was really gone. Matvei would never know my parents or view the photo that defined their love, their humor.

In the kitchen, we glared at each other waiting to see who would push the mother bashing farther. I had a number of Katya offenses left in my arsenal. Katya loved her son best of all, more than her two daughters Laura and Anna, and like any good mother she punished her beloved by treating him badly. One night during sex, Matvei told me that as a little boy in Moscow, Katya repeatedly abandoned him on subway cars. He'd chase after her calling for his mama and Katya would turn around and say, "I am not your mother. I am Nadia." The whole subway ride "Nadia" ignored Matvei, disregarding his tears, allowing him to suffer. "Nadia" moved from seat to seat as Matvei bit his fist and followed. She did this to teach him not to be afraid.

Still brave from my afternoon of vodka, I decided to push the argument.

"What about 'Nadia'? Isn't she responsible for you having panic attacks every time you ride the Red Line?"

"I don't tell you things so you can use them against me." Matvei picked up a Granny Smith apple from the counter and tossed it at me. "I think you have a pie to bake."

Ilya greeted us at the train station. I was surprised to see him out of his pajamas, dressed in a blue wool suit, an orange silk tie knotted tightly at his neck. His thin goatee perfectly manicured and his chest puffed out in strong Cossack bearing. We kissed on both cheeks and I could smell the gingery musk from cologne I'd given him years ago. He lifted the aluminum foil shielding my apple pie and said, "You are as American as this." Ilya took Zinaida's suitcase, and as their hands brushed together, a jolt of static electricity sparked between them. Zinaida jumped and laughed. Ilya led us to his car.

While Matvei and I sulked in silence in the back, Ilya and Zinaida practiced her English in the front seat: "Thanksgiving is a time for family. I miss family in Russia. Someday, I will return to Russia with new family."

Katya welcomed all of us into her home, the home she alone had saved and paid for, the home she'd twice mortgaged in order to send her children to college, the home she cleaned with yellow gloves and generic bleach, the home she'd paid a fortune to expand when her husband insisted he needed an office. As she greeted us, Matvei reached around my waist and drew me in close to his side. Matvei kissed my cheek before saying hello to his mother. Katya hugged Zinaida. "What joy to have you with my family." I wondered what Katya had in store for Zinaida—where she'd hide her next.

I joined Laura and Anna in the kitchen and watched as they took turns basting the fresh-kill turkey. Matvei's sisters were much younger than him, and since both were still away at college, I'd managed to meet them only a few times. They were sweet girls with milky complexions and oversized chests. Too old for me to think of them as my students. Too young for me to talk to them seriously about life. One of the curses of being an only child was that I didn't understand the bond between siblings. I could not bring myself to relax around these bubbly, well-meaning girls. When Laura offered me a drink, I took the bottle from her hand and poured myself a tall tumbler of Georgian wine.

"So what do you think of Zinaida?" Laura asked.

"She's nice," I said, gulping the sweet wine.

"I think she's way too Russian." Anna, the younger, tossed miniature marshmallows onto a casserole dish filled with yams. "What does Matvei think of her?"

"You'd have to ask him." Though I rarely smoked, I wanted one of my mother's life-affirming Lucky Strikes.

Laura stole a handful of marshmallows from her sister and said, "Matvei only likes varsity girls."

Before I could stop myself, I asked, "What do you mean?"

Anna said, "Matvei only dates cheerleaders—blondies with perfect skin. No babushkas for our brother."

True, I was blond. I had small pores and a tiny waist. I'd briefly been a drum majorette in junior high. "Do either of you smoke?" I asked.

"No," Laura said. "Our mother would kill us."

At dinner, I was seated at the foot of the long table—a full place setting away from Laura on my right and Anna on my left. The only one with a view of the kitchen, I felt like I'd been exiled, like I was sitting at a de facto kiddie table. Matvei waved at me from the other end. Ilya stood and made a toast welcoming Zinaida and calling all of the Kalinnikovs "pilgrims." I'd never seen him look so happy.

"I am close," he said, "to finishing my book. Soon all of you will know story of our family's greatness." He sat down and Katya led her family in a round of applause.

"Will you read to us after we eat?" Katya asked.

Ilya passed the platter of turkey to his son and said, "We shall see."

We feasted on maple-glazed acorn squash; roasted corn; cucumber and dill; grilled asparagus; string beans with almonds; garlic mashed potatoes; a salad of fresh figs, star fruit, and strawberries; cranberry-orange relish; oyster stuffing; ginger carrots. The dinner was much more than I ever could have prepared. Katya was right to insist on being in charge. I wanted to thank her, to let her know that I appreciated her effort.

"Everything is so wonderful," I said. "Thanks for going to all of this trouble."

"Well." She smiled. "We know you don't feed Matvei. He is like twig."

At my far end of the table I could reach out and touch no one. I felt distant. What I needed at that moment was for Matvei to stand up and say to his mother, "Let me tell you why you're wrong." He said nothing. Had my parents been alive, had my mother and father been seated next to me at that table, they would have risen, wineglasses in hand, and toasted me, proclaiming, "Our daughter is an excellent cook, a loving person, and your family is lucky to know her."

Zinaida cleared her throat and said, "Lucy very good in kitchen. She make for me breakfast every morning."

Matvei changed the subject to talk about the universal communicator he was working on at the lab. "When we're finished, we'll put you out of business, Dad. No one will ever need a translator again."

Ilya shook his head. "Computer always put me out of business. Canadians build software they call Chinook—beats everyone at checkers. Canada kills great sport. No more Flying Kings. No more Petrov's Triangle. No more checkers champions."

"Chinook is a type of wind," I said. "And a tribe of people. I think their language is extinct."

"You have to know a lot as a teacher." Laura smiled. "How hard is it?"

"Hard," I said. "The kids are great, but the big problem is money. There's just not enough. Not enough for books and technology. Not enough to keep the buildings from leaking. Not enough to pay for good teachers."

Katya interrupted. She brandished a wooden serving spoon and said, "When I go to school in Soviet Union, we have no heat in building, no playground, no magic markers. We share book. Teachers paid nothing. I study. Learn math, science. Problem not money."

I laughed. "So you think education was better in Soviet Russia."

"I think it was good. Good enough to make Sakharov and Solzhenitsyn. Good enough for me."

Despite the fact that Sakharov and Solzhenitsyn had spent their adult lives discrediting the Soviet system, Katya had a point about sacrifice and hard work. I couldn't argue with her. "Why don't you come to my class?" I offered. "Matvei is visiting next week."

"Preaching the joys of MIT and putting on a snowflake laser show. I'm going to turn Lucy's classroom into Siberia." Matvei smiled at me. "Mom, you should join me and talk about computer programming. We'll dazzle them."

Katya stared at her son. "I'm very busy at work. They plan more cutbacks. I cannot leave to talk to children."

"You should do it, Mom," Anna said.

I heard a scratching on the back kitchen door. No one else seemed to hear the sound. I heard it again and before I could say a word, Katya stood up and said, "We need more rolls."

From where I sat I was the only one with a clear view of Katya opening the back door. She greeted a man with slick brown hair wearing a shiny black leather coat. When I saw Katya whisper hello, saw her kiss this stranger on both cheeks, saw her begin to usher him out of the kitchen and presumably up the stairs, my first thought was, *She's having an affair.*

I was mistaken. Katya had no lover. The stranger's name, I'd soon learn, was Walter Richmond. Walter had spent his adult life importing wicker chairs from the Philippines. At forty-two he decided to begin his search for a wife, not by barhopping or joining a health club, but by paying a human trafficker five thousand dollars to send him photos of a dozen contenders. He'd chosen Zinaida from a stack of Polaroids.

I trust now that Katya had a specific plot in mind. She would sneak Walter Richmond into her home, hide him in a closet, and hold her breath. That night, while Zinaida dreamt in the Kalinnikovs' guest bed, Walter Richmond might have swooped down in his leather coat and repossessed his unfaithful beauty. This is what the KGB would do when they wanted you. Take you in the night. Or maybe Katya believed that she could counsel the couple. At the time I couldn't imagine what she was up to. I didn't know that she was hoping to save her own marriage.

I sensed from Katya's cloak-and-dagger move, from her attempt to sneak a stranger up the staircase, that some secret plot was being hatched. I knew she'd return to the table with more dinner rolls and a false grin. Since I was the only one with a view, I was the only one who could contest her lie. I cleared my throat loud enough for Katya to look up and see me seeing her. I stared at Katya and the stranger as they paused on the black-and-white checkerboard linoleum. She put a single finger up to her lips. She'd seated me here at the end of the table not as a punishment, but as a privilege. I was her sentry. I smiled and made my move, calling out, "Katya, who's your friend?"

My mother always said that women were cruel to one another because of men. "Mothers never give up their sons. Not without a fight. Wives will endure every sacrifice and humiliation just for the honor of holding their unfaithful husband's unfaithful hand." I didn't mean to be cruel to Katya. I didn't know that she was learning to trust me, that I was in some way her accomplice.

Zinaida locked herself in the bathroom while Walter Richmond sat slumped on the living room couch. He kept repeating to himself, "I made an investment. Where's my dividend?" I was torn between calling the police and heating up my apple pie. Katya and her daughters disappeared into the kitchen portioning out our half-eaten dinner into color-coded Tupperware. Through the thin bathroom door, Matvei attempted to calm Zinaida. Ilya simply disappeared. I offered Walter Richmond a piece of pie. "She's my wife," he said. "Doesn't that mean anything?"

"You didn't buy Zinaida," I said. "You just sort of leased her." I knew Zinaida would be returning home with Matvei and me.

"Are you somebody's spouse?" Walter Richmond asked.

"No." I smiled. "I'd make a terrible wife."

———

Zinaida, Matvei, and I stood outside in the brutal chill waiting for our train. Matvei pulled his scarf off and wrapped it around my neck. "Are you mine?" he asked.

"I'm no one's," I said. "I'm an orphan."

"Are we ever going to get married?" Matvei looked at me, then looked away. "It's Thanksgiving. Isn't that when Americans get engaged?"

Zinaida stood at a distance from us. I didn't want to receive a marriage proposal in her shadow.

After the Walter Richmond drama, I'd gone outside and noticed Ilya in the backyard gazing up at the cold sky. I thought I'd congratulate him on finishing his memoir and convince him to show me a few chapters, all in the hopes of understanding the Kalinnikovs better. Before I had a chance to speak, I saw Ilya pull something out of his pocket and bring it to his lips. He struck a match. The smoke from the meerschaum pipe glowed white as the rich smell of clove filled the night air.

When the train arrived, I waited for Matvei and Zinaida to enter a car and choose their seats. For a moment, I stood outside the bright glimmering train, watching their framed profiles, considering my life without Matvei, without the Kalinnikovs. I pictured the train pulling away and Matvei pounding on the window and shouting to the conductor, "Wait, wait for my Lucy, my light." I imagined telling him, "I am not your Lucy."

We woke the following morning to find Zinaida gone. I was relieved. I told Matvei about seeing his mother with Walter

Richmond and about watching his father smoke Zinaida's gift. "What a mess," Matvei said. "I'm glad it's not our problem."

"But they're your parents," I said.

"Exactly." Matvei nodded. "And I've spent my whole life recovering from them."

A week after Thanksgiving, Katya came to my class. Matvei was busy trying to set up his snowflake laser show. He bragged that the green, white, and red rays would appear in 3-D. Wonderlanding the students into the squall of a thousand unique crystals. The laser splitter refused to split. Matvei could persuade only a single red beam to cut a straight line through our holiday cactus. As he tinkered with the laser contraption, Bobby and Damien swatted each other with the plastic goggles Matvei had brought to protect their sight.

I was surprised to see Katya and pleased, but before I could introduce her to the class, she dragged me to the back of the room beside the abandoned overhead projector.

"What's going on?" I asked.

"I've been released." Paradime Inc., at the urging of the Human Resources Department, had made Katya redundant. She'd been escorted from her cubicle by a security guard and Zinaida. "Ilya is leaving me," Katya whispered. "He and Zinaida are going back to Russia."

I tried to picture Ilya abandoning his pajamas, returning to the land where he'd once reigned as checkers champion. Where his every move was scrutinized. The mail-ordered Zinaida had found love and was shipping them both back home. My father would have deemed Ilya unworthy, my mother would have labeled Zinaida a home wrecker. I wasn't so sure.

"He said he felt romance translating her letters." Katya looked right at me and grabbed both of my wrists. "I rescued him from Soviets—and now, for him to return, it is like I am nothing."

I feared for a moment that Katya might twist and break the thin bones that held my hands and arms together. Just when I considered saying "Uncle," Katya pulled me into her chest. "You kept her away from my Ilya."

No, I didn't, I thought as Katya hugged and squeezed. I failed her.

The red and green lights from the laser splitter flashed, then fizzled. Bobby Parrilla booed and said, "MIT, my ass. Your boyfriend's straight-up Squanto."

"Quiet, quiet," Katya said, breaking away from me. "My son wants to show you trick. His is not working so I will teach you mine." With all of her classical Soviet training, Katya took a sheet of white paper off of my desk, creasing and folding the document into an impossibly thin fragment. Without scissors or measuring tools, she began with her bare hands to tear the paper, to pull tiny pieces away, to pinch and mince and shred. The students quieted down, leaning in to watch.

"Let me see," Whitney Barbosa insisted.

"I come from far away, like you," Katya told them. "And where I come from"—she unfolded the paper—"we make our snowflakes this big." Katya tossed the lace star in the air. "Do you know this magic?" she asked my class.

"No snow in Haiti." Damien Beauvais smiled. He fanned a stack of papers and began handing them out. "Let's make a blizzard."

Matvei gave up on his laser and guided my students as they crimped and folded their simple sheets into live-action, serious winter art. Katya patrolled the rows of desks, nodding her approval. Disapproving of anyone who demanded scissors. "Pinch it," she'd say, and I thought of the first time she touched me.

Instead of an engagement ring, Matvei has promised me the prototype for his universal translator. Project Polyglot isn't ready yet, but it will be soon. I'll wear my clip-on earring when I instruct the future Damiens and Whitneys, when I argue with Matvei, when I commiserate with Katya. We haven't briefed my probable mother-in-law on our plan to marry. Matvei and I need our secrets. Since Katya moved in with us, almost nothing is private. Katya is always listening. At night when we have sex, I hear the warm breath of her surveillance. Matvei and I joke, "Nadia is spying." I know that Katya wants to detect something in our whispers. Something to give her hope. Something to signal she's part of our family. But Matvei and I have learned to speak the same quiet language, coded and indecipherable, known only to those we both love.

NUMBER ONE TUNA

Malcolm and I stayed in touch only because each of us was privately convinced that the other deserved to fail. We'd been roommates at Haverford, Malcolm's first-choice college, my safety. Since neither one of us really cared for the other, we decided to live together for all four years. "Friends," we assured each other, "make bad roommates." Around campus we appeared cordial, but inside our dorm room we cultivated an exquisite wall of contempt. I just barely tolerated the jizzed condom trophies Malcolm hid under his bed, the skid marks he left on the boxers he borrowed from me, and his insistent declaration that he had J. Crew looks. In turn, Malcolm endured my noisy, bubbling fish tank, my mother's late-night phone calls, and my pathological habit of quoting from *All About Eve*. "Fasten your seat belts; it's going to be a bumpy night!" I'd exclaim every time he brought over a girl from Bryn Mawr.

After college, we both relocated to Los Angeles. Malcolm

used connections I never knew he had and finagled a studio job. An uncle of mine wheedled me an assistant to a paralegal position at a law office in Brentwood. Malcolm and I had stopped living together at this point, but we kept in touch. Once a month, Malcolm destroyed my tennis confidence, then later made nice by taking me out to a new sushi palace. I was mostly friendless in L.A., and I kept hoping that Malcolm might invite me to a glitzy premiere, introduce me to a horny starlet, or better still, arrange a job interview for me at Paramount. Then the worst thing in the world happened. Malcolm sold a screenplay.

He grossed a hundred thousand dollars for the first one. I comforted myself by doing the math: the taxes he paid, his agent's cut. I figured Malcolm took home thirty-five thousand. I could live with that. It wasn't much more than what I made in a year. It never occurred to me that his film would be produced. The film, of course, earned seven Oscar nominations. While it lost Best Picture to that movie about the glow-in-the-dark children and the nuclear winter, Malcolm himself won for Best Original Screenplay. Three minutes after his victory speech, his agent unloaded his second screenplay for a million dollars. In quick succession, Malcolm had a development deal, a production company, and a twenty-thousand-gallon aquarium filled with baby sharks he'd netted in Fiji.

The party invitation simply stated: "Welcome the Stingray." Malcolm lived in a glass mansion high in the Hollywood Hills. As I drove up the narrow curving road, I marveled at the hazy view that stretched from downtown all the way to the beach and out farther to the pounding and polluted Pacific surf. His house, while not enormous, was exceptional. The front entryway boasted a soaring glass atrium. With a push of a button, Malcolm could frost the clear glass, tint it blue, or drop steel curtains down on every wall.

Malcolm had hired the requisite valets to park cars outside his glass mansion. The car jockeys were on a cigarette break when I pulled up in my Ford Festiva. Knowing that the valets would finish every last drag before coming to my aid, I climbed out of the car and lit up a Camel. One of the valets moved close enough to fling a plastic ticket at me. He motioned for my keys. I tossed my key chain at him, then finished my cigarette, slowly. I'd spent two hours in traffic driving from Tarzana. I was in no hurry.

I'd never been to a party for a fish before. At a loss for what to wear, I'd cruised the vintage stores on Melrose and purchased a blue-and-white-striped seersucker suit. The waifish shopgirl used the words "dapper" and "Jazz Age" as I modeled outside the dressing room. I quoted the last line of *The Great Gatsby* as she swiped my debit card: "So we beat on, boats against the current, borne back ceaselessly into the past." She said something about the scene in the book where Mia Farrow fondles all of Robert Redford's dress shirts. For a moment, I actually considered inviting her to the party. I'd been dateless for months, but Malcolm would have sneered at the waif's narrow hips and flat chest and asked me, "Where do you keep her tits?" As I made my solitary stroll to Malcolm's glass house, the dark lights on the pathway brightened, glowed, and dimmed as I passed them.

The stingray was Malcolm's new pet and his newest pet project, the title of his latest screenplay, an intellectual action film, with a marine biologist/chemical weapons expert for a hero. The film would mark Malcolm's directorial debut. He'd bought himself a giant fish to celebrate the studio green-lighting the project. He already owned a Corvette Stingray with a vanity plate that read STUNG.

Dazzling female bodies wrapped in gauzy gowns, and male bodies covered in colorful, collarless shirts pushed and pulled in small schools in the foyer's atrium. The centerpiece of the room was an octagonal aquarium, approximately eight feet tall, with thick glass walls and an open top. Four adolescent sharks, a giant sea turtle, and an enormous winged stingray patrolled the waters. I watched the stingray flutter and float above the sharks' bodies. The stingray, silvery and menacing on top, was a creamy pink on the bottom. As the ray flashed its belly against the glass, I saw its mouth arched in a perfect smile. The perma-grin on his underside gave the stingray a comic, strangely human quality. When I left Haverford for L.A., I gave up my own gurgling fish tanks. Flushed my collection of hatchetfish, triggerfish, and tailbar lionfish. I had no one to give them to, no way to keep them.

I spotted our host's bald head. He'd shaved his scalp for the Academy Awards and now kept his head tanned and polished. In college, Malcolm wore his hair in a blond Afro. I had to admit that his big, shiny noggin looked, in a certain light, like a polished Etruscan phallus. Like Yul Brynner in *The King and I,* Malcolm commanded authority. Bareheaded with bare feet, outfitted from head to ankle in white linen, he kept the party spinning around him. A leather cord lassoed around his neck was punctuated by a broken piece of shell. I used to wear a necklace like that my freshman year in college until Malcolm told me the Bryn Mawr girls were questioning my sexual orientation. The woman hanging on Malcolm's arm wore an orange sheath dress. Large gold earrings complemented her tawny skin. This woman didn't seem to be aware that there was a party going on. Before I could interrupt and say hello, she turned to Malcolm and let loose her husky voice, "I'm going to love you like nobody's loved you, come rain or come shine."

Malcolm held the woman's shoulders as she sang. Her voice was otherworldly. Smitten guests paused their own chatter. I heard someone whisper, "That's Quincy Jones's daughter." I couldn't remember who Quincy Jones was, but I knew he was someone important. When she finished, Malcolm took her by the hand, spun her around, and pulled her into his chest. I needed a drink.

The bartender was a redhead named Desi. "Like Desi Arnaz?" I said. She frowned at me. "Short for Desire," she said. The catering company had dolled her up in a blue-and-green batiked sarong. I wanted to rub her bare shoulders and count the freckles on her back. Instead, I asked for a gin and tonic, and stared down at the uneven cuffs on my new vintage trousers. I kept going to Malcolm's parties because he kept inviting me. He kept inviting me out of guilt.

The screenplay that Malcolm won an Oscar for was based on a series of telephone conversations he had with my mother during our sophomore year. That year, I'd scored a job as a projectionist for the Bette Davis Film Festival. The first night we screened a double feature: *A Stolen Life* followed by *Of Human Bondage*. Bette Davis was magnificent in *A Stolen Life*. She played twin sisters who fall in love with a lighthouse inspector on Nantucket. The bad twin wins Glenn Ford's heart, only to die in a boating accident. The good twin must decide whether to pose as her bad twin in order to reclaim Glenn Ford's love. When I got back to our dorm room, I discovered Malcolm on the phone with my mother. He was taking notes.

Malcolm's first screenplay opens with full-frontal nudity, a shot of a young man running naked through the snow. In the background, the audience hears gunfire, barking dogs, men cursing loudly in Russian. We witness the man being captured, being forced to dig his own grave. Then we flash forward to a shot of this same man, decades older, dressed in a gabardine business suit, dining at the Four Seasons in Manhattan. The man in question was my maternal grandfather, Vadim Kaminsky. A minor Soviet dissident who claimed to have once played chess with Trotsky, who then survived the Holocaust, escaped from the gulag, and rose to fame in the United States as an accomplished neurosurgeon. I'd heard the story numerous times. It never occurred to me that my grandfather's life was sufficiently cinematic. My grandfather hadn't been buried alive, merely threatened. Malcolm had my mother's full permission to write anything he wanted. He never actually met my grandfather until after the script sold. My grandfather was a muscular man, and rambunctious. A fierce handshaker. He appeared with Malcolm on *Charlie Rose, Today,* and *E! News.* He made a special appearance at the Golden Globe Awards with John Malkovich, his older screen self. Malcolm made my grandfather happier than I'd ever seen him. When my grandfather died three weeks before the Academy ballots were due, I knew that Malcolm would win one of those gold bald statues.

I hadn't expected to see my mother at Malcolm's party, but there she was, wearing a killer Armani suit. Flaunting cleavage. My mother had been a Philadelphia housewife and high school substitute history teacher until Malcolm fixed her up as a consultant for his production company. She had a condo in Santa Monica and a cottage in Palm Springs. I watched from a distance as she hugged Malcolm. My mother rubbed her lipstick off his cheek. My grandfather had been married six times—one of the facts left out of the film version, where he falls in love with Björk at the Black Sea in 1931 and marries her in Brighton Beach in 1950. The man had a stable of children. Even though he was wealthy, he kept forgetting my mother was one of his daughters. She never really had money until Malcolm. My mother had offered to ask Malcolm to get me a consulting position as well, but I'd just been promoted to full-fledged paralegal, so I had to turn her down.

My mother pointed out a yellow stain on the right lapel of my suit and asked if I'd heard anything from my father.

"He got your last check."

"Tell him he should come out and visit." My mother took a sip from my gin and tonic, leaving the rest of her lipstick on my glass.

"That's one hell of a stingray," I said.

"Did you bring anyone?" she asked. "I've been seeing a golf pro."

My mother not only looked young, she looked better than me. I wanted to tell her that she was radiant, that California was good for her, that my father, a hapless actuary, had never appreciated her. I wanted to ask her out to lunch, and I wanted to pay for the meal.

"How's the new film?" I smiled. "Are you and Malcolm working your magic?"

Mom described an action sequence involving a dozen scuba divers, a fleet of Jet Skis, and a pair of manatees. I half listened, thinking instead about what kind of mother she'd been and what kind of son I was. When I was ten, I gave her a black lacquer music box for Mother's Day. It was the only gift I could remember giving her. Every time my parents fought, I'd sneak into their bedroom, find the music box, and play it. I'd crank the key and hear "Beautiful Dreamer." The box was lined with red felt. When I lifted the lid, a small plastic man and an even smaller plastic woman popped up on a tiny plastic post. The man and woman held each other, pirouetting to the music. I'd watch the dancers and imagine my mother and father as Ginger Rogers and Fred Astaire in *Top Hat,* Judy Garland and Fred Astaire in *Easter Parade,* Leslie Caron and Fred Astaire in *Daddy Long Legs,* Cyd Charisse and Fred Astaire in *Silk Stockings.* Mom caught me with the box twice. The first time she asked me if I wanted dancing lessons. The second time she checked her underwear drawer, counted her high heels, and asked me if there was anything special I wanted to tell her.

Mom was still gushing about Malcolm, calling him an auteur and promising that *The Stingray* would revolutionize filmmaking. I held up a cigarette and said, "Sorry, Mom, I need a smoke."

As I passed through the crush of guests, I felt a hand on my arm. I turned around and saw Malcolm's shining head.

"You're maudlin and full of self-pity," he said. "You're magnificent!"

"What are you talking about?" I asked.

"*All About Eve*. You were always quoting it in college. I finally saw it the other day. It's a little long but worth remaking."

I said, "I can see your career rise in the east like the sun."

"Excuse me?"

"Another line," I said, "from the same movie."

"I'm thinking of remaking it," he said. "Updating it. Make the ladies movie stars instead of stage actresses. I'm thinking Sharon Stone and that girl from *American Beauty*. It's time to revive their careers."

"Bette Davis will find you and kill you." I tossed an unlit cigarette into my mouth.

"The original won six Oscars." Malcolm pulled the cigarette from my lips and put it behind his ear. "I figure I can win ten."

I snatched my cigarette back. "Promise me you won't remake it."

"I've been thinking you should go to law school." Malcolm gave me a smile and a wink. "I mean, legally, how long can you stay a paralegal?"

"Don't worry about me. I'll surprise you yet."

Malcolm grinned. "Your mom says you're coveting my life. Are you?" A clutch of admirers closed in around him before I had a chance to choose my answer.

The back courtyard was landscaped with a koi pond, fruit trees, and a narrow lap pool with special jets that re-created stressful water currents. I needed a cigarette, but my lighter wouldn't work. A woman standing under a lemon tree held a lit cigarette in one hand and a blistered yellow fruit in the other. She dragged on the cigarette, exhaled, brought the lemon to her face, inhaled. She saw me notice her and said, "I'm testing out my senses."

This woman had the tiniest waist I'd ever seen. She also had lustrous brown hair, large round eyes, a long and delicate neck. Audrey Hepburn, only not in a cultivated don't-I-look-like-Audrey-Hepburn way. As she smoked, she hummed "I Wanna Be Sedated" by the Ramones. When I asked her for a light, she stopped humming and smiled. "Don't you hate L.A.? Don't you hate that no one smokes? That no one smokes the way they did in the old movies?"

We chatted about smoker's guilt, about sneaking butts in our offices. "I'll take two puffs, tamp the cigarette out, and seal it in an envelope for later. I have dozens of cigarette envelopes waiting for me in my file cabinet," Audrey Hepburn admitted. We debated nicotine gum versus the patch versus hypnosis. Placed bets on our lung cancer odds. She pouted. Blew smoke rings.

"What I really hate about L.A. are actors who know nothing about films," I said.

"All of these bombshells and boneheads want to be stars, yet none of them have ever seen a real movie," she said, rolling the lemon in her palm. "Not *Whatever Happened to Baby Jane?* or *Roman Holiday* or *Badlands*. Not even *Klute*. At best, they cried during *Schindler's List* or sniffled through *Terms of Endearment*."

"Have you ever noticed that no one in L.A. owns any books?" I asked.

"Why would you, when the mansions don't have bookshelves? People don't even pretend to read."

We introduced ourselves. Her name was Naomi and she worked at Fang & Moon, a talent management agency. I'd interviewed there for a position less than a year ago. I'd been called back twice, and I was really hopeful, but the job had gone to someone with an MBA and a JD. Naomi was the kind of woman I'd look forward to seeing at work every day. After years in L.A., I was stunned to finally meet the girl I'd most likely been looking for. As a child, I loved musicals. I thought being happy meant breaking out into song and tap dancing. I imagined serenading Naomi with "'S wonderful, 'S marvelous that you should care for me." I'd pull her in close and we'd twirl and splash in Malcolm's koi pond. Like we were Audrey Hepburn and Fred Astaire in *Funny Face*. Pretending that we, too, were magical.

When Naomi introduced me to her boyfriend, Clay, I had a hard time focusing on his face. Clay had blond, sculpted hair. My hand disappeared into his paw as we shook our greetings. Naomi explained to me that she and Clay worked together. Clay had joined the agency less than a year ago.

"Are you talent or production?" Clay asked me.

I hesitated. "I'm behind the scenes."

As Clay wrapped his arms around Naomi and kissed her long, delicate neck, I realized that this guy had my job and my girlfriend. It was one thing to be jealous of Malcolm—I knew I couldn't compete with his fame or his level of success—but my envy of Clay was unacceptable.

Yukio, Malcolm's private chef, accosted me outside the first-floor bathroom. He was at the party as a friend, not in any professional capacity. Yukio wanted to know if I thought Malcolm looked healthier now than he had at Haverford. I said that I thought Malcolm looked healthy but that he'd confided in me earlier that he kept finding blood in his stool. "Don't mention it to him," I said. "He's very sensitive."

"Does he have colon cancer?" Yukio asked.

"You didn't hear it from me."

Yukio promised that he wouldn't betray my confidence. "It might be the mercury in his diet. Malcolm loves fish: swordfish, yellowfin, eel."

I told Yukio that I was especially fond of yellowfin tuna. "I might well be one of the foremost L.A. sushi connoisseurs," I said.

"You've never actually tasted real yellowfin." Yukio laughed. "In order to get real number one tuna, you need to know someone in Chile, a fish boss who can set aside steaks from the Japanese sushi mafia. You, friend, have no idea how good it really is."

As I stalked the party, double-fisting gin and tonics, I heard snippets of conversation.

"It's all about stripping away artifice."

"Who's your blood donor?"

"The Dalai Lama really cracks me up."

"All I want to do is find something fourteen-year-old boys want, and sell it to them."

"He's not just my ex-husband, he's my best friend."

"Is she still eating? I thought she'd stopped."

Malcolm kept a white grand piano in the atrium. I sat down on the piano bench. As I stared at the keys, I thought about what I might play, if I knew how to play the piano. The theme from *Dr. Zhivago,* the theme from *Ice Castles.* A skinny guy in a purple-and-white-striped seersucker suit stood next to the bench. His suit was tailored and the seersucker looked fine and crisp, as though it had been made from something other than seersucker. I recognized him from the movie. He'd played my grandfather as a teenager.

"Aren't you somebody?" he asked me.

"Afraid not." I smiled.

"Everyone kept telling me that there was someone else here wearing a suit like mine. I was hoping for a fashion cat-fight."

"Sorry if I'm not perpetuating the Hollywood myth for you."

"At least you're gay," my young grandfather said. "Malcolm always promises me beautiful boys. Never delivers."

"I'm not particularly gay," I said.

"Well, lucky for you, I'm not particular. Do you play piano?" He sat down next to me and played the opening to "Moon River." A wave of guests surged toward the piano player. Malcolm's tawny chanteuse began to sing. I found myself pushed off the bench.

One of the catering waiters stood on a stepladder and tossed platters of frozen meats into the aquarium. The sharks swam to the top of the tank, the high water churning purple. I counted four small-sized sharks, each one dark gray with black spots. Their rows of teeth flashed white as they dined. I hummed the theme from *Jaws*. The sea turtle swam to the bottom of the tank, avoiding the feeding frenzy. The stingray made his rounds in the middle of the pool. When his tray was empty, the waiter climbed down from the ladder and left.

I suspected that the sharks did not get enough to eat. The stingray's wings were stained with blood from the frozen meat. When the first shark nipped the stingray, I was surprised that his teeth left almost no impression. The second shark bit the stingray's tail. I pounded on the glass. "Stop it. That's not fair." All four sharks made passes, attacking the stingray. I climbed up onto the ladder, stared down at the blurry fake ocean, and jumped into the tank.

I couldn't see much underwater. The sharks were silver shadows. As I tried kicking at their heads, my loafers fell off my feet. I dove down and searched for the stingray, eventually grabbing hold of his tail. I pulled the stingray close to my chest and swam to the top of the tank. The fish did not sting me. When I broke the surface, I balanced the ray against the edge of the tank, pulled myself up onto the ladder, and carried the injured fish down to the marble floor. The skin felt slippery and cold. Bitten and bloody, the stingray was still smiling its perma-grin.

While it's true that almost everyone would like to make a movie, only a few people know what that film would be. Some know the title. Others have pre-picked the sound track. They've fantasized about casting Angelina Jolie as an android or making Steve Buscemi the romantic lead. Only a small percentage of people know how their film would begin, and only I would start with a tracking shot of a man driving a Ford Festiva through the Hollywood Hills. Hardly anyone knows how their film would end, but most would want their ending to be happy.

Soaking wet, I carried the stingray out to Malcolm's backyard and dumped the bloody fish into his koi pond. A crowd of guests was gathering around me. Yukio chided me for putting a saltwater fish into freshwater. The actor who played my young grandfather joked about stingray sushi. My mother was saying, "How embarrassing," and telling me that I would catch pneumonia. Malcolm walked up to me, smiling sadly.

"You're a good guy," he said. "But face it. The stingray's dying. It's about to die. What were you trying to cast yourself as? Comic relief?"

"No," I replied. "I'm the hero."

Some of the guests began to snicker. Malcolm walked back toward his glass house. The crowd began to thin. I stepped into the pond and saw the stingray lying on its back and smiling up at me. I overheard Naomi saying to Quincy Jones's daughter, "I met him earlier, but I didn't catch his name."

ASSEMBLING THE TROOPS

THE SIDEKICK

The playground is where you cultivate your future. Stake out the boy crouching in the shade far away from the monkey bars. The one drawing in the mud with a stick. His name is Bobby Mopes, and though there is nothing wrong with him a Kleenex couldn't fix, he is a target. Watch the Monkey Bar Boys circle. Let them tower over Bobby. Let Arnold Talon break the boy's stick. Intervene moments before the first fist threatens to strike Bobby's runny nose. You are a grade older, three inches taller. You hold the school's Presidential Fitness Record for chin-ups. All you need to say is, "Hey," and the would-be attackers scatter. This is how you breed loyalty, accountability, fear. Bobby won't say thank you. He'll hand you half of his remaining stick. In the wet dirt, sketch a rough map of France. Point to Omaha Beach. Say, "I'm enlisting you for Operation Overlord." On the morning of June 6, 1944, while Nazi soldiers scanned the horizon, the full moon guided your grandfather's transport ashore. The tide so low and the waves so clear your grandfather could see the German bombs hidden underwater. Bobby will nod. He'll clutch the butt end of his rotting twig. Holding the trigger of kindling in his left hand, he will point to the swing set, the giant metal slide, the roundabout, cocking his thumb and firing. You are Danny Riley, World War II historian/schoolyard diplomat.

THE EARLY CASUALTY

Start a food war in the middle school cafeteria. Throw a milk carton at the acne-flaming Arnold Talon's cheeks. You have a sniper's aim, a quarterback's arm. Hit your mark, then duck as Bobby Mopes continues the charge, flinging pizza squares and sugar cookies. Marvel at the chaos you create, at the power you have to unite, divide, and conquer. Laugh until a metal lunch tray slices through the air, striking Jennifer Donner on the base of her skull. Try to hit Rewind. Try to pull the tray from its midair flight. You are not the thrower, but you are still to blame. A week later the vice principal will cancel the annual spring talent show to hold a school assembly on luncheon etiquette and head traumas. The year before, Jennifer won third place for tap dancing to "Boogie Woogie Bugle Boy." In the future, you will judge all women by the standards of Jennifer's performance: her skinny legs, the bounce of her blond ponytail, and the blue sequins sheltering her budding breasts. The vice principal will frighten his audience with stories of spinal fluid leaking from Jennifer's ears. Someone will whisper, "Jenny Donner is a goner." Jennifer will disappear until high school, when you'll see her wheeling down the hallway in a chair motorized by the force of her breath blowing through a long plastic straw. Offer to push her chair. Listen as her blinking eyes refuse your request. Recall how she tripped up the stage on the way to accepting her third place ribbon. How she caught herself before she fell. You are Danny Riley, troublemaker/aspiring problem solver.

THE TALENT

Steal a yellow moped. Get caught skidding past a traffic cop down the hill on Goodson Street. Steal a black leather jacket from the Salvation Army. Get caught by the eager security guard posted at the side exit. Steal a box of DD batteries. Give them to Bobby Mopes along with a massive boom box you swiped from the music room. Shoulder the blame when Bobby dismantles the radio, spray-paints the batteries red, and secures the wired unit to a school locker with a note that reads DETO-NATE. Go to court. Go to a juvenile detention center. Meet a kid named Brian Chang. Watch him blow smoke rings in iso-late halos. Stand guard as he breaks a counselor's jaw with the flat of his left hand. Give him your cigarettes, your copy of *Thrasher* magazine. Brag about what you would do with all of these railings and concrete stairs. Say, "It's not a prison. It's a fuckin' skate park." With his wide feet and narrow hips, Brian will mime switch stance spinners, nosegrinds, and McTwists. Ask him if he's ever stolen a car. Ask him if his grandfather fought for the Red Army. Listen when he tells you that Chang is one of the oldest and most noble family names, that his ancestors invented the crossbow, that he is the descendant of sharpshooters. Ask him who invented the arrow. You are Danny Riley, petty thief/culture warrior.

THE STAR

Sneak into the Goodson Street Movie Theater. *The Right Stuff* will light up the screen in celebration of some moon race anniversary. Be awestruck by Chuck Yeager as he breaks the sound barrier with his broken ribs. Feel sorry for this war hero when he misses out on becoming an astronaut because he lacked a college degree. In the darkness of the theater make decisions about your future. Decide to become a soldier. Decide to graduate from a university. Lose interest in the film once the Mercury Seven astronauts are chosen and the space race begins. You know that the Russians will beat America, that Gus Grissom will die on liftoff, that only Alan Shepard will make it to the moon. Admire the actor who plays Chuck Yeager. You'll want to stay for the credits to find out his name, but the movie is more than three hours long and your mother is inclined to call the police when you're late for dinner. Pay attention to the actor's mannerisms. To the artful way he rides a horse. To the cocky way he chews his gum. Notice how much he says through silence. You are on the verge of becoming either handsome or homely. Emulate this man. Grow out your brown hair, buy a leather bomber jacket, chew gum while others speak. Try to become this actor, this hero. You are Danny Riley, stargazer/moviegoer.

THE GIRL

As her small pixie face broadcasts over the metal sheen of the Firebird Brian Chang boosted from Goodson Street, tell her she'd look better with short hair. She's sixteen. You're a week away from joining the army. Listen to her when she describes how her father died in what will eventually be known as the First Gulf War—a flipped Jeep, a broken neck, a body rotting in the desert. Notice the silver stars she's painted on her fingernails. Tell her she should wash her face less. "You're stripping away the good oils and causing all those pits." Another girl would raise a hand to hide her chin, her cheek, but this one stares back, unflinching. "Take me somewhere." She climbs in the stolen backseat, expecting a chauffeur. She says her name is Margaux with an *x*. Tell her she's full of shit. You know that her real name is Kelsey and that she's angling for a seduction. If you had money for gas, you'd drive her to the coast, frolic with the sea lions, but there are no beaches here, only man-made lakes. Let her call the shots. "Go left at the light," she'll say, luring you out of town. She'll choose all the turns, goose chasing you in a circle. Fail to kiss her. Fail to drape your arm around her willing neck. You are still perfecting your silence. Drop Kelsey off where you found her. Decades later, when you finally sleep with her, she'll reveal how she wanted to bring you home and introduce you to her uncle, the one who liked to bathe her. You were always only minutes away from the split-level colonial where she kept her father's Beretta wrapped in a baby's blanket. You are Danny Riley, virgin.

THE LIEUTENANT

In Bamberg, Germany, discover a love for discipline. Cruise
tanks over Bavarian hills. Assemble an M16A2 with a towel
muzzling your face, tear gas burning your sight. Learn to crack
clavicles and shatter tibias. Hope for a war. Pray to your dead
veteran grandfather. Wake up every morning at 4:30 A.M.—not
to kill or hunt but to help run the military postal system. Under your guidance, care packages and ammunition make their
way to Kitzingen, Würzburg, Ansbach, and Vilseck. You will
be tempted to steal, to profit off your position, but for once in
your petty life you'll pride yourself on your honesty, your
ability to move the mail where it needs to go. This will impress no one. Begin to fear that you might be unremarkable.
That you are not Chuck Yeager or the actor who plays him.
Finish your tour of duty and return home to the States. Four
years later, on a rainy November morning, attend a Veterans
Day picnic. Make note of a familiar face. Lieutenant Arnold
Talon will brag that he pushed heroin and ecstasy through
your Bavarian channels. Nod. Pretend that you knew. Offer
him a patriotic can of Budweiser. Ask Lieutenant Talon what
he's up to these days. When he brags about his life as a military
consultant/mercenary, smile. You are Sergeant Daniel Riley,
adrift/plotting.

THE PROFESSOR

The G.I. Bill means you can take classes in philosophy, bio-
engineering, poetry. You were always a good student. This is

your secret. If you'd had a father or a trust fund you might not have needed the army. Challenge your modern history professor. Claim that the First and Second World Wars are in essence the same conflict. Tell her they should be renamed the European Civil War 1890–1945. Discount the twenty-year cease-fire. Downplay the Treaty of Versailles as just an intermission, a bathroom break during the theater of war. When she asks to see you after class, tell her you're busy, say that you'll probably drop the course anyway. Her name is Dr. Siobhan Porter and even from a distance you can smell the cedar, the juniper, the forests she's splashed on her wrists, her neck. You can see the sparks of blue sequins in her eyes. You could love this woman, but you are not her equal. Recognize this. Allow her to take an interest in you. Impress her with your army German. Your meager Italian. Your memory for military trivia: the Winter War (180,000 Finnish troops recruited; 25,000 Finnish widows created), the Phoney War (2,500 French tanks deployed; 0 German tanks deployed), the Battle of Berlin (280,000 Soviet soldiers wounded; 1 fuhrer dead from self-inflicted wounds). At the end of the semester, Professor Porter will nominate you for a fellowship and though you've never won anything, with her recommendation you manage to score the necessary cash to travel to the Ardennes. Invite her to go with you. When she declines the offer, say nothing. Throw yourself into your research. On a trek between Germany's Siegfried Line and France's Maginot Line, consider the nineteen thousand Americans who died during the Battle of the Bulge. Break the low-hanging branch of a larch tree. Mail your mentor a cluster of golden green needles. Add a note and sign it, Dan Riley, the one who pines for you.

THE FAMILY

When your mother dies a year after you leave the army, use the life insurance to pay for a steel casket, a granite grave marker. Her cancer keeps the casket closed, but you make sure her photograph appears on embossed prayer cards along with an image of a glowing Virgin Mary. In the picture your mother is young, blond but not virginal. Your father, Isaac, a trumpet player you've met twice, snapped the photo. Your mother was pregnant with you at the time. You wonder if your father blew his horn in celebration, in regret. When Isaac dies from an embolism, two years after your mother, you will discover your half brother, Jacob, a man who benefited from your father's music, your father's pious Judaism, your father's love. You are the product of your mother's off-key singing, her passive Catholicism, her loving mistrust. Jacob will give you your inheritance: a Hohner harmonica and a bill for cremation. Be a good son. Pay for your father's ashes and wonder what to do next. You are Danny Riley-Schwartz, orphan.

THE NEMESIS

After the president declares war, pay attention. Know that this may be your chance for advancement. Wait for victory to be declared. Call Bobby Mopes, Brian Chang, your brother Jacob. Ask them to join you in the reconstruction. Bobby will leave behind his new bride, Brian will bail on his stint as a B-movie stuntman, Jacob will say no, then maybe, and finally yes. Arnold Talon has founded his own security company—agree to help him take it international. It's up to you to guard the profiteers—the men who want the oil, the government aid, the democracy. For five hundred dollars a day Bobby and Brian will each drive poorly armored Humvees at 90 mph along the Baghdad Highway as you and Jacob at four thousand dollars a week sweep the scopes on your M4 Carbines. You stop for nothing. On a run to Sadr City, the road before you disappears in an explosion of asphalt and dune. Shoot your weapon into the dust. Breathe in the carbon. You'll wonder why the men who flaunt their rifles in your face decide to kidnap and not kill you. Hug your knees and thank somebody's god that your body wasn't dismembered and set on fire by cheering children. You wouldn't blame anyone for your death. It's your own fault for coming here. Think of Professor Porter. If you were her student now you might argue that there was really only one Gulf War—1990–present. Resist thinking of yourself as a casualty. Remember that you are a former soldier, that you've spent a lifetime marshaling your own troops. This is your American moment. Bobby Mopes will have to die for it to happen, but he's always wanted to die for you. You gave him Operation Overlord and introduced him to his wife, Kelsey. She is carrying their child. If you had a choice you would have chosen Arnold Talon to be the one to perish, but he's too busy, in Dubai, laundering money. The enemy you face wants to videotape a war crimes confession so they can upload you and your pleas for forgiveness. So they can broadcast Brian and Jacob, hooded and silent, over the Internet. You are Danny Shit-for-Brains, an outgunned hired gun.

THE REPORTER

You'll know her name before she shares it with you—an Australian woman showboating for an American network. You've seen her interrogate dictators, commandos, clerics, and thieves. She has a beauty mark on her chin that she conceals with makeup. "This won't hurt too much," she'll say as a stranger attaches a microphone to your collar. Try to learn something from the interview. Wonder what it is precisely that you did. You've always suspected that you might be required to kill. A criminal at heart. You have it in you to slit a throat, bash a groin, murder someone else's child. Let the questions barrage you. Acknowledge all your war crimes, the real and the imagined: confess to paralyzing Jennifer Donner, confess to disappointing your parents, confess to loving no one, confess to loving war, confess to leading your best friend to his death. You were able to escape only because your captors fell asleep. Though Brian Chang and Jacob wanted to flee, you stood over the slumbering body of a boy half your age and noted how he cradled his weapon, noted how his beard hid the split lip of his cleft palate, noted how easy it would be to slip his gun into your own embrace. Feel around your neck for your old dog tags, for your name.

THE BODY

When you kill someone, you feel his life pass through you.

THE LEADER

You don't have a Rat Pack or a Brat Pack or a Frat Pack. Not a Mod Squad or an A-Team. There are no Dirty Dozen, no Ocean's Eleven, no Mercury Seven, no Fantastic Four, no Three Musketeers, no Wonder Twins. Neither a Justice League nor a League of Distinguished Gentlemen. Not even the usual suspects. What you have left is shell shock, a friend with shrapnel, a half brother who regrets having met you, a pregnant widow, a ghost in a wheelchair, a best friend blasted dead by an improvised explosive device, a boss who's managed to escape with your fortune. In another lifetime Professor Porter would have taught you how to tell your story, but what you're left with now are merely fragments. Sharp pieces of metal. Professor Porter is married to a heart surgeon. They have two children. You always wanted to be a part of something. You've spent a lifetime assembling yourself. The second time you met your father he brought you to an amusement park and lost you. You were six. A troop of Campfire Girls found you defeated beside the Sky Wheel. You recognized the power in their numbers, their organization, their uniform. You were grateful that they weren't Girl Scouts or Boy Scouts or Brownies. That they were sanctioned pyromaniacs. The troop leader, an older woman with a shelf of cleavage, told you not to worry. She buried your head in her bosom and you cried over the loss of your father and the pleasure of a stranger's breasts. When the man you'd only twice called Dad finally reappeared, he gave the troop leader ten dollars for her troubles, then whispered to you, "I would have left you to the wolves, Danny, but the wolves said they wouldn't raise you."

THE BUTCHER, THE BAKER,
THE CANDLESTICK MAKER

Margaux Mopes will weigh four and a half pounds when delivered. By the time you hold her, she'll be healthy, plump, and prone to crying. Make this child your own. Tether yourself to her future. You are Danny Schwartz, father/father figure. Sing her every nursery rhyme you know. Wonder how you learned them all. Imagine that your off-key mother taught you "Rub-a-dub-dub three men in a tub." Listen in the hopes that Margaux might sing back to you. Realize how alone you are. Sleep with her mother, Kelsey. Come quickly, then retreat to your side of the mattress. Apologize. In the morning, stand over Margaux's playpen. Tell her that you spent your entire life in search of a getaway driver/a demolition expert/a sharpshooter/a seductress/an inside man/a whiz kid/a kung fu master/a badass motherfucker/a man named "the Wolf." An army to make everything all right. You kidded yourself that you were the man with a plan. Hoping the whole time for a shoot-out, a heist. A score settled. You needed her father, your sidekick, because you knew that you couldn't do, whatever it was you planned to do, alone. Bring Margaux Mopes to the playground. Wipe her runny nose. Hold her as she swings on the monkey bars. Do not enlist her in Operation Overlord. Put away your broken sticks, your borrowed crossbows, send home your tanks and stolen cars. Let the war go on without you.

MERCHANTS

Mr. Cho and I sit before a low glass table. He crunches handfuls of small dried fish that silver-speckle his lips and fingertips. Kettlefish, Juno calls them. Mr. Cho is Jung-Kil and Mrs. Cho is Soon-Yi. I've nicknamed them Killer and Sunny. Killer and I exchange smiles in silence. Juno's parents understand more English than they can speak. This means that if I prattle on about the weather in Portland and my job at Powell's bookstore, Killer, even if he comprehends, can only nod and grin. We pantomime. I signed up for language lessons over a year ago, but Juno made me quit. "Emily, I speak Korean like a ten-year-old," he said. "If you learn, you'll be better than me. That's disgraceful." I told him he was wrong. I thought I would learn just enough to show I cared.

Killer rises and walks over to a large standing globe. He lifts up the northern hemisphere and reveals a bar stocked with Chivas and Johnnie Walker. I've seen this bar globe once before, in the pages of an upscale catalog. That's where I first became acquainted with most of the apartment's furnishings—the vibrating leather massage chair, the brass harbormaster telescope, the lamps with the silver beaded shades. Everything in the apartment is new. The building, after all, is called The Future. Red digital letters blaze the words across the entryway.

Juno likes to say, "My parents live in the future," but more often, he complains about the lack of family heirlooms. Nothing remains from their time in Pusan and Seoul save a few photographs. Nothing from the big move to Asunción, Paraguay, except a straw basket that Juno wove at trade school when he was six. Nothing from the illegal years in America spent working up the East Coast from Disney World to Flushing to Thirty-second Street and Broadway. The neighborhood where Manhattan becomes Korea. Where restaurants serve toasted silkworms and pastry cakes filled with sweet red beans. The Chos own the largest store on the block. They sell discounted electronics, overpriced sneakers, sheets of roasted seaweed, ceramic jars filled with fermented cabbage, vitamins made from shark fins, gold pills that promise to turn shit into gold.

Killer holds up a glass and nods to me. Wrapped snug in a blue silk robe, he's freshly showered and smelling of sandalwood. I shake my head and say, "No, thank you." His hair slicked back, Killer looks like a gangster, and even though I know he has a mistress and that I'm not supposed to like him, his confidence charms me. In South America the Chos lived in a one-room house with a clay floor and traveled around together, all four of them, on only a motorcycle. I picture Killer revving the engine with Sunny seated behind him, their daughter, Yung-Ran, tucked into his lap, and Juno, the youngest, balanced over the handlebars. I think of this father, steady and self-assured, and of the entire family leaning in unison, shifting their weight around winding dirt roads, bodies braced against speed and wind, eyes fiery with dust. If I could talk to Killer, I would ask him how—how do you go from having nothing to being an entire floor of lights on the New York City skyline.

A dozen or more blooming white plants stand guard on various flat surfaces. Creamy hooded creatures with pink freckled faces. Juno explained that orchids rarely have a scent and I laughed, because neither does he. "Even when you sweat, there's no smell. Nothing to remember you by." I think I hurt him when I said this. The truth is, Juno does disappear for me sometimes. Even when he's standing in front of me, I can't always see him. I blame his thick black eyeglasses and the shaggy bangs that fall over his forehead. "You're hiding," I tell him.

Juno's real name is Hooju. As a little boy in Pusan, he was Kyushu to his grandmother. Kyushu means "my little chili pepper" when used affectionately and "cocksucker" when spoken in anger. In Paraguay he was Rico in the hot sun, tanning his skin and rolling his *r*'s. In the States his parents tried calling him Richard, after the great American president, until they discovered that Nixon wasn't so great. For a time he was simply "come here" and "do this" and "stop that." When he turned eleven his parents let him reinvent himself. Juno—goddess of light. "But that's a girl's name," I said when we first met. "Or are you the capital of Alaska?"

Juno enters in Killer's tuxedo, arms locked at his side, feet waddling in his best penguin imitation. Sunny trails behind him, dusting the jacket with a velvet lint brush. A tiny woman with a halo of sable hair.

"He looks great. It's a good fit," I say, smoothing down my cashmere sweater. "Suddenly, I'm underdressed."

"Jealous?" Killer cocks an eyebrow.

"I look like a con man from an infomercial." Juno throws his arm around my shoulder. "You too can have beautiful women."

This is the first time Juno has touched me in front of his parents. I wait for a reaction on Sunny's face and I'm pleased when she reaches for a camera. The flash strobes and I know that in this picture I will tower over Juno like a Polish giantess. His clunky black frames have slid down his nose. I reach over, remove the glasses, and fit them onto my own face. I pucker my lips and kiss my boyfriend's cheek. Sunny laughs, cupping a hand over her mouth to hide her dentures. Killer stands before me, bows, and lifts the glasses from my ears. He turns to Sunny, holding up his son's nerdy frames. I know what will happen next. Sunny doesn't want to wear the glasses, and she raises the camera in protest. A flash. Killer, all smiles, coos a coaxing phrase in Korean. He tries to force the glasses on over Sunny's head, and in the struggle the nose rest twists and snaps, leaving two halves.

Amid the shouting and hunting for tape and glue, I feel responsible. "I'm sorry," I tell Juno. He palms a lens and grinds the glass into the corner of a dark marble table. I hear a splinter, then a crack. Juno lifts his hand and brushes sparkling shards across his jacket sleeve. Small red cuts appear across his skin, and Juno raises the bloodied palm to his mouth, sucking on the heel of his thumb. He looks at me then closes his eyes and says, "They've been acting like children."

Without his glasses, Juno cannot see. He might as well have cataracts, glaucoma. "I'll be your eyes," I promise. He stumbles into his shoes, and I sense that he doesn't want to leave his parents alone. Sunny helps me into my wool coat and says, "Tomorrow we go for soup."

"It's a Korean thing," Juno explains. "A New Year's soup for health and luck."

"Sounds great." I lean down to hug Sunny. Her arms and back are solid muscle. On Thirty-second Street, she's feared. Juno claims that the other merchants call his mother "the Dragon Lady," the woman fellow shopkeepers approach for loans. For this reason, she has no friends of her own. Most days she comes home from work, cooks Killer's dinner, cleans their clean apartment. As we leave I watch her clear Killer's plate of kettlefish and refill his whiskey glass. She props his feet up on a pillow. Around her neck, she wears a chain of repeating diamond stars.

Everyone likes Juno. My coworkers call him easygoing and tell me that I'm lucky to have found such a nice guy. He's forever inviting new friends over for dinner, disappearing into our kitchen, searing yellowfin tuna and roasting red peppers, while I take stabs at entertaining strangers. Athletes, mostly. People Juno meets in the park playing Ultimate Frisbee. Tall white lawyers and computer jocks who try cajoling me into their sport, not realizing that I am independent, cynical: a girl with no interest in games. Juno hardly speaks to his new friends, preferring instead to serve them lavish meals and accept their compliments. If I weren't dating Juno, these men might think of me as loud and arrogant. With Juno as my boyfriend, I am a nice girl. Sweet, even.

On our way down in the elevator, I ask about the building's name.

"When it was built, they touted it as the most modern co-op in the city."

"Call something the future, and then the future's already passed."

"You know, my dad wanted to live on the thirty-third floor because he and Mom had been married that long. A year for every floor. Now he tells me he's moving away. Moving in with his mistress. Maybe go back to Korea."

"It's just a midlife crisis," I say.

"You know what I think. I think he's finally become an American."

The party takes place in a private bar beneath a restaurant. A speakeasy run by Juno's childhood friend Ray Kim. We make our way through the darkness, guided only by swinging strands of ruby lights beaming off brick and concrete. A live band plays bad guitar. The crush of bodies bouncing makes the floor shake. Juno hasn't seen his friends in over a year, so I give him time alone to catch up with his buddies. I wander, drink in hand, amid sleek Asian women, testing my skill at a game Juno calls "Chinese or Korean?" Back in Portland at the bookstore, Juno would quiz me on the ethnicity of customers, laughing at my attempts to identify shiny-haired girls as Thai, Filipino. After several tries I defended my failure by pointing out that I couldn't tell a German from a Swede. Juno replied, "You could if one of them was your enemy."

At the party, Juno neglects to introduce me to his friends and none of the women approach me. Even so, I'm happy being the only white person until this blond guy wearing a bolo tie sidles up to me and kisses my ear. "Happy New Year," he hollers. I'm stunned, as much by the bolo tie as by the kiss, and the stranger, sensing my confusion, leans in and says, "It's all right. I'm with her." He points to a short woman—Vietnamese, I think—her cleavage showcased in a tight orange evening gown.

"It's awesome, isn't it," the cowboy says. "To be with someone who can make you feel exotic."

"I wouldn't know."

"But aren't you with that little guy?" He nods toward the bar where I see Juno holding court over a row of spiky-haired Koreans.

I feel incriminated by Cowboy's whiteness. He may feel like some rare exotic bird, but to me, he looks like a target. Cowboy begins to shadow me, so I escape to the bar.

Ray Kim plays bartender, pouring champagne into plastic flutes. As I approach, he says, "So, Emily. I got a question for you."

"Don't start." Juno's face has turned red and blotchy from the alcohol.

"What is it?" I ask.

Ray says, "I have this theory. White women your age date Asians for two reasons: they've dated them before"—he pauses—"or they're crazy."

The Korean boys make spinning loco rings with their fingers and slap Juno on his back. A challenge has been issued.

"What if I told you that I, too, was Asian," I say. "I have a Mongolian patch."

"What is she talking about?" Ray hands Juno a fizzing glass.

"On my ass. I have a small blue birthmark. Shaped like a horse. That means I'm a Mongol and I conquered your people in the thirteenth century."

Ray laughs. "She's crazy, all right."

I take the champagne glass away from Juno. "Dance with me," I say.

On the empty dance floor, I twirl my boyfriend dizzy until he begs me to stop. I drape my arms around his shoulders. *He's blind,* I think and steal a good hard look at him. His eyes have glints of orange, and his lips are full and pillowy. Across the room I see the Vietnamese girl. Her round face and pale skin suggest to me that she is half white. I think of the child that I see some nights sleeping between Juno and me. A little girl with thick black hair, a small flat nose, and maybe nothing of mine except the way she kicks the blankets in her sleep and snaps her tiny teeth. He's the first man I've thought to have a child with. I want her to come true. I tell him, "Let's get out of here."

We walk up a set of stairs to a vestibule and then, just like that, I have Juno against the wall. There are doors on either side of us, but I don't care if someone walks through. We'll have to sleep in separate rooms tonight, and I want this now. We kiss, and I pull Juno around so that he's covering me against the wall. I reach in under his cummerbund and stroke him. I unzip my pants, but I have tights and thermal underwear on, and there's no way to get to me through all that silk and wool. Juno gently lifts my hands away from his chest and groin. Still I continue. Then a door opens, a throat clears, and Cowboy says, "Showing off your Mongolian patch?" He and the Vietnamese woman push through the exit, blasting us with cold air.

"It's all right," I say.

"No." Juno shakes me off. "You are too much. There is too much of you."

I learn that New York City cabs are scarce on New Year's. We begin to walk the twenty blocks home. I'm cold and hungry and I beg Juno to stop in a café. He strides in front of me, angry and silent. I'm worried he'll run off and leave me stranded. I try to latch arms, but he pulls away. Finally his blindness catches up with him. He trips over a rough patch of cement and sprawls to the sidewalk, landing on his hands and knees. I lean over to help. As I pull him up, the pebbles and grit on his palms press into mine. I ask, "Why are you mad at me? What have I done?" I say that everything will be better, once we get back to Portland, once he leaves his parents behind. "I'm not going with you," he says. "I'm not leaving."

The first night Juno and I slept together, he told me that his sister Yung-Ran, or Anger, as I call her, had been raped as a child in Paraguay. Before I could say how sorry I was, Juno lit a cigarette. He smoked and described how his turn to be raped came in America. It happened early in the morning, on the roof of a row house in Queens. Juno was ten. The white man was tall, with blue sneakers. "When it was over, I couldn't explain to my mother what had happened," he said. "I wanted to. I didn't have the words. Not in Korean or in Spanish or in English. I didn't have the words for *ass* and *bleeding*."

Had Juno told me this story before we dated, I might have

been afraid to touch him. Had he preferred to wait for a few months, I might have feared that I'd been touching him all wrong. But since he shared the story during our first night, I never had an opportunity to worry. Maybe his pain made me love him a little more. Maybe his pain made me want to protect him.

Juno has told me other stories about his family and moving and always being poor. He's called himself an immigrant, a fresh off the boat—FOB—and he's taught me things. Like how to season a slice of cantaloupe with black pepper, how to throw a Frisbee into a breeze and have it come back to you, how to make a bed while you are still under the sheets. I wouldn't say that any of it felt exotic. In exchange I told him stories about my family and growing up a different kind of poor. My mother bought all of our clothes in thrift stores. Our shoes, even. When I needed a pair of snow boots, Mom purchased an old set several sizes too big. She wrapped empty bread bags around my feet to keep them dry, and stuffed more in the toe to fill up the difference. Roman Meal bread bags. I remember the plastic wrap's emblem, a man with a sword and a shield. My sacred family crest.

I tried to convince Juno that we shared a history in common. My grandparents had owned a store as well. A Polish bakery.

"That's not the same," Juno said. "My parents are merchants. They sell anything. They're always trying to sell something."

Back then, Juno was waiting to hear from medical schools. When he didn't get into any, or at least not the ones he'd hoped for, he quit his job at Powell's and moved in with me. His parents started sending him monthly checks.

"It's for med school," he said.

"But you aren't going," I said.

"They know that."

Later on, Juno explained the principle of *kibun*. In a Korean family, every effort is made to maintain harmony and a sense of well-being. The way I understood it, his parents were helping Juno save face. When Juno's parents realized he'd been raped, they brought him to a doctor. The doctor sewed him up. Then his parents took him to the zoo. Juno still remembers how the animal smells made him sick. The fur and the sawdust and the shit. But his parents bought silver balloons and pointed at polar bears and took pictures of their son petting a goat. A family in a zoo is normal and safe.

Juno wants his parents to divorce. That's what he told me the morning we arrived in New York. We went to the shop and I watched Sunny sell thousands of dollars' worth of video equipment. She is the brains behind the business. Killer stood alone, relegated to the back of the store by the stereo speakers, smoking a cigarette and staring at his own image in a security monitor. I imagined Killer together with his mistress, a middle-aged Korean woman he'd met on a business trip. I liked that she wasn't some young thing. What bothered me was his carelessness. According to Juno, his father charged expensive gifts on his Discover card and made daily phone calls to Korea, knowing that Sunny would tally the bills and see the invoices. Watching Killer puff smoke rings, I shared his desire to be caught.

In bed one night after sex, Juno peeled the yellow skin from an Asian pear, sliced the fruit, removed the core and fed me slivers. The fruit was all crispness and water. Later I found a box of pears in our refrigerator, each plump fruit wrapped in a special white-netted holder to shelter the skin from bruising. I stole several that day, sneaking a pear each day after, until Juno found me emptying the carton. "Those pears cost two dollars apiece," he informed me. Was that just pettiness on his part? I replaced the missing fruit, not letting myself eat another pear and wanting more.

Even though we are still several blocks away, I can see the red lights of the Future. Juno tells me that his decision to stay with his parents is final. I walk ahead of my blind man and duck into a coffee bar. I find a table. Juno sits at the table next to mine. He rubs his eyes and holds his head in his hands. The café is empty. One of the waiters mops the floor around us. I play with the raw sugar packets.

"I have to take care of the family." Juno touches my arm. "My mother needs me."

"Your mother is stronger than all of us," I say.

"Then I need to be away from you. There's so little of me. I know your face better than my own."

We order coffee, and the waiter brings us free almond cookies. The coffee is bitter, and the cookies are hard and stale.

"Emily, you have no idea how difficult it is for me just to say words. I'm never sure about the tense, the emphasis. I learned how to talk to you by watching your favorite movies."

No one has ever said a sadder thing to me. I get up only to sit down again.

"Emily," Juno says, "you think we're the same, but we're not. You weren't poor like me, and you aren't afraid like me."

"I can't believe you're staying here," I say.

"My family is breaking up."

"It's not," I say. "I've seen your mother. She won't let that happen."

Back in the apartment, there is evidence of a fight. Two of the orchids are overturned. Patches of soil stain the carpet. In the kitchen sink I find an empty wine bottle and a shattered goblet. Juno begins to clean up the mess and then stops himself. In the dark I can see the broken flecks of glass that he brushed into his jacket sleeve. He reaches out to touch my cheek but settles on my shoulder. "I care for you," he says. I think of all the things he cannot tell me. When he leaves the kitchen, I do not follow him.

I wait until Juno has washed his face and gone to bed before wandering into the living room. Even though it's after midnight, the red and green lights of the Empire State Building are on, and I think of the Korean word for chili pepper. *Kyushu.*

I head over to the bar globe and I find Korea. Before Juno, I thought Korea was an island in the South Pacific. I run my finger over the cracked map paper, past a saffron Thailand and a yellow Indonesia. I note the distance between Borneo and Burma and realize that I would have placed them much closer together. Following the northern polar pull, I discover Korea above Shanghai, a peninsula attached at the shoulder to China, a barrier between the Yellow Sea and the Sea of Japan. I shiver and look up to see Sunny standing before me in silk pajamas. She holds out a blanket. "My house is cold," she says.

The building sways. I have never slept this high up and been part of the sky. I want to tell Sunny this, and other things, too, but I worry that she won't understand. Then I decide that "son" and "love" are words she knows. I'm ready to declare myself when Sunny makes it easy for me.

"You like Juno?" she asks.

"Yes," I say. "Very much."

"Juno is soft. Not like his father. Or me."

"He looks like you," I say.

Sunny has worn her diamond necklace to bed. The gems are her own fortune. Even though we have just met, I know that I will miss her when I leave and that I will miss her always for being part of Juno.

"Tomorrow," she says, "we will find luck. Oxtail soup."

Sunny is promising me magic. I want to believe her. In two days I will leave New York without Juno. He will stay and take care of his parents' marriage until it too turns to ruins. We will not call or write each other.

Five years will pass before I see Juno again, and then, only by accident. He'll spot me outside a bookstore in San Francisco, and though both of us will say hello, neither one of us will cross the street. A young Korean woman will be at his side, and I'll wonder if she is Yung-Ran, Anger. I'll be wearing a pink dress with white flowers, and even though I'll be alone, Juno will know by the bottle of wine I swing in my arms that I am on my way to meet someone. This will happen. There is nothing more I can do.

Sunny shows me to the place where I will sleep. Halfway down the hall she reaches out and fits her hand into my palm. Her fingers, curved and held together, feel like a fish. I close myself around her, not wanting to let go.

SORRY, YOU ARE NOT
A WINNER

Matt parades around his fortieth-floor apartment decked out in tight red boxer briefs, his naked chest, limbs, and face coated with a glossy emulsion that's gradually darkening his skin from winter white to a tropical shade of orange. "Dazzle and shine, Genie," Matt instructs, as he snaps the straps of my denim overalls. His girlfriend, Jordan, traipses about the apartment in a paper bikini and coconut bronzing gel. I watch her reflection in the dirty windows as she twists and knots her shimmering black hair high up on her head. Jordan pursues her boyfriend from kitchen to wet bar, her makeshift ponytail fluttering and flinching like a crow's broken wing. She whispers to Matt in her forceful baby voice, loud enough for me to overhear, "Cinderella can't come to the ball."

On this Saturday afternoon in April, I'm busy washing Matt's windows, polishing the glass interior with vinegar and the Arts & Leisure section of the *Times*. My client and his girlfriend have just returned from a preparty tanning session upstairs at their swanky health club. They are sticky and glistening. As far as code names go, Cinderella is an ironic one for me. From Matt's bedroom, I can glimpse the primeval penthouse where I grew up. I can point to the rooftop garden where I spent my childhood evenings smoking hash, aiming water balloons at strolling lovers, and threatening to jump. At sixteen, I dated one of the princes of Thailand, modeled Ralph Lauren formal wear for *Town & Country,* blew my French teacher on Tuesdays and fucked my drug dealer on Wednesdays. The summer between my junior and senior years of high school, I reached the status of class legend by running away to Bangkok on my mother's American Express card. Now, at twenty-six, slender and full of regret, I take care of my dying, impoverished parents and clean apartments for the nouveau riche. I barely warrant an invite to one of Matt's trendy dating parties.

Jordan bounces over to me and I get a good look at her disposable bikini. The bandeau top and high-cut bottom are constructed from a heavy waffled tissue. The same tissue that's used to make the hospital gowns I laced my father into five days a week for six weeks during his radiation treatment. If I wasn't her boyfriend's cleaning lady, if she and I were equals and friends, I might tell Jordan about my dad, about the brain tumor that smoldered, undetected, in his frontal lobe for almost a decade. About the years he spent estranged from his family, dissipating our wealth. About his subsequent, penniless return. I might tell her about the seizures, the craniotomy, the Gamma Knife. If she were my friend and not my boss's lover, she might say, "How awful for you," and then reveal some noteworthy tragedy of her own. A brother lost to schizophrenia, a sister dead from self-inflicted wounds. Something terrible to bond us forever.

Jordan inspects the windows and says, "Genie, be a good Eskimo and run out for some ice."

"The caterers are bringing bags and buckets." I claw my fingers through my spiky hair. "They might even chain-saw a frozen swan."

"Caterers always promise more than they deliver." Jordan steals my spray bottle and sniffs the air. "Why does this place smell like coleslaw?"

"Vinegar," I say. "It makes the windows gleam."

"Matt." Jordan laughs. "She's douching the apartment."

Jordan is a real estate broker. She sold Matt this corner of high-rise about a year and a half ago. Seduced him with the sunken living room, the floor-to-ceiling windows, the unobstructed views of New Jersey. On the day they closed the deal, she asked him out. Matt likes to joke that Jordan uses her job to screen potential boyfriends: "I hadn't paid for the first date, and already she knew my net worth and my earning potential. She ran a credit check before she ever said, 'I love you.'"

Matt owns and runs an upwardly mobile social club called Friend of a Friend. My boss claims to have invented the group date. Instead of matching people up individually, Matt emphasizes the cluster dynamic—meet as many people as you can before pairing off. Members pay an exorbitant sign-up fee for the privilege of spending more money to attend champagne tastings at the Rainbow Room, guided tours through the Museum of Sex, touch football clinics in Central Park, or tonight's event: a Connect Four tournament.

Matt busies himself setting up card tables while Jordan positions the yellow slotted game traps on their blue stands. Twenty or more elite professionals will be arriving shortly to compete for the title of reigning Connect Four champ. When Matt graduated from Dartmouth, his father handed him a cigar box loaded with cash. Four tidy bundles worth ten grand each. A note inside the box read, "That's it. No more." Matt plowed through a stash of money that summer: bankrolling a fraternity brother's foray into professional wrestling, squandering a small fortune on laser hair removal, splurging on a Tahitian snorkeling adventure. One night in Tahiti, Matt bought a round of mai tais for a team of scuba divers and a squad of internationally ranked lady surfers. As Matt watched the hammered divers lick body shots off the sporty surfers' chests, he realized that what he truly enjoyed in life was introducing one set of friends to another. Bringing strangers who belonged together, together.

Matt extended tonight's Connect Four invitation to only his most attractive and successful clients, reassuring all of them that their challengers would be equally gorgeous and ambitious. "Rich people," he reminds me, "love to play games. Especially Connect Four. It takes them back to their childhood."

I restrain myself from suggesting more appropriate diversions: Risk, Operation, Life.

Matt was my first. Searcy Lighthart, a former best friend from my formerly prosperous life, set us up. I was nineteen, temporarily fatherless, a high school dropout in need of a job. Searcy could have helped me directly, could have given me money and never missed it, could have insisted her own father create a comfy post for me at his public relations empire. Searcy who taught me how to shoplift designer cosmetics, how to diet with chocolate-flavored laxatives, how to insert jumbo tampons. Searcy who totaled my Saab on our way home from the Head of the Charles Regatta. Searcy who owed her enviable reputation to rumors I'd spread about her fellating one of the Beastie Boys. Searcy, who claimed she would always be there for me, told me she thought it would be best if she didn't help directly. "This way you won't feel like you owe me."

Searcy knew Matt from weekends in Bridgehampton. His social club was just getting started. Searcy thought I could assist around the office, answering phones, charming prospective members. Unfortunately, Matt had already hired a busty receptionist from Queens. Still, Matt was willing to help his summer fling's best friend. When Matt asked me what skills I had to offer, I quickly surveyed the messy confines of his Park South workplace, picked up a stack of invoices, and lied: "I'm obsessive-compulsive."

In the past seven years, I've cleaned Matt through three apartment upgrades and two office spaces. In turn, Matt, my accidental fairy godfather, has set me up with my own roster of cleaning clients. I work almost exclusively for unmarried businessmen. Grateful slobs with no shame. Men who don't bother tidying up before I come over. With rare exception, the guys I've worked for are far too preoccupied to scrutinize and critique my cleaning. Often, too inattentive to flirt. While on the job, I make myself plain—beige clothing, no makeup, minimal chatter. My clients want two things from me: order and invisibility. The relationship between a man and his maid must be, for him anyway, low maintenance.

I never work for professional women. They are too demanding. Whether single or married, women feel guilty about hiring help, and, in turn, compensate for their guilt with criticism. The women I've worked for claim that if they had the time to clean up after themselves, if they weren't so busy marketing and launching, supervising and demoting, then they would certainly do a better job of housekeeping than I ever could. Women insist I purchase and use organic disinfectants: cleansers that cost three times as much as my favorite chemicals. Women buy me special grout brushes. They demand I use Q-Tips to dust the accordion pleats on their lampshades. Women think they can teach me how to make a bed.

When I tell people I'm a maid, their first response is almost always, "But you're white." I explain that because I'm white I can charge more for my services. A lot more. White people will spend a great deal of money to have another white person clean up after them. The money I earn pays for my parents' medical bills, for private nurses with lilting Jamaican accents. Some days I'll vacuum in front of an audience of former classmates. I'll start sweeping the kitchen linoleum only to have my client's girlfriend show up to inspect my work. Soon, she's on her cell phone gossiping, "You'll never guess who's over here cleaning my boyfriend's apartment. Remember Eugenia Bigelow, yeah Genie, the would-be princess? Well, she's here right now, wielding a mop."

"What color am I?" Matt holds out an arm for Jordan's inspection.

"You're all streaky," she says. "You're like a giant dirty carrot."

Matt's face and entire body are darkening in comic, uneven swirls. The party is only a few hours away.

"I was going to wear short sleeves." Matt turns to me. "What should I do?"

Jordan folds her own coppery arms across her chest and gives me a look, daring me to solve her boyfriend's latest problem.

"Vinegar gets out almost anything." I pick up my spray bottle. "I can wet you down and Jordan can rub you clean."

The three of us convene in the bathroom. Matt stands in the tub, holding court, describing his visit to the high-tech tanning box while I douse his face and arms. "I went into this closet and it was just like a car wash. All of these nozzles and hoses moving up and down spraying this caramel-colored mist."

Jordan nudges me out of the way and begins to swab baby wipes over her boyfriend's forehead. "Did you rub the cream into your skin?"

"Wasn't I supposed to?" Matt asks.

"The spray needs to dry evenly on its own." Jordan inspects the skin on her arms and tummy. "Does my fake tan look natural?"

I sit on the toilet and watch the happy couple.

My parents met on a blind date. They were set up by a mutual friend who mistakenly believed that my father, Oliver, loved opera and that my mother, Sheila, could have been a great singer. The friend gave my future parents his own private box at the Met, never guessing that the sleepy couple would abandon *Madame Butterfly* at intermission to catch a late-night showing of *Rosemary's Baby*. My father was a budding real estate mogul. During the scene in the movie where Mia Farrow has sex with Satan, Dad gossiped about the film's setting, the Dakota apartment building, and detailed how none of the residences received enough light. Oliver had gotten rich buying up old warehouses downtown and turning them into fancy artists' studios. My father insists he invented the loft space. When I was little, he'd take me with him through the narrow gallery-lined streets of SoHo pointing out buildings he owned. "That one's yours," he'd tell me. "Better than any dollhouse." Back then, my brawny father had silky, auburn hair, but in my memories, I see him then as he is now: frail, bald, a crescent-shaped scar carved into his skull.

At the time they met, my mother didn't have cirrhosis of the liver. Her nose and cheeks were not marred by ruddy tributaries of broken blood vessels. My mother did not slur her speech or fall on her ass after three tumblers of gin and tonic. My mother never passed out at five o'clock in the afternoon, only to wake up howling and hung over by ten o'clock at night. That evening at the opera, the cirrhosis that she didn't have had not developed into inoperable hepatocellular carcinoma. When my parents met, Sheila was narrow waisted and raven haired. She lived with her family in Tuxedo Park in a mansion my father worshipped. With her brazen good looks, her athletic prowess, and her working knowledge of French, Spanish, and Italian, my mother might have been a corporate spokesmodel, a professional golfer, a translator at the UN. Her parents had protected her from ever having to work. Dad proposed after their third date.

In the bathroom, Jordan continues to wipe Matt down as his skin becomes red and irritated. "Genie, we need some space," she says without a glance in my direction.

I leave, closing the door behind me. The outdoor window

washer is late. If he doesn't slide down on his silver cord with bucket and squeegee in hand, the view of Jersey City will be hazy and smudged tonight. All my work will have been for nothing. I stack the red and black Connect Four game pieces that Jordan has left strewn about the coffee table. This game is not strategic like chess or nimble like checkers. It lacks the elegance and simplicity of tic-tac-toe. I think about the witty comments I might make tonight, if Matt invites me to his party. I could tell jokes about my family's housekeeper, Esmeralda, who insisted on scrubbing our floors with juicy halves of tangerines. Esmeralda dusted the bookshelves and mantels with old pairs of my father's silk underwear. She perfumed every drawer in our home with sachets of sandalwood. Even the knife drawer. When I was little, I would shadow Esmeralda with my own miniature broom and dustpan cleaning up the thin line of debris she could never quiet sweep away. I think about myself and how I'm an erratic cleaner, how I sometimes fall asleep while folding laundry. How I often spend hours on a client's couch watching his cable TV. How I pocket loose change and sample leftover Chinese noodles right from my clients' refrigerators. I think about my parents and how I've caught Mom stealing Dad's painkillers. Pilfering opiates from the man she once loved. Then I hear them. Jordan and Matt are fucking in the shower.

I still need to vacuum Matt's bedroom. The Dirt Devil drowns out their sex. I leave the machine on even after I've finished. The engine blare masks the shudder and squeak as I open Matt's sock drawer and reach deep into the back corner. The little black velvet box I pull out hasn't moved since the first time I found it, nearly three months ago. I snap open the lid and there she is: a two-and-a-half-carat emerald-cut diamond set in a sleek platinum band. The ring has weight and heft. This is not a trinket. This ring is serious business. I slip the bulky band onto my finger and speculate. What makes a man buy an engagement ring and neglect to ask the requisite question, "Will you marry me?"

I've learned a lot about people from straightening up their messes. Not from snooping. From cleaning. I'm half forensics expert, half intuitive gossip. After careful examination of his bed linens, I've surmised that Matt's emergency method of contraception is withdrawal followed by ejaculation onto a pillowcase. Having vacuumed under his bed, I know his private stash of longings include *Volleyball Goddess, Fortune* magazine, and *Shaved Asian.* In light of his recent requests for unscheduled cleaning appointments, coupled with the long curly blond hairs I've found on the sheets and in the bathtub's drain, I am certain that Matt has been aggressively cheating on Jordan.

I don't clean for Jordan, so I don't know her that well. We banter and snipe, but in truth, I kind of like her. She's tough, smart, and works in the same business my dad did before he decided to leave my mother. I was seventeen when my father fled to the West Coast and bought a failing vineyard in Sonoma. He ran off with a woman he'd met the one time he accompanied me to my orthodontist's office. His mistress had an overbite. Her name was Gloria Tepperman. Their affair lasted for nearly three years, until one day, as Gloria put it, "Your father came home from San Francisco wearing an orange bedsheet." For a week he ranted at Gloria about the Three Marks of Existence, the Four Noble Truths, and the Thirty-seven Factors of Enlightenment. My undiagnosed brain-tumored father decreed to become a Zen Buddhist monk.

I hear the bathroom door swing open and I look down at the diamond ring on my finger. The ring is slack and wobbly. My mother sold her own wedding bands a few years after my father left. She pawned the gold settings first, then the stones, neither for what it was really worth. I'm annoyed at Matt and Jordan for fucking within earshot. For making me feel like the hired help. It occurs to me that I could return Matt's ring to its hiding place or leave it out for Jordan to see. With one careless gesture, I could force a discussion that would change their lives. I shove the velvet box under a pile of black nylon socks, then slip the engagement ring off of my finger and into the pouch pocket of my overalls. For safekeeping.

Matt comes into the bedroom freshly showered, a bulky towel around his waist, the skin on his face, arms, and belly a slightly lighter shade of orange, the clear amber of a plastic medicine bottle. I turn off the vacuum cleaner.

"Genie," he says, water beading down his chest and legs, "I really need you to stay for the party."

"The vinegar worked." I hand Matt a fresh new T-shirt.

"Our real problem is Jordan. I can probably put some makeup on my face and wear a long-sleeved shirt, but Jordan got stained. Her skin looks like someone marinated her in soy sauce and roasted her over an open flame. She's on the phone right now threatening to sue the health club."

I motion to go help, but Matt blocks the door. He snaps the white T-shirt over my head and belts it around me, drawing me in close to his wet chest. Matt lowers his voice. "Be my date tonight."

I've slept with Matt off and on throughout our years as boss and cleaning lady. Sex with Matt is sporting and competitive, like we're each fighting to see who can take more pleasure away from the other. Though Matt prefers me to pivot and pitch on top of him, I like it best when his heavy muscular body is weighted against my thin frame, when I feel a little crushed and pinned down. While I have almost no desire to be his girlfriend, and while I can't imagine being anyone's wife, when Matt bites my neck and squeezes my ass, I feel less like a housecleaner and more like a home wrecker.

The intercom buzzer sounds off.

"That must be the caterers," I say, pinching his right nipple and backing away.

"Be my date." Matt pulls the T-shirt over his head, the bright white clashing with his bronze face. "When was the last time you treated yourself?"

I catch myself saying, "I have nothing to wear."

"Jordan has clothes. Borrow whatever she was going to show off. We'll have fun." He smiles. "I'll introduce you to some great people, and if you tidy up a little before you leave, it'll make cleaning tomorrow easier for you."

A year before Dad deserted Mom, I went to a Valentine's Day party and met the prince of Thailand. The prince attended the same prep school as my drug dealer. After selling me a bottle of baby aspirin filled with lavender quaaludes, my dealer introduced me to his Royal Highness. Earlier that evening, Searcy Lighthart had attacked my hair with a crimping iron. The prince, fascinated by the wavy pattern, asked, "May I touch?" I sat beside him on a velvet love seat as he examined my feathery hair, testing the softness between his long thin fingers. The skinny prince wore a tailored red jacket with overstuffed shoulder pads and an embroidered royal crest. I imagined a toy crown covering his lustrous blue-black hair. As the quaaludes sang their sweet song to me, the prince spoke in a quiet halting voice about his love for American music: "Your rockabilly, and your punk, but most of all I dig the heavy metal. Americans make the most beautiful noise." I nodded in agreement. He hadn't stopped stroking my hair. The prince and I smoked cigarettes wrapped in gold foil, and just when I thought he might bow his neck to kiss me, the prince asked if I'd come listen to him play electric guitar at his school's spring talent show.

The prince and I never did much more than make out and hold hands. Early on, I tried to show him my breasts, but he wouldn't touch or look at them. "You are too precious to me," he said as he worked the pearlized buttons on my blouse back into their holes. For his love, I mostly stopped screwing around with my dealer and my French teacher, having grown out of the role of teenage slut and into the near drama of palace concubine. The prince consistently rejected the hands I placed on his thighs and groin. "We don't need that yet," he'd say, forcing down his erection. Though we went on dates to Eurotrashy nightclubs, the prince mostly just wanted me to hang out in his school's music room and listen as he played Metallica covers with Imelda Marcos's grandson and Baby Doc Duvalier's nephew. Preferring me as an audience, wishing not for a kingdom of subjects but for an adoring crowd of groupies. I was the one who named the band the Benign Despots.

The theme of Matt's dating party is Indoor Recess. Catering waitresses in schoolgirl uniforms—tight white blouses and microminiskirts—twirl trays of oversized cookies and midget cartons of milk spiked with Kahlúa. Peanut butter and jelly finger sandwiches compete with smoked salmon pizzas. Matt has replaced the architecture magazines on his coffee tables with nursery rhyme coloring books and sleek tins of crayon pencils. He's propped a sizable chalkboard against the mantel to keep track of the Connect Four tournament results. Matt has also set up individual games of Battleship, Hungry Hungry Hippos, Masterpiece, and Clue. He's lowered the lights to conceal the bright glow of his tarnished tan. In the spirit of the party, many of the female guests have worn their hair in loose braids or pigtails adorned with grosgrain ribbon. None of the men bothered to costume themselves. The women resemble grade school coquettes, while the men in charcoal suits and business ties could easily pass for their doting fathers. Jordan is hiding her discolored body in Matt's bedroom. I adjust the flimsy straps on the pink-and-green Pucci sundress she grudgingly loaned me. I am an imposter.

The first Friend of a Friendster I chat with, a redheaded corporate raider, asks me right off what I do for a living. I say, "I clean up other people's messes."

"Oh," he replies, "so you're like a bankruptcy lawyer."

I explain that I literally clean apartments, that I'd cleaned this one just today.

"I have a maid," he says. "Mine's a live-in. Fabulous woman named Yvette. She used to be a journalist in Haiti. Do you know her?"

What I like most about my job is that I get to spend so much time in lavish apartments pretending that I'm home. Early on in my career, I'd bring my mother along, settle her down into a comfortable recliner, pour her a vodka and tonic, and hand over the remote control. I knew if she was able to drink and watch travel adventure shows in a setting similar to her own lost penthouse that she would never have to fully come to terms with her missing husband. Sheltered in our borrowed residence, we could both pretend that we were waiting for Dad to barge through the door, plotting to take us out to a revival showing of *Rosemary's Baby,* a bouquet of downy peonies cradled in his arm, a kiss for each of us.

There are forty-two holes in a Connect Four game board—seven across and six down. My strategy is to flirt with my male opponents and outmaneuver my female ones. I prefer to go first, controlling the center, but I can win as easily from the number-two position, building up from the sides and trapping my opponent. I'm especially adept at something I call the Pyramid of Victory. Two diagonal lines of four that meet in the middle to form a triangle. An upside-down V. So far, I've beaten the vice presidents of two competing cable news networks, a balding geneticist, an heiress to a frozen-dessert fortune, a recently divorced state senator, and a former Miss Westchester County. I've managed to make it to the semifinals. My next challenger is Searcy Lighthart.

Of all the debutantes I grew up with, Searcy is the third to become a handbag designer. She fashions leather and vinyl into revolutionary versions of the rectangle, the square. Searcy has invented something she calls "the grab bag," a variation on the clutch purse. Each of these soft leather purses has a one-of-a-kind secret treasure—Tibetan prayer beads, a freeze-dried seahorse, an antique decoder ring—sewn into a concealed pocket of the lining. On certain afternoons, I've found myself in Bergdorf's inspecting the grab bag display models, fingering the hidden seams. Searcy is the first of the pocket-book baronesses to position herself as a lifestyle guru. We haven't spoken in five years. Not since she asked me to wait tables at her father's sixtieth birthday party.

Tonight, my former best friend wears a white backless apron top with a plunging neckline. An embroidered trio of ripe cherries blossoms over her left breast. Her skin is expertly artificially tanned. Searcy twists a ringlet of curly blond hair around a finger and says to me, "I'm no longer limiting myself to accessories. I'm thinking clothing line, morning talk show, an appointment as a goodwill ambassador. But first, I'm working on a perfume. It's all about branding an image."

The longer Searcy speaks, the lazier her left eye becomes. It's a minor flaw, imperceptible to a stranger. I see it only because I know her so well. When Searcy was ten, she had an operation to fix the wandering eye. She had to wear bandages, a patch, blurry goldfish-bowl glasses. The operation had limited success. As Searcy brags about her dominance of the Asian markets, I watch her one imperfection list and loll.

"What you need," I say, "is the right scandal. A sex tape. A media embarrassment that will launch you into Middle America's lap."

"Any specific suggestions?" she asks, rubbing the lucky cherries on her chest. "Advise me, my scandalous friend." Searcy drops a black disk into the blue frame, blocking my victory pyramid.

"I have my own empire to worry about." I bare my teeth in a showy grin. "Plenty of money to be made in filth."

Searcy demonstratively rolls her eyes and wags a manicured

finger at me. "I love how you managed to stay in this world. I would have just married someone. But you built a real business. I'm proud of you."

Matt sends a miniature Nerf football spiraling past Searcy's head.

"He's such a prank." She toasts Matt with her Kahlúa milk carton.

Matt waves and gives us the thumbs-up. Years ago, when Searcy first introduced us, she bragged about my own notoriety. "She's the Genie behind the Genie Job." Matt laughed. A girl I'd gone to junior high with had secretly taken a snapshot of me and given it to her plastic surgeon. My narrow, tapered nose was her ideal, and she convinced the doctor to model her own new nose after mine. The operation was a success and soon other girls requested the Genie. The plastic surgeon got hold of my phone number and asked my mother if he could make a plaster cast of my face. I obliged. On seeing me, Matt gave me a quick once-over and said, "I think I dated someone with your nose."

Earlier tonight, I called my mother to tell her I'd be back late, to let her know that I'd arranged to have her dinner delivered, to remind her to check on Dad. When I asked how she was doing, she said without irony or self-pity, "I'm always dying." Then she added, "I hope you didn't order Thai food." I left high school three months before graduation in order to take care of my mother, who was suffering from severe liver damage. That was nine years ago. Right before he left us, my father confronted my mother about her drinking. Mom bellowed back, "I drink because I'm lonely. I drink to bring the day to an end. I drink because our daughter's a whore. I drink because my husband ignores me." My father calmly replied, "You drink because you're an alcoholic."

My father returned home after almost a decade of drifting, bringing his orange robes, his clay Buddhas, and his diagnosis. A brain tumor was the primary cause of his personality transformation. It seems obvious now that there was something medically wrong with Dad, but at the time, my mother maintained that his affair and, later, his meditative monk shtick were just pathetic attempts to stay out of jail. There were questions about Dad's business dealings. Mom had to answer all of them alone. She was forever bankrupted by his disappearance.

Out of loyalty to Mom, I rarely bothered to contact Dad. I kept tabs on him through Gloria Tepperman, until Dad came under the influence of a charismatic monk, a tiny scoundrel who forbade my father from communicating with his family. If I mentioned Dad, Mom would say, "He is dead to us." When I told Mom about Dad's cancer, that it was nearing stage four, that there would be an operation and radiation, but that his condition had gone undiagnosed for too long, she got up from the comfort of her own deathbed, poured herself a shot of Absolut and joked, "So, he means to upstage me."

Searcy and I are well-matched competitors. She wins the first two games, I take the next two. By the fifth and final bout, I know all her weaknesses. She can't anticipate my next move, or set up an ambush for me to fall prey to. She stubbornly attempts to pile up towers of four. A small crowd of onlookers forms to watch us. I wonder if anyone will meet the love of his life tonight. It occurs to me that Matt might still set me up with a worthy guy, or that perhaps he simply wanted to bring Searcy and me back together. Matt is forever grateful to me because I came up with the name Friend of a Friend. His business used to be called Love Made Easy. Prospective clients would mistake it for an escort service. As I cleaned his office that first day, thankful for the chance to work and earn my new living, I commented on the fact that while close friends like Searcy rarely offer life-changing help, acquaintances like Matt were often willing to throw their support behind people they hardly knew. "A close friend can't stand to see you succeed, while an acquaintance enjoys taking credit for your success. It's my friend of a friend theory," I said. Matt smiled, grabbed me around the waist and kissed my rouged cheek. "That's our new name," he said. "A best friend will never hook you up with a great love, but a friend of a friend can help broker a lasting connection."

Searcy fluffs her blond curls and I realize that she is literally responsible for the clumps of hair I've collected from Matt's drain. They are screwing around again or maybe their love affair is more serious. Maybe she's the reason behind the engagement ring. I'd been kidding myself that Matt had some small intention of springing a proposal on me. "You are the only person who can give me what I need," I imagined him saying as he knelt on the bamboo floor I'd just finished polishing. Of course, I still would rather have a prince. Someone to rescue me. There is no way I'm letting Searcy win. As I drop the plastic disks into their chambers, I connect my own chains of four. "*Rosemary's Baby*/my parents/sex/me." "Me/Searcy/Matt/Jordan." "Matt/Jordan/engagement ring/mistress." "mistress/

orthodontist/my father/cancer." "Cancer/my mother/loneliness/ me." I can connect anything.

For my final victory over Searcy, I orchestrate a blatant four down, right in the center column of the board. My enemy never saw it coming. I tap the line of triumph and whisper to Searcy, "For my sake, next time you fuck Matt, change the sheets."

Searcy tosses her blond mane over her shoulders. "Like you've never slept with him." She narrows her eyes. "Personally, I think he's cheating on all of us: you, me, Jordan. I think the only thing he truly loves is being a matchmaker."

"What do you love?" I ask.

"I love flying first class on someone else's dime." Searcy smiles and leans in close. "I love the power I have over older men. I love losing weight without trying. How about you?"

I gaze into Searcy's imperfectly focused eyes and smile. "My work," I say. "I love taking care of people."

Searcy pulls Matt away from a game of Pay Day with Miss Westchester County. I wonder why my former best friend didn't bother to ask about my parents. Searcy always loved the way my mother would sneak us maraschino cherries, dredging the vermouth- and whiskey-soaked fruit from the bottom of her Manhattans. Searcy used to call my father deadly handsome and joke that someday she would be my evil stepmother. I turn my back on the party. If there is one thing I'm good at, it's washing windows. The outside window washers came through for me after all. Through the highly polished glass, I can see the party's mirrored reflection. So many couples have united to flirt and tease. The frozen-dessert heiress brushes her bare shoulders against the state senator and challenges him to a

game of Boggle. A well-dressed fat man plays Chinese checkers with a pair of advertising vixens. The handsomer of the
two TV vice presidents bets a sexy catering waitress that he
can eat all of the cookies on her tray. Nothing will come from
these brief encounters. Maybe a few weekends in Montauk,
or even a trip to the Berkshires, but nothing that will lead to
happiness.

I look down at Jordan's Pucci sundress. The expensive
swirls of pink and turquoise remind me of a child's abstract
drawings. We are here tonight, all of us, pretending to be kids.
I want to shout at Matt's party guests, "Why aren't you at home
taking care of your parents?" Why aren't these healthy children
playing gin rummy with their alcoholic mothers, or helping
their skeletal fathers into flimsy pajamas? Why aren't they sort-
ing Tegretol and OxyContin into plastic containers labeled
with the days of the week? Why aren't they kissing night
sweats off their mothers' foreheads or holding their fathers after
a grand mal seizure? Why aren't they researching the sowing of
radioactive seeds into brain tissue? How many of them even
know what palliative care means? Why aren't they watching
their parents sleep?

I lose in the final round of the Connect Four tournament
to a green-eyed magazine editor who wants to write a story
about my life. "You were practically an heiress, and now
you're a charwoman. I bet we could sell the film rights." He
keeps toasting me with his wineglass and praising my self-
sacrifice. "You gave up college, a career, any future of your
own, all to keep your parents from self-destructing. Horatio
Alger in reverse. A life of luxury squandered. Do you even
have time for a boyfriend?" Just when I'm convinced that he's
hitting on me, when I begin to plot the menu for our court-

ship, my editor asks how much I charge for a house call, and whether I'd be willing to come over next Thursday to dry-mop his hardwood floors. When he mentions Murphy Oil Soap and asks for tips on removing beet juice from Formica, I figure that it's time for me to leave.

Matt shakes the journalist's hand and makes a grand show of presenting my rival with a towering gilded trophy. As the members of Friend of a Friend cheer, Matt kisses my ear and whispers, "I forgot to get a consolation prize."

The party dissolves and I make a halfhearted show of chucking milk cartons, coloring books, and broken cookies into a Hefty bag. I stick the Hungry Hippos back into their box and close the hard plastic lids on the Battleship games. Matt escorts Searcy and a few other guests down to the lobby.

When I go into Matt's bedroom to change out of my borrowed party clothes, I find Jordan, wearing a white nightgown, clutching my overalls to her chest, examining Matt's engagement ring. Her flesh is shiny and brown like the toasted skin on a Peking duck.

"Sorry," she says. "I just moved your clothes and it spun out of the pocket. I had no idea you were getting married."

"It's a nice ring," I say. "You can try it on if you'd like."

Jordan hops onto Matt's king-size bed, fanning her body over the satin comforter. I kneel on the mattress and slip the ring on Jordan's wedding finger, rolling it, with difficulty, over her knuckle. She admires the sparkling stone, holding the diamond up to the light. The ring is too tight on her.

"I apologize for being an idiot earlier," she says. "It's not that I didn't want you here tonight, just that I knew Searcy was coming. Matt's hoping you two can be friends again, but I've heard the way that woman talks about you. It isn't right."

"I can handle Searcy." I climb off the bed. In one swift motion, I slither out of Jordan's dress, hugging my tiny breasts. Jordan does not avert her eyes but rather surveys my body for age and imperfection. I give my ugly stepsister what she wants, unshielding my arms as I reach for my black tank top, slowly stretching the shirt above my head and over my teardrop tits. I turn and give her a good look at the taut muscles of my lower back, my smooth thighs. Cleaning keeps Cinderella in shape.

Jordan says, "Searcy only cares about money. That's why she makes purses. She doesn't understand that luck can change. Look at me." Jordan waves her lacquered arms. "I'll probably have to miss work on account of my failed tan. I'm actually supposed to sell a building your father used to own."

I pull on my overalls.

"You know," Jordan says, "I'd love to meet him sometime, pick his brain about the business."

"Jordan, his brain has already been picked."

As Jordan realizes her mistake and slaps a hand over her mouth, I tie my sneakers and get my bag.

"Tell Matt I'm furious." Jordan stands up. "He never even bothered to check up on me tonight."

"He was working." I wonder if Matt is downstairs, fondling Searcy. I pause and turn around. "Is Matt a good boyfriend?"

"Is there such a thing?"

"There might be," I say.

"I'll tell you what he does that I hate. He fucks me in his sleep. I'm serious. In the middle of the night, he'll roll over on top of me, screw me, and not even wake up."

"Zombie lover. That's a new one."

A moment passes between us, and Jordan who grew up in

Kearney, Nebraska, Jordan who was the first person in her family to attend college, Jordan who has no birthright to her fancy job or to the disingenuous world she's entered, Jordan raises her scorched arms over my shoulders, squeezes our bodies together, and gives me her interpretation of a hug.

Jordan twists the engagement ring off. "Don't forget this." She places it in my palm. "You never told me who the lucky fellow is."

The metal is warm from Jordan's body and I know that if I steal this ring from Matt, a part of my life will be over. "I used to date a prince. A long time ago. This was his promise to me." I tuck the ring into my pocket.

I take the subway back to Brooklyn, to our brownstone in Fort Greene. My mother bought the nearly derelict building when she couldn't afford to keep our penthouse, when she couldn't pay the back taxes on the mansion in Tuxedo Park, when the banks and lawyers who claimed my father owed them money threatened to take everything. The neighborhood wasn't much then, but now it's hip and the renovated brownstone is worth three times what she paid. My father praises Mom on the foresight of her investment. But mostly, they don't talk, at least not in front of me. Dad and I share the ground floor. Mom moved up to the second in protest when Dad returned. Sometimes, I'll come home early and catch my mother downstairs heckling a bad movie on the Lifetime network with Dad asleep by her side. It took my parents' dying to bring us home together.

For patients who are nearing death, my parents are both pretty healthy. Mom still leaves the apartment to stretch her edema-swollen legs in the meager asphalt park across from our home. She eats five small meals a day and alternates between gin and vodka. She quotes her oncologist: "Some people with liver cancer feel entirely well." Dad still meditates. We'll walk our neighborhood, his orange robe twisted and saronged around his wasted body, and he'll tell me how much each building was worth back in 1976. Some people with brain cancer feel entirely well. My parents' doctors have told me that nothing more can be done. Their diseases cannot be cured.

When I ran away to Bangkok, I never expected my parents to follow me. They'd been split up for months. Even as a small child, I'd often encouraged my parents to divorce, convincing them individually to seek legal counsel, cheering on his threats, her allegations. For my part, there was a certain element of sport involved, a desire to see how far they'd take the frenzy. Before their split, I was unaware of Dad's infidelity, and when I ran away to Thailand, I had no idea that a tumor was slowly altering my father's temperament, his sense of smell and balance, his sex drive. As a teenager, I mocked the sad sight of my father as he ranted about real estate conspiracies, insisted that something was burning, and tripped over his own feet. Back then, I believed in always having a good time. My parents weren't having one. Divorce was my mantra. I goaded them on.

Three months after my father abandoned us, the Benign Despots were out late one night after a gig at a club on the Upper West Side. The prince had invented a fusion of new age, funk, and speed metal he called Buddhist Discord. As the boys cut through Central Park, wired from their performance, hoping to score a drug that would help calm them down, they were approached by three men, two of whom had knives. Baby Doc's nephew handed over his TAG Heuer watch, the Marcos grandson gave up his gold money clip, but the prince being the prince refused to surrender his Stratocaster. Chose not to empty his pockets. The muggers, disappointed with their take, threatened the prince with their serrated weapons, and when he did not waiver, stabbed him. A dozen slicing blows over his beautiful slim body, the body I was not permitted to explore or touch. As his friends stood by, my prince bled to death on the great green lawn of New York City. One of the muggers pulled the prince's nylon wallet from the inside pocket of his red crested jacket. This man tore open the Velcro closure to discover five dollars and a picture of me in a bikini, tan and happy. So much for once upon a time.

A century ago, the kings of Thailand were allowed to marry and bear children with as many women as they pleased. Consequently, the current royal family is overrun by hundreds of lesser princes and princesses, sired by distant cousins to the reigning king. I didn't know this then. I thought my prince was the king's own son and I assumed his tragic end would make the headlines. I imagined that as the official girlfriend, I'd be interviewed by the *Post,* flown over at the kingdom's expense, and treated, during the funeral, like a noble widow. The prince's father, a second cousin to the king, was the black sheep of the royal family. He tried and failed to be the first person to export rare Thai orchids to America. He then unsuccessfully attempted to invent the world's first Zen travel agency. I never met the man, but his business dealings, like my own father's dealings, were highly suspect. He paid the bare minimum to have his son's body flown back to Bangkok without fanfare or accompaniment.

Searcy convinced me to run away to Thailand. She sympathized with my loss at first, but then she grew bored by her own show of empathy and dared me to steal my mother's credit card and jet-set away. I was in a rage of mourning, unable to catch my breath, clutching a pale green Lacoste polo shirt I'd stolen from the prince's dorm room. Searcy ordered a car service and rode with me to the airport, convincing me that I was on a quest, that my prince would want me there at his funeral. Back then, I knew nothing about Buddhist burial ceremonies. Had no idea that I was supposed to bathe my prince's scarred body and decorate his coffin with paraffin candles and sage incense. I was unaware of the many days the mourners spent lingering beside the coffin in the prayerful company of monks. Or that during the final procession to the crematorium, how I could walk slowly, clasping one of the many long white ribbons the singing monks had secured like arteries, lifelines to the prince's coffin. Someday, I will do all of this for my father.

My mom could have thwarted my plan by canceling the American Express card I stole from her sharkskin wallet. I chose the Amex because I knew it had no limit, because I wasn't certain how long I'd be gone, and because I figured when I did return I'd placate Mom with the argument that I'd added enough frequent traveler miles to her card for a first-class upgrade. The trip would have paid for itself.

When I arrived in Bangkok after a twenty-six-hour flight with a layover in Taipei, I was struck by the speed of life, the rapidity of foreign speech, the relentless clattering traffic. Buzzing motorcycle taxis cruised the airport, picking up trusting backpackers. I paused outside the airport terminal, unsure of my next move, terrified to negotiate with a cabdriver, afraid that I might simply turn around and fly back home. Then I saw a white van, a hotel shuttle. I did as my prince had always told me to do and went straight to the Oriental, "the greatest hotel in the world." My mother's dwindling fortune would save me from any misadventure. The driver maneuvered through the frenetic expressway, dodging three-wheeled open-air *tuk-tuks,* taking me deeper into the city of modern glass towers and ancient golden temples. I tried to imagine my calm prince negotiating this madness. On our approach to the hotel we drove beside the Chao Phraya River, blue longtail boats floating calmly in the water. I pictured my prince sailing past me, waving his hello, his good-bye.

The lobby of the Oriental was magnificent, white marble floors, chandeliers like crystal birdcages, an endless pool of lily pads and ginger-colored lotus flowers. I've never quite recovered from that opulence. I checked into the Joseph Conrad suite, where the legendary writer may or may not have stayed. My room was dominated by a teak, curtain-draped four-poster bed. Like a cursed princess I slumbered for two days, dreaming of having jet-lagged, drowsy sex with murdered royalty. My plan, after I'd first smoked a long pipe of opium, was to storm the palace and demand an audience with the king and queen. I wanted them to know how much I'd loved my prince, how I was haunted by the sensation of his hands fluttering over my hair, the feel of him buttoning and rebuttoning my clothes. I felt as though there was something here for me to claim. When I woke up, my prince was still gone, but my separated and bickering parents were standing over the hotel bed, each holding a different guidebook. My dead rock star prince bringing us all together. "So," my dad said, "what do we hit first? The Buddhas or the baby elephants?"

Some days, when I'm cleaning, I'll begin my shift by imagining that I am boarding a plane, a train, or a bus. I consider how far I could travel in the time that I have to scour somebody else's disaster. I've made it to the customs desk at Heathrow, to the drive-thru at the Canadian border, and as far as the eroding beaches of Cape Cod. I've cleaned my way to the West Coast, down the Mississippi, and over the Atlantic. My imagination takes me as far as the journey, but I never actually daydream my way into a vacation. I've never made it back to Thailand. Years after my prince died, I followed a story in the newspapers about an elderly Thai prince who lost his life when his young bride poisoned his coffee with insecticide. The princess, whom everyone called Luk Pla, or Baby Fish, had been adopted at age four by a thirty-five-year-old prince nicknamed Than Kob, or the Frog. Before marrying her, he put her to work as his housekeeper. After years of abuse, the Baby Fish poisoned her Frog in order to be with her true love, a poor chestnut seller. Proving that there are all types of fairy tales. Any number of willing or unwilling princesses.

I often blame my trip for triggering something in Dad. Our first day together in Bangkok, we went to the Wat Pho temple, the oldest and largest of all the Buddhist temples, home to the giant reclining Buddha with his golden plaster and his enormous inlaid mother-of-pearl feet. We stood before this statue, the three of us together holding hands. The sideways Buddha, pausing on his way to nirvana. The temple was filled with young holy men, their heads newly shaved, their starved bodies seated in prayer. Dad joked that I might find a new boyfriend among these monks. "True believers," he said. "They seem like nice enough guys." My mother turned to me, still holding Dad's hand. "We're going to punish you later," she said. "But for now, we should enjoy our family vacation."

On my way out of Matt's apartment building, I run into Searcy and my boss in the lobby. The night deskman looks the other way as Matt presses Searcy up against the granite wall, squeezing the cherries on her skimpy blouse. I ignore them, but they call out to me.

"There's our girl," Searcy says. "Isn't she something?"

"She's the best," Matt chimes.

I move swiftly to the revolving door before turning around to face my master and his mistress. "Who would have ever guessed," I say, "that I'd turn out so well."

When I get home from Matt's party, my parents are asleep in the living room—one ghost on either end of the outdated Ultrasuede couch. The blue glow from the television makes their jaundiced skin look healthy and tanned. Each one breathes in his or her own distinctive heavy wheeze. I don't want to wake them. As difficult as life has been with my parents, I keep waiting for the moment in this fairy tale when everything goes decidedly wrong. When my father's organs begin to shut down, when my mother slips into a coma. They will die soon, I know, and then my life will begin. I'll be awash in medical debt and life insurance benefits. Their deaths my legacy.

I collapse onto the couch between my mother and father. Their decaying bodies throw off heat and the familiar, pungent reek of vinegar. I reach out and lift their hands, the ones closest to me, resting their palms in my lap. If I knew any prayers, we could pray together. My father knows many prayers. He will sometimes sit cross-legged on a small cushion in the middle of this room chanting a low sweet song. My mother knows how to plead. She will sometimes beg me for hours and hours to buy her booze. I take Matt's ring out of my pocket. This engagement ring was not meant for me or for Searcy or for Jordan. The ring slides on smoothly and fits my mother's finger. Neither too tight nor too loose. In the morning, I will tell her that it is a gift from Dad. That he's always wanted her to have it. My father will smile, unsure if I am lying. As a child, I was always lying.

I should carry my mother up to her apartment and settle my father into his bed. *Not yet,* I think. *Not yet.* This is what I have been looking forward to: the brightest part of my day. I am tired now. I could rest here.

AFTERNOONS IN THE
MUSEUM OF CHILDHOOD

The chatty concierge who checked us in last night bragged about the hotel's indoor pool—the largest in all of Scotland. I woke up early to investigate the deep emerald waters, the spring-action diving board, the arched glass atrium. I couldn't escape our suite. Dad snored, stretched out on a cot he'd wedged against the door, still fully dressed in gray trousers and an argyle sweater. My vigilant, slumbering bodyguard. All morning, through the room-serviced scrambled eggs and the bad British television, I've been camped out in my turquoise two-piece begging my parents to let me swim. I'm the only one who packed a suit. Mom dials the front desk desperate to speak to anyone who can hunt down a size-sixteen Lycra tankini. I smile and tell Mom that she can watch my butterfly stroke from the comfort of a lounge chair. She bites her blistered lips and shakes her head. "No, Amanda," she says, afraid of what might happen if she isn't in the water with me. Afraid that I might dive under and disappear. I need Mom and Dad to let me out of their sight, to forget the brainwashing, and to accept that the man who calls himself Messiah can no longer harm us. Dad holds up a pair of dark blue boxer shorts and asks, "Can I get away with these?"

Scotland in January was my father's idea. According to him, Mom and I are here to relax while he does business with a biotech company—the one that cloned a sheep. In truth, we are hiding from the cunning photographers, the prying journalists, and the handsome man who kidnapped me.

The elastic in my bathing suit pinches my waist and digs into my shoulders. The suit is from two summers ago. I've grown almost five inches in the time I've been gone. I have breasts. Hips. My voice has lowered from soprano to alto— from melody to harmony. I've gotten my period. When Dad came to the police station in Tucson to identify me—alone so Mom wouldn't get her hopes up—he didn't recognize his elder daughter. Not at first. He didn't run, tearful and expectant, into my arms. He restrained himself and studied my round, curvy figure, made note of the worry lines etched into my forehead. He wanted to be certain I wasn't a hoax, and so I let him look. I knew he was my dad despite the thin thatches of silver hair that fell over his eyes, despite the layer of stubble that shadowed his gaunt cheekbones. Before my disappearance his hair had been thick and brown, his face soft and full. Dad asked, "Is that you?" Asked, "What's our dog's name?"

"Wylie," I said. "Like the coyote."

The cops exchanged nervous glances, waiting for Dad's response.

"Good girl." He leapt forward, pressing me into his chest. "Forgive me for doubting."

I told my hysterical father that he smelled like cigarettes.

"I had to do something while you were gone." He then broke the news that Wylie, my Alaskan husky, had been run over by a well-wisher. "We'll get you a new dog."

More than nine months ago, I was abducted from our home in the desert. Stolen from my bedroom while my parents nodded off to Jay Leno, while my little sister Belle dreamt in our top bunk bed, while I fidgeted at my computer desk, patchwork plagiarizing an essay on *Dr. Jekyll and Mr. Hyde*. I was fourteen. Within the first month of my disappearance, I was as famous in America as those celebrity teenagers whose dyed platinum hair matches my natural blond, the ones who sing and dance like sexy robots, the ones whose posters my sister Belle fun-tacked to our walls. My friend Trisha has described how the tabloid news replayed home movies starring me petting a llama, playing the cello badly, and dancing on a pink beach in Nova Scotia. Mom insisted that Larry King stop broadcasting a clip of me in a diaphanous nightgown opening Christmas presents. The white lace and cotton too risqué. I was gone but I was everywhere. Gracing the cover of *People* magazine, featured on Nancy Grace, prayed for by the president at the National Prayer Breakfast as he led his fellow sinners in morning grace. Sea-World sponsored a Find Amanda Stevenson Day and circulated postcards of me holding a plush toy manatee. According to Belle, I was deemed too important for a milk carton. When I turned fifteen, five months into my captivity, the entire state of Arizona celebrated my birthday with a candlelight vigil. America loved me and wanted me home. I was never an international story.

Morning turns into afternoon and we still haven't left the hotel suite. I change out of my bathing suit and ask if there is any hope we might see the city.

Mom looks at Dad and shakes her head. "Your father has to meet with his cloners."

Dad and I laugh, but Mom misses her own joke.

"Can't I go with you, Dad?" I ask. "Or can't we all go together?"

"My meeting is top secret. The company is hidden out in the countryside. I have to go alone."

My father is a geneticist and a businessman. He believes in mapping genes and making money, and the life he has created for us is a good one. When I disappeared he didn't mess around with meager sums. Though the FBI warned him to start small, right away Dad offered a hundred-thousand-dollar reward for information leading to my return. Arlene, the single mother of three who eventually spotted me shopping in Bashas' supermarket in Carefree, Arizona, claimed she recognized me by the mole, what she called the beauty mark, above my lip. She told my mother that I looked angelic in the boxy blue-and-white pinafore Messiah insisted I wear. Arlene made it clear to both my parents that I had been sent to her by the Lord himself, and that she was Christ's own messenger ordained to bring me home. Then Arlene asked my dad if any portion of the reward might be issued in cash. She won't get paid in full until Messiah is convicted. Arlene saw me that day in Bashas' only because I watched her slap her youngest son in the face after he snapped open a tube of Poppin' Fresh dough. As I helped clean up the mess of spongy lard, I considered telling a grocery store cop that a woman was harming her child.

The three of us take the elevator down to the lobby to wait for the private car that will shuttle Dad to his meeting. The desk clerk on duty, the same one from last night, wears a bright red uniform with epaulets and brass buttons. He looks ready to invade a nation. Instead, he waves at me.

"Did you fancy our pool?" he asks.

"Still no luck with the swimsuit." My mother smiles and pulls at my arm. She has gained over fifty pounds since my abduction and I'm not used to the feel of her fleshy swollen hands.

Outside, a black Mercedes with tinted windows waits for my father. We kiss him good-bye and watch as the driver secures a black blindfold around my father's eyes.

"Security precaution," the driver says. "We can't have anyone knowing where the compound's located. They'd blindfold me too if they could."

"How do I look?" my father asks.

"Handsome," I say. "Like a handsome hostage."

My father's jaw drops and I think of a ventriloquist releasing his dummy's mouth.

"We'll see you at dinner." Mom helps Dad into the car, guarding his head from the doorframe. Dad has arranged for us to dine at an inn where our ancestor, the writer Robert Louis Stevenson, once lived.

As we watch the Mercedes pull away, I know I have only a moment to convince Mom to ask the doorman to hail us a taxi, to sneak us off into the city. To make a break for it. When she demurs, I say, "We don't need Dad." I smile and wrap my arms around her thick waist. "You can protect me."

The cabdriver explains that Edinburgh was built on a volcano.

"That's why she's fiery and full of force."

All the ornate buildings seem to be covered in a layer of volcanic ash.

"It's soot. From burning coal." The cabbie offers to drive us around the city, to give us the royal tour.

"Do you want to see the castle or the palace?" my mother asks.

"I want to see the volcano," I say.

The castle sits on top of what is now a very dead and indiscernible volcano. The reddish-brown walls of the fortress match the rocky cliff it's built upon as though the whole walled compound and all the buildings were carved from this stone. The view from the top is vast, breathtaking. I imagine that a person could spot an enemy approaching from miles away. The cabbie offers to stop, to let us out, but Mom orders him to keep driving.

"It's a tourist spot," she leans in whispering. "An American might recognize you."

"What's the difference between a palace and a castle?" I ask my mother.

"I think a castle is a kind of military fortification and a palace is where the monarch lives."

"What would you rather be?" I ask. "A palace or a castle?"

"After what we've been through"— she looks at me, tucks

my hair behind my ears—"I think I'd be a castle. One with lots of guards and secret passageways."

I shake my hair loose and pull several long strands across my face. "I'd prefer to be a palace."

Messiah claimed that he was building a temple in my honor. Even when the police arrived in their bulletproof vests, when they shocked him with their Tasers—in front of me so that I'd know he'd done something wrong—when one jackbooted cop kicked him in the stomach and another in the head, he called out to me, "I'm building you a temple. We'll be safe."

My mother decides that we ought to buy Belle a gift. I ask if I can pick out something for my friend Trisha. Of all my friends, Trisha is the only one who doesn't treat me like I'm haunted or fragile. She's not afraid to call me a bitch or point out that my right breast is smaller than my left. If I ever reveal everything that happened with Messiah, it might be to Trisha. She deserves to know.

The cabbie offers to drive us to a shopping district called the Royal Mile.

"Best place for keepsakes," he claims.

Belle is staying with our grandmother in Scottsdale while we're here in Scotland. The only person in our family who didn't change while I was gone was Belle. She stayed small and elflike. She still wears her auburn hair in long beribboned braids. Still insists on eating only yellow foods—chicken fingers, macaroni and cheese, corn on the cob. She still begs me to play with her unicorn collection while she croons the same Disney songs about failed princesses and sinking mermaids.

During our trip, I've considered hurting my mother with the irony that she'll happily abandon one daughter in favor of another. "Belle could be stolen too," I keep myself from saying. But there is something fearless about Belle. No one would dare take her. She's like those dreadful Disney heroines she admires so much. If someone held a knife to her throat, she'd kick and sing, punish and convert her attacker. After all, Messiah had a choice between the two of us and he chose me. I'm not even sure he had a knife.

As we sit in traffic, I notice that the buses in Edinburgh don't advertise TV shows or perfume or sporting equipment. All of the buses are black and red and along the side of each bus are different messages in bright white letters: z, ZERO TOLERANCE, and MALE ABUSE OF POWER IS A CRIME.

"What do they mean?" I ask the cab driver.

He looks out the window at the buses. "You'd have to ask my wife."

The main streets along the Royal Mile are a narrow hilly maze with even narrower, steeper side streets. The storefronts decorated in bright cheerful blues and purples. As we leave the safety of our taxi, Mom takes my hand and guides me as though she knows where we are headed. My mother was once a college psychology professor and she still has a studied authority. A few days after my return, she tried to explain to me about brainwashing. She promised me that even girls who score in the ninety-eighth percentile on their PSATs might fall victim to mind control.

Messiah warned me about brainwashing. He told me not to trust anyone who would use that word. He explained that the brain is a delicate organ but one that cannot feel pain or emotion. He insisted that he could open a hole in his skull, stick a knife down into the gray matter, and the tissue would feel nothing. The brain would not respond. But if he plunged a knife into his own chest, the heart would writhe with jolts of pain. "It's your heart I'm after, not your mind," he'd claim.

Mom pulls my wrist and says, "Let's not get lost."

For Belle's souvenir, we choose a store that sells crystal figurines and wind chimes. My mother scans the aisles in search of the perfect unicorn. The shop reeks of patchouli and vanilla. I'm surprised to see a young woman, with hair hennaed just like Trisha's, smoking behind the register. She sees me stare and holds up her pack. "Want a cig?" she asks. I nod and take a slim brown cigarette. "They're vanilla flavored," she says. My mother is at the very back of the store by a shelf marked BONNIE BARGAINS. I have terrible asthma and my eyes swell from the sweet stench, but I need this. Messiah used to burn vanilla incense when we prayed.

Outside, a canopy of black clouds threatens to rain ash. Pedestrians dash under shop awnings. Across the street a large metal sign with the silhouettes of a boy and girl running hand in hand swings wildly, creaking in the wind. I ask the cashier, "What's that?"

She lights my cigarette. "It's the Museum of Childhood," she says.

I inhale the smoke and cough. Without begging for my

mother's permission or telling her where I'm going, I exit the store and run out into the dark rain.

Admission to the Museum of Childhood is free. This is a good thing because I have no money. Even if I wanted to make a real break for it, to hop a plane back to Arizona, to find the federal prison where Messiah is held, to beg for his release, I couldn't afford to. According to the pamphlet the elderly tour guide hands me, the museum was the first of its kind to be dedicated to the memory and idea of being a child. Glass cases crammed with injured tin soldiers, derailed toy trains, abandoned teddy bears line the walls. Rows and rows of naked cloth and porcelain dolls stare out from dull glass eyes. A crime scene of nostalgia. I'm impressed only by the dollhouses. Large cabinets of miniature life. Inside each dollhouse are families of figurines interacting and leading their own simple lives. Making beds, taming rocking horses, tuning toy pianos. I wish I could shrink myself down and disappear into one of these worlds.

My freedom is short-lived. I'm standing in front of the most impressive dollhouse when my soaking wet mother takes me by the shoulders and shakes me.

"How could you run away?" she asks.

For a moment, I think she might strike me. Part of me wants her to.

"Didn't you hear me?" I lie. "I said that I was going across the street. I came to find Trisha a gift."

Rain drips off of my mother's eyelashes. She takes a deep breath, closes her eyes.

I feel her body count to ten.

"I thought you heard me," I hear myself say. "I thought you said it was okay."

"What is this place?" Mom spins around, spraying drops of water.

"It's a museum for people who want to remember their childhoods."

My mother stares at the enormous dollhouse. Inside the home a tiny father pours his daughter tea. The card beside the dollhouse describes how the home was built by a bachelor cabinetmaker to advertise his business. He had no children of his own.

"It's sort of scary," she says.

"Yes," I say. "Who would want to remember any of this?"

Mom and I walk over to a case that holds a giant automaton dressed as a dentist. The mechanism keeps the dentist's hands moving as he hovers over his patient, a small child.

"I need to know," Mom says. "You have to tell me what that man did to you."

The caption for the automaton reads OPEN WIDE.

My mother asks again, "What really happened?"

I could tell her what she fears. That I went with Messiah because I wanted to. That I'd met him a week before the kidnapping when Trisha and I ditched school to shoplift Mother's Day presents from the Galleria. That we made him buy us hot pretzels and smoothies. That we joked he looked like Elvis. Messiah claims all of this. Claims I told him where I lived. That I left the downstairs window open for him.

Or maybe Mom is asking something else. Maybe the psychologist in her wants me to describe how Messiah spoke about God as he slowly lifted my pinafore over my head. I could tell her how terrifying it was the first few times. How I got scared and anxious. How I cried when it hurt, and it did hurt. If I thought my mother really wanted to know, I would explain how the rape became routine, the way I imagine sex in a marriage becomes tedious, perfunctory. How at nights, after I made Messiah dinner, after he complained that I only seemed to know how to cook yellow foods, I would think, *Not this again*. What I can't tell her is how I learned to coach Messiah, to coax his fingers into touching and rubbing me. How over time, I managed to take control. Teaching him to slip his tongue inside of me so as to stop the sound of his preaching.

"I'm okay, Mom," I say. "I'm sorry you didn't hear me."

The worst thing about being the miracle child, the one who returns from the scene of the crime, is how easy and dull coming home becomes. Half an hour after my reunion, I was already restless. As happy as I was to see my family, I could not give them all they needed. I couldn't make myself appear and reappear for them. My return was magic but I myself was not dazzling, not magical. I wanted to sleep, to watch television, to be left alone. Only Belle seemed to understand this. Only Belle is not interested in what happened.

I used to think Messiah was sexy. With his jet-black pompadour, his full red lips, he was my Elvis. I had no idea that he dyed his hair. I know this now from seeing him in his orange prison jumpsuit with his ashy gray mop. He looks ruined and this makes me think of how he's ruined me. How a part of me wanted to believe that I was truly chosen.

The cab ride to the restaurant is long and quiet. We are driving toward the coastline and I open a window to breathe in the salt air. Mom shows me the glass horse she bought for Belle.

"It's not a unicorn, but the ears sort of blend together to make a horn."

"It's nice," I say. "She'll like it."

"We should have looked for a department store. For a place that sold bathing suits."

"It's okay, Mom," I say. "I don't have to go swimming."

"Do you remember," Mom asks, "how when you first learned to swim, you begged me always to take you to the community pool?"

"Did I really?" I ask. "You know I don't remember much from before."

My mother wraps her fake unicorn and puts it away. The harbor opens up before us and in the distance I can see a long suspension bridge.

"We went swimming almost every afternoon. I taught you the breaststroke."

"Sounds like a nice memory," I say.

"Maybe you're lucky for not remembering. Some people spend their whole lives trying to recover from their childhood."

"That was mean," I say.

"I'm sorry." My mother looks out the window at the blue-green water.

"No, it's a good sign," I say. "If you think you can be mean to me then maybe the next step is letting me go."

"I'm learning to," my mother says. "I'm slowly learning how to let you out of my sight."

The Hawes Inn is not as posh as Mom had hoped it would be. The outside is all whitewashed walls and dark beams while the inside is decorated with faux antique bric-a-brac—spinning wheels, lanterns, horseshoes, a flaccid set of bagpipes.

"I wanted Amanda to have a nice meal." My mother puts down the menu. "Not this pub grub."

"It's fine," I say. "I've never eaten under a bridge before."

The inn is tucked underneath a famous bridge across from a famous lighthouse.

"We're on the Firth of Forth," my father says as he finishes his whiskey. "Or maybe it's the Forth of Firth. Just a fancy way of saying we're by the North Sea."

From the pub's front windows we have a view of an orange sun descending over the dark wine harbor. The lighthouse strobes its beam into the rising night.

Dad asks how we spent our afternoon and though I'm prepared to lie, Mom isn't.

"We had an adventure," she says. "Took a tour of the city."

"See anything good?" Dad asks.

I describe the castle and the volcano. Mom mentions the museum.

"It was for adults, really," she says. "A museum of childhood but not for children. I think Amanda was frightened."

"Were you?" my father asks.

"Frightened?" I can hardly believe they would think this. "I've seen worse."

The waiter brings Dad his fish and chips, warns Mom that her chicken potpie is very hot. He serves me a grilled cheese sandwich and smiles. I smile back. He has pock-pitted skin and crummy teeth, but he's tall and I like that men seem always now to notice me. He brings me extra lemons for my Diet Coke.

During dinner Dad can't stop talking about how he can't talk about the cloners.

"There's so much I wish I could tell you both, but I signed a dozen nondisclosure agreements. They'd kill me, then sue me if I breathed a word."

"Did the cloners really clone that sheep?" I ask. "What was her name?"

"Dolly," my mother says.

"I mean, how would anyone know for sure that it was a real clone and not just another sheep?" I take small bites of my grilled cheese.

"It's a simple DNA test," my father says. "And yes. They're the real deal. Just a few cells and that lab can reproduce outside a womb."

"Could they make a new me?" I ask. "A spare child?"

Mom and Dad stop eating.

"Did you ever consider it while I was gone?"

My father pats my knee. I don't mean to, but I pull my leg away, knocking the table and nearly spilling all of our drinks.

"I'm sorry," he says. "We never considered it seriously, but there was this one night."

My mother bites her raw lips. "Your father ransacked the house for brushes and combs. He searched all of the photo albums."

"Your mother was convinced that she'd saved a lock of your hair."

"For a while, it was the only thing that gave us hope."

I can't imagine what it must have been like for them. To have been so frightened when so often I was simply bored.

"Belle would love this country," I say, looking down at our dinner plates. "All of the food in Scotland is yellow."

After dinner my father asks our waiter to give us a tour of Room 13.

"We're related to Robert Louis Stevenson," he tells the waiter. "I want my daughter to see where her ancestor wrote *Treasure Island*."

"I can show you Stevenson's room." The waiter smiles. "But he didn't write *Treasure Island* here. He wrote *Kidnapped*."

I know if my parents laugh at this mix-up, everything from now on will be okay. That if they can grin and have a sense of humor about bringing their kidnapped daughter to a place famous for kidnapping then we can all get on with our lives. But my parents don't laugh or chuckle. Mom hides her mouth with her hands. My father shields his eyes with his arm. For a moment, I think that I should block my ears so we can speak and see and hear no evil.

Before Robert Louis Stevenson wrote his bestsellers, the Stevenson family was already famous for their lighthouses. I learn this from a plaque in the inn's lobby while we wait for a taxi to ferry us back to our hotel. The Stevensons modernized their intelligent beacons. Giving each lighthouse its own shuttering system, its own signature way of blinking. A ship aware of the lighthouse's code could identify its location. Tracking itself against the coastline.

While I read about my ancestors' accomplishments, my father stands behind me. He smells my hair. I want to pull several strands from my head and hand them to him. Want to say, "Here, make more of me if you like."

"I'm so sorry," my father finally says. "I feel as though I can only fail you."

"Which would you rather be?" I ask my father. "A lighthouse or a volcano?"

"A lighthouse," he says. "So you'd always be able to find me."

"But isn't a volcano a kind of lighthouse?" I say.

Back at the hotel I imagine that there might be enough guilt and goodwill for me to finally get what I want.

"Let me go swimming," I say. "Let me go downstairs by myself."

I try to explain that it will help me to be alone. That what I need most is to build back my sense of independence. My autonomy. "I need to feel safe with myself. Fifteen minutes is all I'm asking."

My parents are tired. I have aged them more than they care to acknowledge. My father surrenders his cell phone.

"Call us if you need anything."

Before they have a chance to change their minds, I pull on my turquoise swimsuit, throw on one of the hotel's terry cloth robes, slip on a pair of slippers, and bolt down to the lobby. I wave at the desk clerk in his red coat.

"Pool's closed," he tells me.

"No," I say. "Please," I beg.

"Sorry," he says. "We close her up at 9 P.M."

The clerk is short and pale. He's at least five years older than me. My friend Trisha would call him an albino troll but he has a kind, thin-lipped face.

"But you were the one who told me I had to take a swim."

"Sorry," he says, and I think he really means it.

"Do you know who I am?" I don't wait for him to say no. I touch the top of his hand with my fingertips. "I was stolen."

He listens to the short version of my story. The one where I'm held against my will and rescued. Even before I finish, he's opening a drawer and pulling out a set of keys.

"You can't tell anyone," he says. "Or I'll lose my job."

The pool covers the length of a small stadium, the arched glass ceiling a brilliant mantle of night. Our voices bounce off the water and into the glass, echoing and reverberating between us. My clerk calls the room a natatorium and I decide that I could love him for using such a beautiful word.

"Come swim with me," I offer.

"I have to get back to the front desk."

I drop my robe on a chaise. My suit is tight and uncomfortable, and right there, in front of my new pale friend, I struggle to take off the top then slide off the bottom. He doesn't say anything. Just unsnaps the brass buttons and throws his red jacket off, a victorious matador. His chest, legs, and ass are even paler than his pale face. His body goes from pink to blue. We dive into the water without touching each other.

My greatest gift is buoyancy. Mom taught me how to float for hours without kicking or paddling. I fold my arms behind my head, cross my feet, and drift in the warm green water.

"How do you do that?" my accomplice asks.

"I think my bones are hollow."

"Were you really kidnapped?" he asks.

"I was shipwrecked. I floated in the Indian Ocean for months on end."

"Seriously," he says. "Were you ribbing me?"

"I was taken by a man who fell in love with my friend Trisha. He meant to kidnap her but couldn't find her house. He settled for me."

I dive under and swim toward the desk clerk.

"Did he hurt you?" he asks.

"He made me cook for him."

"Did he ever tell you that you're beautiful?"

"He told me I was lost."

My mother, the psychologist, believes I need to accept that I'm still the same girl I was before Messiah. "You have to get over this idea that you were okay and then something bad happened that divided your life and you were never okay again." But something bad did happen, and I feel as though I'll spend the rest of my life searching for more bad things to come.

"You should go," I tell the desk clerk. "You don't want to be fired."

He squints at me, then splashes his way out of the pool. I watch him put on his clothes, glance at his penis as an afterthought. There's no way this one could do me any harm.

Finally, I achieve what I've wanted every day since my return: to be alone. I float on my back and gaze up at the glass ceiling. The stars of Edinburgh offer scant light. Somewhere in the world, a volcano erupts, forming an island in the South Pacific. Robert Louis Stevenson died in Samoa, far away from his famous family. He is part of me, my distant relative. He too liked to disappear. Enjoyed a good anonymous adventure. I miss my disappearance. I was never so important as when I was gone. If I had a choice between being a lighthouse or a volcano, I would choose to scorch mountains, destroy homes, and use my ash to block out the sun. Part of me longs for the tabloid camera crews that once camped outside my home. I want them to capture my disaster footage. Record my pain. I want proof for my mother, want her to see who I was before I was taken.

That I was quiet, studious, and desperate to do wrong. A shop-lifter, a plagiarist, a negligent sister, an indifferent daughter.

Upstairs in our hotel suite, I know my parents are having sex. Quick, anxious, affirming sex. "Our daughter's going to be okay," they keep telling themselves as they slide into each other. Relief sex. They deserve this after all they've been through. Maybe I've brought them closer together. True, Dad notices Mom's chubby belly slap hard against his chest. Mom remembers that Dad used to be muscular and toned. That he once had a beautiful head of hair. Still, they are grateful for each other. I will wait down here long enough for them to finish. Long enough for them to tidy up their mess.

I am naked and floating under my chosen stars. Their lights blinking me ashore. This pool my temple, my museum. Sometimes when I pray to Messiah, I imagine him inside of me stirring my devotion, making me question my guilt and in-nocence. Sometimes when I pray for myself, I remember those distant afternoons when my mother first taught me to swim. How she held my back as I struggled to stay afloat. How she smiled above me as I learned how to slowly drift away.

NOTES TOWARD AN
ANATOMY OF PAIN

**Fragment #1: From a Journal of Pain the Patient Was
Unable to Keep, Cape Cod, 1990, Spring**

Whether I'm sitting, standing, or lying down, my foot and calf
dart up and out in a constant kick. My knee pops while my
thigh pivots from side to side. My forearm oscillates back and
forth, striking my chest like a tree branch tapping a window
during a storm.

I. BREAKTHROUGH PAIN

The shaking began in the Patient's left leg. The foot kicked
first, the calf and thigh followed. This happened shortly after
the Patient, age thirteen, arrived home from a private ballet
lesson at Mrs. Stevenson's School of Dance. The Patient, with
her straight blond hair and long torso, was about to star in a

production of *Alice in Wonderland*. That day, she'd practiced falling down the rabbit hole. Mrs. Stevenson, swank in her low-cut leotard, ordered up grand jetés and arabesques, and chided, "You're tumbling, Toots. Tumble." Exhausted from her workout, the Patient lounged on a pink velvet chaise in her parents' bedroom, watching *The Love Connection*. After the first commercial break, she lost control of her body. She wishes now that she'd been viewing a television show with greater cultural ambition, or better still, reading something in French.

Jean-Jacques Rousseau, *Emilius; or, a Treatise of Education*, **1768**
Except pain of body and remorse of conscience, all our evils are imaginary.

By dinner, the shaking had spread to her arm.

Charles Darwin, *Expression of the Emotions in Man and Animals,* **1872**
Great pain urges all animals, and has urged them during endless generations, to make the most violent and diversified efforts to escape from the cause of suffering. Even when a limb or other separate part of the body is hurt, we often see a tendency to shake it, as if to shake off the cause, though this may obviously be impossible.

II. MULTIPLE PAIN SITES

A young neurologist, Dr. Gibbons, diagnoses the steady shaking along the Patient's left arm and leg as an involuntary kinetic tremor. Dr. Gibbons is a small man with a short red beard and spectacles. As Dr. Gibbons softens his voice, his shoulders rise close to his ears, shortening and obscuring his neck. The Patient's instinct as a dancer is to push these shoulders down, to raise the doctor's chin and tilt his head back.

"Tests need to be performed," the doctor says. "I'd like to do an EEG to evaluate the electrical activity in your brain and an EMG to monitor your nerve conduction time. Depending on the results we may have to do a cerebrospinal fluid analysis."

The doctor smiles.

The idea of these tests comforts the Patient. She is good at tests. But she's confused. The doctor has yet to ask her where or how she hurts.

An Interview with the Patient's Mother on the Fifth Anniversary of Her Daughter's Pain
"The tremors were there even when you slept."

An Interview with the Patient's Father on the Tenth Anniversary of His Daughter's Pain
"Hey, guess who I am." (Father shakes left leg uncontrollably.)

III. (THREE)

There are three types of pain:

1) Transient
2) Acute
3) Chronic

There are three types of pain:

1) Injury
2) Depression
3) Puzzling

There are three types of pain:

1) Mild
2) Moderate
3) Severe

There are three types of pain:

1) Mechanistic
2) Localized
3) Empirical

There are three types of pain:

1) Somatic
2) Visceral
3) Neuropathic

There are three types of pain:

1) Individual
2) Departmental
3) Organizational

There are three types of pain:

1) Root canal
2) Breaking a leg
3) Having a baby

There are three types of pain fibers:

1) A-beta fiber
2) A-delta fiber
3) C fiber

There are three types of painkillers:

1) Acetaminophen
2) Anti-inflammatories
3) Narcotics

IV. THE AUTHOR ON PAIN

The funny thing: pain can't be shared. Pain is singular. The closest you can come to sharing pain is inflicting pain. When I describe my pain to you, you may feel something, but what you feel is not my pain. A mother giving birth knows a pain incomprehensible to the child she delivers, just as the child cries for reasons the mother cannot entirely understand. The mother may mistake her pain for punishment from God. She may justify the labor pain as an act of purification, as a spiritual transformation, or as a test.

While reading a story about pain, my hope is you become more aware of your own. The stiffness from clenching a telephone against your shoulder and shouting "motherfucker" into the receiver (pain in the neck). The tender ache that arises when sitting too long in a train depot, waiting for someone you no longer love to arrive home (pain in the ass). The weight of sadness you feel when hugged hello (chest pains). Take pains to justify the pain. Or better still, take pain for what it is, a warning.

V. LAW OF SPECIFIC NERVE ENERGIES

A male technician attaches electrodes to the Patient's scalp with a paste that smells sweet and metallic like canned peaches. The Patient sits in a cushioned reclining chair, her feet elevated and level with her hips. Her leg rocks and jives, and she's really starting to worry about permanent muscle damage. Dr. Gibbons explains that the electrodes won't shock her. They will record her brain waves. The Patient is a perfectionist and wants to understand all the technical aspects and perform the tests exactly as directed. As the doctor discusses the frequency of alpha waves and delta rhythms, the technician parts the Patient's hair and secures the small wired instruments. In the left corner of the room, there is a computer and a printing mechanism with a scroll of paper. This machine will trace one hundred pages of brain activity. The Patient wants to tease Dr. Gibbons. Tell him that she might not have a full hundred pages to give, but since she's tired, sore, and female, the joke will probably come out wrong.

The technician tells the Patient to close her eyes, relax, and remain still. The Patient rubs her good hand over the erratic knee. The technician points to the Patient's leg. He says, "You'll have to stop that."

"It's why I'm here," the Patient replies.

Dr. Gibbons and the technician begin an initial recording with the lights dimmed and the Patient resting in the chair. They do another run under what the doctor calls "stress-producing" conditions. The Patient is asked to breathe deeply and rapidly for three minutes at a time. As the girl starts to feel faint, the men shine bright lights on her. Air-raid attack.

Fragment #2: From a Journal of Pain the Patient Was Unable to Keep, Children's Hospital, Boston, 1990, Spring

The next test is even stranger. I'm asked to undress and change into a paper robe.

Dr. Gibbons explains that a needle electrode will be inserted into a series of different muscles and that a mild electrical shock will be administered to stimulate a particular nerve. I'm surprised that after promising not to shock me, he sends a charge straight through my muscles.

"We'll fluctuate the voltage, and if you feel any severe discomfort, we'll stop."

"What about regular discomfort?" I ask.

Dr. Gibbons brandishes an instrument resembling the cordless shaver I bought Dad last Christmas. On this device, instead of three rotating heads, a single needle shivers. He pierces the needle into my right thigh and places a metal plate underneath me. The pain. Words leave me. Quickly, I try to remember the four muscles that make up the quadriceps. I can remember only one. Sartorius. The longest muscle in the human body. The one that allows the legs to rotate and cross during fouettés and piqué turns. Heat surges along my thigh as a small amplifier registers a sharp piercing note. I try to correlate the shock to the noise, but it sounds like an indecipherable language only neurologists and shih tzus can decipher. He switches to the left thigh and asks, "How long have you been a ballerina?" I tell him that he is trying to distract me from the pain.

Johannes Müller, *Handbuch der Physiologie des Menschen für Vorlesungen*, 1835

The same cause, such as electricity, can simultaneously affect all sensory organs, since they are all sensitive to it; and yet, every sensory nerve reacts to it differently; one nerve perceives it as light, another hears its sound, another one smells it; another tastes the electricity, and another one feels it as pain and shock. One nerve perceives a luminous picture through mechanical irritation, another one hears it as buzzing, another one senses it as pain.

Lewis Carroll, *Through the Looking-Glass*, dated 1872 but actually published in December 1871

At any other time, Alice would have felt surprised at this, but she was far too much excited to be surprised at anything NOW. "As for YOU," she repeated, catching hold of the little creature in the very act of jumping over a bottle which had just lighted upon the table, "I'll shake you into a kitten, that I will!"

VI. RELIEF

The Patient's pain entitles her to comfort. Her mother buys her a Walkman. A fancy yellow one with an auto-reverse function. The Patient doesn't know anyone else who has a Walkman this nice. In bed, she slumbers to the score from *Alice in Wonderland* all night, uninterrupted. A click in the mechanism signals that the music has switched sides. She choreographs her tremors to the flutter of flutes, the drawl of clarinets, and the jazz of cymbals flashing. When she wakes in the mornings, the immediacy of her shaking startles her less. Now there is music to accompany her strange dance. Her mother has yet to tell her that, in the part of Alice, Mrs. Stevenson has replaced the Patient with the Mock Turtle.

Bands the Patient Wishes She Could Have Listened to with Her Walkman
PAIN
Pain Station
Pain Emission
Slow Pain
Pro-Pain
Pain Killer
Pain Teens
Sweet Pain
Pain?
Iron Maiden
Pad of Pain
A Band Called Pain
House of Pain
Pain of Salvation

Tattoo of Pain
Circus of Pain
Jam Pain Society
Born from Pain
59 Times the Pain
Ecstasy, Passion & Pain
Morphine
Ether
Codeine

Barbra Streisand, in an interview with Barbara Walters, *Barbara Walters Special*, September 13, 1985, ABC, 30 min.
How can you really feel anything if you're not allowing yourself to feel the pain? It is part of being human and alive to feel all kinds of feelings.

VII. PAIN TREATMENT

The phenomenon of pain is best studied after battles. Soldiers injured during the American Civil War often experienced a chronic burning pain, causalgia, in their hands and feet that bore no direct relationship to their wounds. What shocked the doctors was the lack of cause. By one account, a survivor of the Battle of the Wilderness was overheard shouting, "My hands. My hands." He'd been shot in the chest. The severity of the pain across the palms of the hands and the tops of the feet lasted even after the soldier had healed. He was no longer able to hold cups of tea in fine porcelain china, polish his rifle, bury the dead, stack firewood, balance on branches with tools, catch children thrown high above heads at picnics.

The common treatment for causalgia: amputation.

S. Weir Mitchell, *Injuries of Nerves and Their Consequences*, 1872

No history of the physiology of stumps would be complete without some account of the sensorial delusions to which persons are subject in connection with their lost limbs . . . Nearly every man who loses a limb carries about with him a constant or inconstant phantom of the missing member, a sensory ghost of that much of himself, and sometimes a most inconvenient presence, faintly felt at times, but ready to be called up to his perception by a blow, a touch, or a change of wind.

Conversation with Classmate Dino Savistano, on Patient's Return to Wareham Intermediate School

Dino: Where are your scars?

Patient: I don't have any.

Dino: But they told us you had tumors.

Patient: Tremors. I had tremors.

VIII. CALENDAR OF EVENTS 2001–03, AMERICAN PAIN SOCIETY (PARTIAL LISTING)

International Anesthesia Conference

SPONSOR: Pakistan Society for the Study of Pain

DATE: September 7–9, 2001

LOCATION: Islamabad, Pakistan

CONTACT: www.people.goplay.com/conference2001

Fibromyalgia Conference: Reversal of Fibromyalgia with Guaifenesin
SPONSOR: Presbyterian Hospital and Albuquerque Fibromyalgia Support Group
DATE: October 27, 2001
CITY, STATE: Albuquerque, NM
LOCATION: Presbyterian Hospital Savage Auditorium

Headache Now 2002!
SPONSOR: American Headache Society
DATE: January 18–20, 2002
CITY, STATE: Bal Harbour, FL
LOCATION: Sheraton Bal Harbour
CONTACT: American Headache Society
PHONE: 856-423-3195

American Academy of Pain Medicine, 18th Annual Meeting, Review/Refresher Course
SPONSOR: American Academy of Pain Medicine
DATE: February 27–March 3, 2002
CITY, STATE: San Francisco, CA
LOCATION: Hyatt Regency at Embarcadero Center
CONTACT: American Academy of Pain Medicine
PHONE: 847-375-4731

6th European Headache Congress
DATE: June 17–22, 2002
LOCATION: Istanbul, Turkey
CONTACT: www.bthehf.org

44th Annual Scientific Meeting of the American Headache Society
SPONSOR: American Headache Society
DATE: June 21–23, 2002
CITY, STATE: Seattle, WA
LOCATION: Sheraton Seattle Hotel & Towers

10th World Congress of the International Association for the Study of Pain
SPONSOR: International Association for the Study of Pain
DATE: August 17–22, 2002
CITY, STATE: San Diego, CA
CONTACT: IASP Secretariat

6th International Symposium on Pediatric Pain
SPONSOR: American Headache Society
DATE: June 15–19, 2003
LOCATION: Sydney, Australia

IX. PAIN SPOTS

1) What is the function of the "Patient"? How is this character revealed in the story? What is the author's purpose for writing? If this story is autobiographical, how does it compare to other autobiographical works we've read? For example, Montaigne suffered from gallstones and kidney stones and spent his adult life in agony searching for curative waters.

2) To ask the question above in a different way, i.e., restate it, what kind of a woman is the Patient? What are her concerns

and desires? How would she compare to other female pro-
tagonists (Cassandra, Clytemnestra, Courtney Love)?

3) What power does the author attribute to the imagination?
What is the relationship between mind and body? What is
the author afraid of?

4) Why does the author insist that there are "three types of
pain" and then go on to list twenty-one? Which terms are
privileged and why?

5) Why does the author talk so much about physical pain?
What is the relationship between pain and the ability to
write?

6) Does the author successfully avoid any unnecessary puns
involving Thomas Paine? Are there any hidden quotes
from Paine? For example: *These are the times that try men's
souls.*

7) Returning to the question "What is the author afraid of?"
Why are there no references to Saint Vitus' dance? Epi-
lepsy? Cerebral palsy? MS? Was there really anything wrong
with the Patient?

8) Similarly, are the references to Rwanda and trepanning in
Bulgaria necessary?

9) Pose your own question and answer it. Then share your
insights with others.

X. TREPANNING

Trepanning, Exhibit A
Apollinaire, not his real name, was injured in the head during
the First World War and survived a trepanning operation, only

to die from the Spanish flu. The only records of his pain are poems.

Fragment #3: From a Journal of Pain the Patient Was Unable to Keep, Cape Cod, 1990, Spring

The pain was so bad last night I had to leave the house. I walked down to the beach in my nightgown barefoot. Part of me shaking the whole way. There was snow on the ground or maybe it was sand. I would cut off my arm and leg to make this stop. Dr. Gibbons can't find anything wrong with me. "Too much electricity," he jokes. "If I could climb inside you, then I could switch it off." I'll never dance again. I haven't cried yet. *Switch what off?*

Exchange Between the Patient and Her Father as Recalled by the Patient's Mother
Patient: Dr. Gibbons thinks I'm crazy.
Father: A gibbon is a small tailless ape.

Trepanning, Exhibit B
Jonathan Bousfield and Dan Richardson, *Bulgaria: The Rough Guide*, 1999
Considerably more interesting is the Museum of Medical History, ul. Paraskeva Nikolau 7 (Mon–Fri 10am–4pm with an unpredictable lunch break), sheltered within the sandy-coloured nineteenth-century building that once housed Varna's first public hospital. . . . An array of tenth-century skulls on the ground floor reveal that one in three of the local population had been subjected to a symbolic form of trepanation (the practice of drilling holes in the skull)—in which the bone had been

scratched and dented but not actually pierced. Archeologists presume that this had some kind of ritual purpose—but quite what, no one knows.

One in three raises the question of whether or not the remaining two held the patient down and drilled the hole or whether they were busy taking an unpredictable lunch break.

Dr. Gibbons on the Patient's Prognosis
"The shaking may stop as mysteriously as it began."

XI. SOMETIMES WE GO A LONG WAY FOR OUR PAIN

From pp. 46–47 of *Rwanda: The Bradt Travel Guide*, 1999
   Meningitis
   Sexual risks
   Ebola
      Useful Contacts
      Central Hospital of Kigali Tel: 575555
      King Faycal Hospital (Kigali) Tel: 82421
   Animals
      Rabies
      Snakebite
   Further Reading

Future Pain the Patient Will Endure
Four impacted wisdom teeth
Allergic reaction to penicillin

Riots (Cincinnati, Ohio, and Cyprus)
Volcanic eruption (Mt. Etna)
Flash flooding (various locations)
Several stubbed toes
Ligaments torn from sternum
Shingles

Future Pain the Patient Will Inflict
During a fight with her mother in a parking garage in
Montreal, the Patient will knock her mother to the
ground. (Her mother has no memory of this.)
  The Patient will advise a friend to get a haircut she
doesn't need. (The friend brings this up on the phone all
the time.)
  The Patient will hit a deer with her car. (The deer
will flee the scene of the crime.)

Brochure: "The Pleasures of Acupuncture"
(third inside flap)
*Following Richard Nixon's visit to China in 1972 the number of US
practitioners of acupuncture rose by ninety percent.*

Lewis Carroll, Chapter X, *Through the Looking-Glass*
  Shaking
*She took her off the table as she spoke, and shook her backwards and
forwards with all her might. The Red Queen made no resistance whatever; only her face grew very small, and her eyes got large and green:
and still, as Alice went on shaking her, she kept on growing shorter—
and fatter—and softer—and rounder—and—*

XII. SURGERY OF PAIN

Three weeks have passed. During an office visit, Dr. Gibbons asks to speak with the Patient's mother alone. The Patient is too weak to be offended. She sits on the examining table and stares out the window to her right at the building across the street. A pair of men cross the roof, holding boxes. When the men reach the edge, they remove a collection of long, thin, white tubes from the cardboard. They drop, toss, and javelin the cylinders down deep into an alleyway. On impact, the shafts explode in brilliant puffs and clouds of white air. Fluorescent lights. Just as one shatters, the men drop another. When they run out of lights, the Patient slips off the table to stand and admire the path of glass. She thinks about Indian holy men who cross over razors and smoke white coals. The Patient stands at the window for several moments before she notices that the shaking has stopped. Her arm rests straight at her side and her foot is pressed hard and weighted into the floor. The muscles feel loose and she practices lifting and raising her leg.

The Patient is not prepared for her cure. She sits back down on the table and kicks her leg up and down. At first she points her foot, but then she decides that it looks better flexed. She snaps her knee and elbow in unison and strokes her thumb across her palm. She considers adding a facial tic but abandons the idea in favor of a shoulder roll. Her version of the tremor is more fluid and has a slower cadence. She rests. With one eye on the door, she waits for Dr. Gibbons and her mother to return. When they enter, she focuses all of her attention on her shaking. The Patient barely hears the doctor when he tells her that she'll have to lie flat for eight hours after the spinal tap. He doesn't seem to register a difference between the previous careless tremors and her own precise choreography. At first the Patient is offended, but then she recognizes the success of her pantomime. She looks at her mother. Even she's convinced.

XIII. THE PATIENT IS THE ONE WHO WAITS THROUGH PAIN

Lewis Carroll, Chapter XI, *Through the Looking-Glass*
Waking
—*and it really WAS a kitten, after all.*

Fragment #4: From a Journal of Pain the Patient Was Unable to Keep, Children's Hospital, Boston, 1990, Spring

The doctor explains that he'll numb my back and then draw the fluid from a puncture made in my lower spine. He says that I might suffer nausea and a severe headache. "Your equilibrium will be gone and you'll have to wait while your body restores the fluid."

The nurse arrives and helps me change into the paper hospital robe. She's a tall woman. An Amazon with short white hair and violet eyes. She holds herself in perfect erect posture. I remember to both tremble and sway my arm and to keep the beats of my kicks quick and sharp. Once I'm dressed, the nurse lifts me up onto the table and rolls me over onto my left side, thinking that the pressure will alleviate the tremors. I continue to twitch. The nurse draws my knees up to my abdomen and bends my chin down until it touches my chest. This woman knows how to hold me. Her exact positioning reminds me of a strict Russian ballet teacher correcting her students at the barre.

When the doctor announces that he is ready to begin, the nurse offers me her hand. The pain of the anesthetic injection is so strong that I squeeze her fingers together like a fin. She begins to take in long deep breaths and I follow her lead, waiting for my back to numb. In a few minutes the spinal needle is inserted and all I can feel is a thrust of pressure. The needle is unimportant. I know that the fluid it collects is clear and warm and beautiful. I'd like to lift my chin off my chest and raise my head with a reverence for this nurse, but I understand that I must maintain my position, motionless. I hold my body close until she says I'm free to go. This test will tell them everything is normal.

THE MASTER OF NOVICES

I. VIA DOLOROSA

That summer, before we lost her forever, my older sister, Rachel, helped me memorize the stations of the cross. While Dad fished his river and Mom tanned her freckled skin, Rachel and I huddled together in her basement bedroom under posters of The Cure and Bad Religion studying our supposed Savior as he stumbled falling once, twice, three times, on the way to his tomb. I was a rising junior at Mercy Academy. Rachel, at twenty-one, had just dropped out of Salem State College. We both agreed that our favorite station was the sixth, the one where Veronica knelt beside Jesus to wipe the sweat and anguish from his forehead. Rachel liked it because she thought it was sexy. "Veronica was a fox. She wanted Jesus. Wanted him bad." I liked the station because the photorealist rendering of Veronica in my *Spirituality Now!* confirmation guidebook looked just like me when I wore my hair pulled back, silhouetted my lids with smoky eye shadow, and bit my lips to make them puffier.

As I sprawled across Rachel's queen bed, cramming for my Catholic confirmation, eager to become a "soldier of Christ," my sister sashayed around the room snapping an orange afghan. "The Veronica is the name of a bullfighting move." Rachel had spent that fall of her junior year in Spain studying Gaudí, El Greco, and a Basque bartender named Enrique. "The matador dances superclose to his prey, grazes the bull with his cape, and then strikes." My long-limbed sister dropped the afghan net over my head and tackled me, slapping my belly, spackling my face with kisses. Mixing her affection with violence.

While at Mercy Academy, Rachel liked to wear a blue bra under the white blouse of her school uniform. Liked to flirt with Father Patrick Burleigh. Liked to fail physical education and get A's in Advanced Calculus. Liked to taunt the nuns with nicknames: Sister Afterthought, Sister Sacrifice, Sister Slippery When Wet.

I still remember Rachel canceling her own confirmation. The night before that ceremony, my sister decided to dye her honey-colored hair a vivid magenta. When I woke up the next morning, the yellow guest towels, the ceramic tiles in the bathroom, the wicker hamper, and the porcelain sink were all stained a murderous red. I was certain that someone had been killed.

A week later Father Burleigh expelled Rachel from Mercy Academy for "godlessness."

With her punky tresses, her buttery skin, her sharp feline features, Rachel was less groupie and more rock star. Her magenta makeover in tandem with her renunciation of God and her glorious schoolgirl expulsion boosted her boastful confidence. After her aborted confirmation, I came home from catechism to find my pink-haired sister tying herself to her bed. Rachel wore a patent leather bustier and army surplus pants as she busied herself, binding her ankles together with strips of silk, securing her feet to the anemic iron rods that fenced in her footboard.

"Are those Dad's neckties?" I asked.

"Help me out," she said. "I need you to do my arms."

I was curious, and so I used a standard square knot to fasten my sister's bony wrists to her head posts. Crucifying her to the bed.

"Is this some kind of game?" I asked.

"Vince McGowan wants to tie me up and fuck me. I need to know how tight to make the knots."

II. RECEIVING THE CROSS

As Catholics, my sister and I had the added pressure of parents who'd both been in their holy orders. Our voluptuous mother joined the convent at nineteen, running away from the constraints of her own devout family. She lasted for almost six years. Neither Rachel nor I ever took our glamorous mother's bout with religion seriously. Curvy and fertile, Mom was quick to warn us: "I got pregnant the first time I had sex." Mom spent every summer of our childhood wearing a bright green bikini, smoking thin chocolate-colored cigarillos, and reading to us from thick paperbacks embossed with golden lockets and paintings of men and women in the onset of arousal. She called us "her bounty" and assured us that we constituted the one right choice she'd made. It was our father the near priest who worried us all. Mom, Rachel, and I each feared that he would eventually abandon us for God.

A well-stocked river snaked behind our modest cedar-shingled house. During the school year, Dad marked his time as a librarian at Bridgewater High in order to spend his vacations fishing. One night during that final summer, Rachel and I stood downstream from Dad, the three of us in khaki waders flicking our lines overhead. Dad and I were strictly catch and release, but Rachel proudly killed, filleted, and consumed her trout. Dad and I listened to Rachel complain about college, about the lack of intellectuals, the crappy dining hall, the dingy dorms. "I'm not hoping for Derrida, not expecting Le Cirque, I don't even demand maid service, but would it be so wrong if every so often someone ran a dry mop over the school?"

"I had maid service once." Our father bragged that he'd lived for a time at what was once the Hilton Hotel of North Aurora, Illinois. This was the summer of 1962. Dad was in his first year of study as a Jesuit. The brick-and-glass resort our dad called home had been erected near an upscale racetrack with the promise that the new interstate would glide right by the hotel's luxury accommodations. The racetrack prospered, but when the roadways were finally constructed, the Hilton was twenty miles from the closest off-ramp. "What if you built a hotel and no travelers came?" Dad joked. "Too much room in the inn." The Hilton Catholics dodged a major financial loss by charitably donating their profitless hotel to Saint Ignatius Loyola's Society of Jesus. "I lived in room 109." Dad jangled a set of imaginary keys summoning a relic from his former life.

"My sliding glass door opened out onto a courtyard with an Olympic-size swimming pool."

"Sounds like the good life." I laughed.

"You should have seen me dive off the spring board." Dad straightened his body, saluting us with his muscular arms, pretending to jackknife into our river. "I gave up that good life for you." Dad pointed to Rachel.

"Does that make me the Antichrist?" Rachel asked.

"This remains to be seen," he said.

III. FALLING FOR THE FIRST TIME

Typically, a man joins the Jesuits right after high school. Our father entered the Jesuits after college. By then he'd had sex with at least two women. Rachel and I weren't supposed to know this. From her basement bedroom, Rachel treasured a box of rotting Bibles. She planned on making an art project— canvas collaged with scraps of gospels, images of slaughtered lambs, wine-stained wine labels, and photos of men with epic beards. Rachel fished out our father's red leather Jesuit journal from the bottom of the decay.

"You know how Mom and Dad oppress us with their virginity? Well, I've got the scoop on Dad's first time. Mom was like maybe his third."

She wouldn't let me hold the impressive journal, or thumb through the gilt-edged pages. Rachel motioned for me to sit and play audience while she deciphered our father's slanted cursive. She read to me about Dad's first sexual encounter. On a stormy afternoon at a friend's beach house in Cape May, a chubby Polish Catholic lost to our father in a marathon game of Sorry. She offered up her virginity as reward. Said, "I don't know how to do this," then squeezed our scrawny, knock-kneed dad hard between her pink-sunburned thighs. Dad thought she'd break him in two.

The best and last of our father's pre-Jesuit lovers was a married Protestant who worked at his parents' grocery store. He often thought of Lois Pendleton on his afternoon walks around the Hilton—imagining the two of them on vacation there together, playing tennis, ordering room service, the only guests in the entire resort. He knew that she was busy back home, stacking cans of stewed tomatoes, counting the inventory on miniature jars of baby food. Lois was tall. She could reach up to the highest shelves merely by stretching her arms. Sometimes, when she did this, her sweater would rise above her waist, revealing the tight muscles of her lower back. Dad imagined Lois in her home at night pouring a shot of rye for her electrician husband, brushing her gray teeth with baking soda, undressing for bed. The final time they had sex, he made her cry out to God, made her entire body shudder and convulse. He stopped, pulled back, and watched her recover on his narrow bed, her toes pointed, her face and chest blushing red. When he asked if she was okay, she rolled over, laughing. "Funny boy," she said. "That's more like it."

Six weeks later, our father joined the Jesuits. He knew what he was missing.

IV. JUDGED BY PILATE

Once I mastered the fourteen stations of the cross, Rachel offered to quiz me on my saints. She didn't know them herself. My sister, her brown hair now sugared with streaks of platinum blond, strutted past me in a familiar pair of white terry cloth shorts and a red-and-blue-striped tube top.

"You look like a patriotic trollop," I said.

"True or false," Rachel challenged. "Saint Innocent is the patron saint of pedophiles."

"Wait a minute." I moved closer to her. "Those are my clothes."

"True, but I fill them out." Rachel shook her ass.

I cinched the back of the tube top, stretching the elastic and exposing the top bulbs of her breasts.

"Perv," she said. "If you want to see my tits, just ask." Rachel shimmied the tube top down past her nipples, flashing her C-cups in my face. "Mom gave me these. What did she give you?"

"Self-respect." I buried my face in my study guide.

Rachel swiped the book away, riffling through the pages. "All of these names repeat. Six Saint Marys, John of on and on, Francis of this and that. Total lack of imagination."

"Father Burleigh claims each one is different," I protested.

"No." Rachel squeezed her breasts together. "Trust me. They're all the same."

V. THE VIRGIN AND THE CROWN

Rachel kept disappearing that summer, only to return from her lost weekends hungover and insolvent. Her skin blistered and peeling. From my bedroom window, I'd watch Rachel kiss off a different deadbeat boy piloting a different rusted beater. The boys hightailing it in reverse burning down our driveway before our father had a chance to shame and menace.

My sister left college because of all the sex she'd had. "I'm the whore of Salem State," she told me one night. She'd misplaced herself among a host of guys: a sculptor named Ephraim, a dorm security guard she called St. Christopher, a struggling actor who impersonated a warlock at the witch trial museum, a bisexual Harvard divinity student, a late-night caller our father referred to as Him Again.

"Ephraim thinks I'm a slut. St. Christopher figures I was abused. The warlock believes I'm certifiable. The truth is I'm just promiscuous. Like Daddy was before he got all full of Jesus." She knelt on her bed and began to bounce. "At least I'm not afraid of sex."

I hadn't so much as kissed anyone. My only crush so far was on another girl. Malaya smelled like lemons and mint. Her family had just moved from the Philippines, where her father owned a matchbook factory. One afternoon, while we waited outside the church for our parents to pick us up from catechism, Malaya dared me to lick the blue tip of her father's strike-anywhere matches. "They taste like blueberries," she insisted. The matches were waterproof, and after we kissed them, we struck them against the church walls, sending a shower of sparks across the limestone.

"I know what's wrong with you." Rachel trampolined on her bed. "You're frigid."

"And you're a Catholic girl cliché." I threw a throw pillow at Rachel and she caught it in midair.

"No," she said, "I'm a revolutionary."

"I bet you have diseases," I countered. "I bet you get pregnant."

Rachel stopped jumping. "I've been pregnant twice already," she told me. "If it happens again, I'll probably keep it."

My parents and I spent the hours before my confirmation searching for Rachel. We checked her walk-in closet, our next-door neighbor's gazebo, under the derelict screened-in porch. I scouted the river, scoured the marshy backyard, turned over Dad's abandoned canoe, and called Rachel's name out to the early morning. When we were kids, Rachel's favorite game involved convincing me to hide while she promised to seek. Fool that I was, I would always agree, tucking myself into a kitchen cabinet while Rachel, my seeker, rode off on her Huffy twin-speed. When I was three, Rachel seduced me into following a leathery black toad as it hopped all the way down into a construction trench. She abandoned me a dozen feet below-ground and feigned ignorance when Mom asked where I was. I was trapped for over an hour before an off-duty mail carrier heard me singing for my sister. At the emergency room, while the doctor set my broken wrist, my father nicknamed Rachel "Bully" and me "Damsel."

As we left for church without Rachel, Dad scribbled a note and tucked it under a Jesus flaming-heart refrigerator magnet: "Dear Bully: Why hast thou forsaken us?"

VI. VERONICA

When we arrived at St. Theresa's, my sister was already there, kneeling in a center pew, purple and gold light from the stained-glass windows streaming down over her penitent face. She'd walked the three and a half miles in plastic flip-flops. Rachel smiled upon seeing us and said, "I came early to pray."

Our father slid gracefully into the pew and knelt beside his elder child. He'd given her a non-Catholic, Old Testament name: Rachel, the beloved daughter of Laban, the favorite wife of Jacob, the younger sister of Leah. Dad told us how Jacob worked seven years for Laban in order to wed Rachel, and when tricked into marrying Leah, Jacob worked another seven years to earn the hand of his true love. Though my name was not Leah, I had a sense of what it was like to be something other than the chosen one. I watched Dad hug Rachel's burnished shoulders as Mom kissed the apple of her cheek. I couldn't help but feel that this day was no longer mine.

The ceremony was a series of prayers and processionals. Our regular and special confirmation names were read aloud by the visiting archbishop. Then each one of us made our way to the front of the church so that Father Burleigh could lay his calloused hands on us, ask us to reject evil, and bless us with chrism. Mom had told me how before Vatican II, the priest would say, "*Pax tecum,*" Peace be with you, and then slap you across your face. Just enough to sting you. Just enough to make you question what it was you were doing.

I wore a white silk gown fitted at the waist with opalescent beads intricately embroidered on the skirt. When I sat, I felt as though I was perched on a pincushion. My mother had woven a crown of fresh lilacs into my blond hair. Malaya sat beside me smelling my purple flowers. I could see the shadow of her brown nipples pressing against her white linen dress. We paid as little attention as possible to the mass, rubbing our stocking feet against the worn leather kneeler. Malaya pulled at my pearls. "You look like a duchess," she said.

I church-whispered, "Want to meet my parents?"

"The nun and the priest?" she asked.

"The sexy nun and the not-quite priest," I said.

When my sister went up to receive communion, she stared into Father Burleigh's jaundiced eyes as he placed the Eucharist in her cupped hands. A moment passed between them. I could feel her hatred, his disdain, and something else. Maybe lust, maybe disgust. Rachel did not bring the sacrament to her mouth. I watched her hide the body of Christ in her hand like a card sharp palming an ace. She returned to the pew and knelt down, inspecting the thin, translucent wafer. Studying the Eucharist like it was some creature she'd caught. A pale moth, wounded and flightless, the white wings pulsing against her skin. She saw me staring at her. Instead of a wink or a smile, my godless sister made the sign of the cross. Rachel had refused her own confirmation because she didn't aspire to be a child of God. "I'll do it if you want," she told our parents. "But I'm not ready to commit." Dad surprised us all by saying that he understood. "You're not eager to be nailed up on that cross."

VII. CYRENE

At the end of the service, my family did not rush to congratulate or photograph me. Instead our father grabbed my sister by the arm, steered her down the aisle and out of the church, her flip-flops slapping against the marble floor. Our mother followed, whispering at my sister's side, "We're near the end with you." When we reached the parking lot, Dad insisted Rachel take the communion.

"You can't hold on to it," he said. "It's not right."

Rachel looked away. Her arm flexed as she tightened her fist.

I wanted to make a joke, defuse the drama, reclaim the

day for myself. I thought of mentioning that I too had always considered smuggling out a Eucharist wafer, just to have it, just in case. I didn't see the problem, but I was still thinking like a child.

Our father held Rachel's face in his hands. For a moment, I thought he might kiss her. A moment later, I wanted him to strike her.

Dad backed Rachel up against our Fiat and squeezed her wrist. Our Mom begged him to stop. Rachel fought him with her free hand, pounding his chest and shouting, "Do this in memory of me." One by one he forced her fingers open. She'd crushed the Eucharist. Our father swept the crumbled mess up from my sister's palm, opened his own mouth, and dissolved the bread on his tongue. Then our angry red-faced father walked away from his daughter, stranding his family in the church parking lot. Abandoning us like we always feared he would.

VIII. THE SECOND FALL

Mom ran off to calm Dad while Rachel drifted downtown. "I need a drink," she said to me as she wandered, anxious for the bars to swing open their Sunday doors. I hailed a ride back home from Malaya. We gossiped together in the backseat of her parents' station wagon, sweating in our white gowns. "Your sister's beautiful," she said to me. "But she needs to be careful about her anger. It will make her old and wrinkled." Malaya's family invited me to brunch but I declined. Afraid of seeming too eager. Afraid that I might covet her parents. When they pulled up to the river house, I snapped off one of the pearls from my dress and handed it to Malaya. "So we remember," I said.

With nothing to do, I sneaked into Rachel's room and read our father's journal. Discovered how that summer at the Hilton Seminary, my father and his best friend, Brother Anthony Santoro, found a movie projector and a cache of film reels in one of the hotel's entertainment rooms. After some wrangling, they instituted an outdoor film festival. Brother Ambrose, the master of novices, the man in charge of shepherding the younger Jesuits on their spiritual course, a man who threatened always to drain the Olympic-size swimming pool, insisted on viewing the films in his private cell before granting his approval. The Marx Brothers were deemed acceptable. The Three Stooges too subversive.

In honor of the North Aurora Thoroughbred Derby, Dad chose to screen the Marx Brothers' classic *A Day at the Races*. In the film, the evil Douglass Dumbrille plots to turn a mental hospital into a casino to benefit his nearby racetrack. Dad joked that Dumbrille's scam was the opposite of the Jesuits' own ploy to transform the Hilton resort into a sacred seminary despite the racetrack.

Earlier that day, a group of Jesuits from Chicago had driven up to North Aurora with a handful of inner-city boys in tow. These urban Jesuits had promised their city kids a spiritual retreat and a trip to the racetrack. My father described how one of these men, a handsome, athletic-looking priest named Dominic, knew Anthony, how this man commented on the heat and asked if anyone ever used the pool to cool off at night. "What do you say we have a midnight dip?" he asked. Anthony laughed. My father said nothing.

Dad had seen *A Day at the Races* several times, but he loved sitting on the warm lawn watching the men in starched Roman collars and the young boys in white cotton T-shirts howl at Groucho's complicated, absurdist portrayal of veterinarian/headshrinker Dr. Hackenbush. One of the Chicago priests, an older, smiling man with a potbelly, passed around a pack of Parliaments, encouraging the boys to smoke. My father thought better of this before succumbing to his own previous addiction. As the boys smoked, the haze from their cigarettes illuminated the projector's column of light. The night was humid but breezy. When Dad lit his cigarette, his first in almost two years, whatever concerns he might have had about these Chicago priests were assuaged by the misadventures of Chico, Harpo, and their racehorse Hi Hat. There was something so pure about these other brothers, the Marx Brothers, and their desire for a good prank, their holy need for fun. My father's attention diverted, he began to hope that another film might be shown, a double feature—maybe *Saint Joan* or *Some Like It Hot*.

The brothers rarely had access to entertainment and hardly ever heard reports on the outside world. The first disruption Dad noted came in August 1962 when Marilyn Monroe died. That night at dinner, Brother Ambrose spoke of Marilyn's overdose as a parable, as an example of how excess would always inevitably be punished, as a warning against wantonness and sacrilege. Ambrose advised in his Irish brogue, "We can all learn a great deal from her passing." Though he was more familiar with the famous men she'd married, and though she'd always struck him as a little dime-store, my father thought shouldn't we mourn, shouldn't we cast our judgments aside? When the old priest sat down, the young, celibate men hunched over their simple meals, bowed their shaved heads in unison, and prayed for their lost platinum goddess.

Later, when my mother and father returned home, when they apologized and promised to fête me with lobster, I pouted and claimed it wouldn't be enough.

"It was my confirmation," I said. "Didn't it mean anything to you?"

Dad nodded to Mom that he would make amends. He invited me out to our screened-in porch, overlooking our river. Dad insisted he was proud of me. Joked that I might carry the cross for all of us. "Maybe you'll be our cardinal. Heck, maybe you'll make it to pope," he said.

"Do you ever miss it?" I asked.

Dad lamented the fact that he never went through with his missionary work in Chile. "I was keen on trolling this one lake famous for brown trout—big as a man's thigh. But then I met your mother."

Having spent the afternoon reading about his past, I quizzed him on leaving the brotherhood, abandoning his pursuit of righteousness. Dad smiled and reached into the beer cooler he kept on the porch. He told me not to take things so seriously.

"That Jesuit stuff was a long time ago. To be honest, I never really bought into it the way some of the other guys did." He twisted the top off the amber bottle. "The self-denial, the kneeling, the silence."

"You didn't talk much, did you?" I asked.

"When we did, we spoke mostly in Latin."

I imagined my father speaking in a dead language with men who had made their desires half dead.

IX. THE DAUGHTERS OF JERUSALEM

After more apologies and my lobster banquet, my mother, father, and I arrived home and noticed the light on in the basement. I went downstairs and found Rachel packing. She confided, "I'm five months along. Due on Halloween." Then she shoved a knot of clothes into a knapsack. "Trick or treat."

I noticed that she'd packed my favorite nightgown.

"Are you keeping it?" I asked, uncertain if I was referring to her baby or my nightgown.

"I'll give my spawn away. A wealthy Presbyterian couple, maybe a pair of devout Buddhists, or a kick-ass family of Unitarians. No fucking Catholics."

"How did this happen?" I heard myself ask.

"Don't you know." Rachel twirled around on her bare heels. "There are only so many stories for women. Be a nun. Get married, get raped, get murdered. Get pregnant and become a mother"—she paused—"or not. I want my own story, an unknown plot."

"I could be an aunt." Even then I suspected I might never have children of my own. "Do Mom and Dad know?"

"Only if you tell them," she said.

My sister didn't leave that night. She disappeared for good a few days after my confirmation. Since she'd gone missing so often, our parents didn't know to take this vanishing seriously. I said nothing. The days became weeks and I fantasized that Rachel had returned to Spain, that she was living in Barcelona earning her keep as a flamenco dancer. I wanted her to send me postcards of men in pink tights fighting bloodied bulls. I'd hoped she might ask me to join her.

As time passed, my mother and I stopped attending mass regularly. It was the summer, and we were lazy from the heat. Mom and I went swimming instead. She bought me my own green bikini. We grew closer and, with every outing, I believed that Mom was on the verge of confessing that I'd always been her favorite, that we were better off without Rachel squawking and flaunting.

"Rachel is her father's daughter." Mom balanced on top of an inner tube, swirling around one of the river's tide pools. "It kills him that they're so similar, so stubborn. I suppose she's like me too, I mean we look the same. But you, you're your own person. I was never as smart and grounded as you."

"I'm like you and Dad in some ways." I dove under, not waiting for a response.

With Rachel's disappearance, I felt free to invite Malaya to the house for sleepovers. The loud bickering space where Rachel preened and prodded was now filled by an elegant, quiet presence. When we changed into our pajamas, Malaya always stripped off her clothes in front of me, not flaunting her body, but unashamed, unafraid to let me see her. I'm not sure if Malaya understood how I felt, we were barely fifteen. Sometimes we'd sleep in the same bed, her front pressed against my back. I'd feel her breath on my neck and hope that she might lean in, might brush her lips against my cheek. I wasn't even sure what women did as lovers, but I thought if there was some signal, some way for us to both agree that we wanted more, wanted to explore, that it might happen, and that both of us would know what to do.

Only my father kept going to mass, kept praying for Rachel's return. Earlier that summer Dad had eavesdropped on Rachel's late-night phone calls. I eavesdropped and heard him tell Mom that he believed Rachel was pregnant. He was certain that St. Christopher was to blame. Dad tracked his missing daughter down to a boardinghouse in Hartford, Connecticut. She'd already left, but the manager confirmed that the woman he'd been renting the back bedroom to was carrying a child.

In the Benedictine convent where I now volunteer on weekends, where I clean the kitchen, stock the pantry, read verses to the dying nuns, there are still young pregnant women who seek shelter before their adoptions. Frightened, silent girls who suspend themselves in prayerful sleep. Wishing to be roused when their pregnancies are over. Hoping to return to their lives with the promise that nothing has changed. During those months before giving birth, I am certain that my sister did not go to a convent or a home for pregnant unwed mothers. I imagine that pregnant Rachel found a willing man on a motorcycle and rode off with him to his lakeside cabin. Maybe she taught him to fish the way Dad had taught us. Even in brown-green waders with her belly swollen, Rachel would have looked irresistible. Though this stranger was not her baby's father, with his Jesus hair and his Rasputin good looks he would make her swoon, pay the bills, and keep her happy until the time came to give up her child. He would beg her to make the baby theirs, promise to turn in his leathers and Kawasaki for driving loafers and a sedan. Rachel would be tempted, but my sister had convinced herself that the child was not hers.

X. STRIPPED OF GARMENTS

One Sunday Malaya and I woke up on opposite sides of my bed. We had planned to go to church together. At some point in the night, Malaya kicked off her blankets. I heard the rustling of nightclothes, the snapping of an elastic waistband, the movement of fingers. Watched her arm saw back and forth, casting rapid shadows on the ceiling. Felt that side of the bed shake as her legs kicked. I wasn't sure if this was some sort of signal. I asked, "Are you okay?" Malaya said nothing. I asked again. She said, "I'm sleeping."

Malaya dressed quickly that morning and insisted on calling her parents. "I'm not feeling well," she lied into the phone. While we waited for her dad to chariot her away, I showed Malaya my father's journal. Together we read about that night in North Aurora, how my father woke up in the summer of 1962 and heard the splashing, the men running across the concrete and torpedoing their bodies into the pool. Dad described how he left his room, slid open the glass door, and spied the naked men and boys at play, the floodlights beaming over their bodies, the boys muscular and taut. The potbellied Chicago priest stood in the shallow end, smiling, his hand snaked down the front of his shorts. None of the naked boys were being touched, but all were being watched.

Dad couldn't believe that no one else had been alerted. He feared that he was stuck in a dream, and so he went and knocked on Anthony Santoro's door, hoping his friend might help him make sense of the evening. In his journal, he noted that Anthony said, "Come in," but my father was forever inclined to barge in unannounced. The door was open—why would a door in a seminary ever be locked? Anthony and

Dominic were not having sex. Their clothes sat piled on the carpeted floor. The blankets and sheets pulled back. The naked men lounged facing each other. A chessboard between them. It was Dominic's move.

"Is that why your father quit?" Malaya asked me.

"No," I told her. "He quit because he met my mother. They left their orders for each other."

"You should have read the part where they met." Malaya seized the book from me and began flipping through the pages. "What's wrong with you?" she asked. "Don't you know how to tell a love story?"

XI. THE THIRD FALL

A week after my father caught Anthony and Dominic together, Dad was roused from his sleep by Brother Ambrose and instructed to hurry to the rectory. Once there, Dad was surprised to see Dominic and several other brothers all standing with their heads bowed. My father was certain that he was in trouble——he'd said nothing about the swimming, about the men and the boys, about his best friend and the handsome priest. This was his chance to come clean. Brother Ambrose looked directly at my father as he spoke, "One of us is lost."

Brother Ambrose handed my father a flashlight, told him to search the grounds. "Check the trees," Ambrose said. "Our brother may be hanging from one of them."

Dominic had come up that night to see Anthony, only to find a suicide note. "I love you. I've left to hang myself." He brought the note to Ambrose, who asked no questions.

Together the brothers cut a path through the loamy woods surrounding the resort. As Dad stepped on wet moss and hemlock needles, he strobed his bright beam over the lush canopies of hackberry and pear hawthorn, their green leaves burning in the moonglow. The men sought a body in the branches. My father did not want to find his friend.

Earlier that evening, half a dozen horses had broken free from their paddock at the North Aurora Racetrack. The thoroughbreds stampeded, galloping into the night, exhausting themselves until they found Brother Anthony Santoro, barefoot and wandering, a noose of rope cradled in his arms. He'd been walking for miles on the traffickless road, praying for a strong tree bough. Instead he found himself corralled by these tired, breathless animals. An approximate sign from God.

XII. RIVER OF NO RETURN

My sister, who never studied for her own confirmation, who didn't believe in demons or priests, etched out her last words, "For God so loved the world that He gave His only Son," in neat schoolgirl penmanship on the back of a Stop n' Shop grocery bag. It was December. Her motel room was not winterized. Rachel left the bag on the bed, wandered out wearing my borrowed extravagant nightgown, and found her way to the half-drained motel swimming pool. I can see her breath fog the air of Barnstable, Massachusetts. Can picture the pool's icy green water. Somewhere there is a bottle of vodka, a purple box of Sominex—the blister packs broken. Does she flinch when her bare hands touch the pool's cold metal ladder? When she first enters the water, does she sink, swim, or float? Does my diaphanous nightgown billow up around her neck, exposing the fresh, stapled scar on her belly, the track marks from where her child was pulled? She'd given up a baby, her only begotten, so that she could die in the awful swimming pool of the Sandpiper Inn a few days after Christmas.

In the Old Testament, Rachel bore two children, Joseph and Benjamin. She lost her life giving birth to her second son. When my father identified my sister's frozen, waterlogged body, he did not think of the biblical Rachel. He thought of Marilyn Monroe dead in her bedroom, and of Brother Ambrose's insistence that anything could be learned from her passing. Marilyn couldn't have children, couldn't be anything other than sex to most people. I know from a television special that Marilyn used to visit schoolyards and longingly spy on children. I like this hearsay. In playgrounds and parks across this country, I have searched for Rachel's child on jungle gyms and swing sets. I have watched little girls and boys kick and pump their legs out to the sky, and I know that my sister is somehow still alive, still present in the world in a way that I am not and never could be.

XIII. *MISSA PRO DEFUNCTIS*

Anthony and Dominic drove up from New York for Rachel's funeral. At the wake, my numb mother introduced them to me as partners. I asked, "What sort of business?" and the men smiled. I knew they were gay, but I wanted them to talk to me, wanted them to recognize some part of me.

"We're your father's old Jesuit friends." Anthony explained that he'd abandoned the seminary for Hollywood, for best boy gigs on low-budget biker flicks.

"It was fun while it lasted." Dominic rolled his eyes. "Now we languish in Westchester and run a multiplex."

Anthony put his hand on my shoulder. "I'm sure you loved her very much."

My sister's open casket was an arm's length away. I'd donated my white confirmation gown for the viewing. The funerary artist had dusted Rachel's pale puffy face with a pink opalescent powder and teased her dull brown hair. She looked like a slumbering bride. Someone had laced rosary beads around her waxy hands. I'd knelt down and kissed the crucifix, certain that my sister would have hated her burial display.

"Do you still play chess?" I asked Anthony. "My father told me that he'd always catch you and Dominic playing chess late at night."

Anthony raised his eyebrows, but Dominic understood. "We play," he said, "as often as we can."

XIV. LAMENTATION

In the decade since my sister's death, my parents have hunted down and blamed every one of her lovers. Have interrogated motel clerks and accused Father Burleigh of driving their daughter into despair. In their pain, my mother and father have often forgotten me. I notice and try not to mind. My job writing grants for Catholic Charities keeps me busy toiling long hours securing funds for Christ. Dad shakes his head at my work. Mom, who has long ceased going to church, considers me a traitor.

A few weeks ago when my father first saw the potbellied Chicago priest on television, he called me at my office. I listened to his story while staring at a brochure pinned to my cubicle. An image of a starving Filipino girl, a bowl of rice her salvation—all for a yearly donation of thirty-two cents a day. Dad met the priest only once almost forty years prior, but he recognized this man's obscene body. In the news clip, the priest wears a black cassock, and though the sleeves are long, they cannot hide the handcuffs clapped around his wrists. Four boys, now men, came forward with a litany of touching over the clothes, under the clothes, in the parish and after sporting games. The priest coached and counseled a youth sports league and the men testified that he offered them gifts and incentives: sneakers, football gear, tickets to Bulls games, trips to the racetrack.

I've never revealed to our father that Rachel and I read his journal. The book went missing at the end of that summer just as Malaya withdrew, claiming I made her uncomfortable. "You want something from me?" she asked. "Don't you?" I'd always suspected that Malaya stole the journal. That she used her father's matches to scorch the Hilton, the horses, the chess game, our friendship.

As I listened to my father over the phone, I considered how difficult this church scandal would make my job. How much harder my campaign, my fund-raising might become in the shadow of more abuse. Then I thought of all the stories that had gone unspoken in our family. The secrets. The omissions. Remembered my mother's insistence that Rachel was somehow a greater reflection of her parents' love. That I was my own person. My own mistake. My father's voice faltered as he said, "I could have stopped this years ago. I failed."

I asked my father, "What did you see?"

He said, "I saw nothing. I saw a man in the pool."

"Who was he with?" I asked.

"There was no one. There were several boys."

"What did you do?"

"I did nothing," he said. "I looked away."

XV. RESURRECTION

For me, my sister is always in Spain, living it up with Saint Ignatius Loyola, a man who began his adult life as a playboy before submitting to his own divine conversion. Rachel and Ignatius are waving the Veronica in a bullring. Rachel svelte and healthy, Ignatius drunk and carefree, the bulls indifferent to their good time. My sister with her pink tiara of hair, dressed in my gauzy stolen nightgown, is so dangerously beautiful that she has the power to keep Ignatius from God. I know that what my father regrets most is joining and then leaving the Jesuits. Had he stayed in his order there never would have been a Rachel. If Saint Ignatius had commanded a greater hold over my father, perhaps Dad would have stayed. But my father knew sex and could imagine a life with my mother, even when she was a young, virginal bride of Jesus. Had Dad never joined the Jesuits, he might have stayed forever with Lois Pendleton, his Protestant secret, a barren woman who died one October evening when her electrician husband strangled her with an extension cord.

My father, the holder of so many stories, could not save his own children.

When I think of that long-ago night at the Hilton, I know that Dad should have joined the swimming boys under the stars. He should have frightened their handsome, dark-haired molester. Dad could have taught the boys how to dive, how to use their bodies as a weapon, how to protect themselves from evil and temptation. My sister loved to swim, loved to hold my head underwater to see if I could go without breathing. The day she left, I almost confessed my crush on Malaya. I know that Rachel would have laughed and encouraged me. "That's great. Kiss her hard. Make me all kinds of proud." If I'd told her my truth, maybe Rachel might have stayed. Instead, I let Rachel disappear, the one person who might have known me. It's easy enough to remain a novice to sex and love, to forgo touch in favor of isolation. I have yet to live up to my sister.

While my father awaits the Chicago priest's verdict, we often fish together in the rapid currents of the Wading River. Sometimes my dad will call out to me in excitement over a golden trout racing on his line. "Rachel," he will say to me. I do not correct him. Instead, I push myself through the water. "What is it, Father?" I ask. "How can I help?"

CAMP

After busting the Andro Boys for scoring an ounce off of Downtown Homeless Pete, we retreated to the roof of the Octagon to smoke the evidence. Sammy Chatterjee—Business and Economics—packed the bowl while Regina Racela—Video and Film Production—described how the buffest offender had offered her a bribe: "Promised me a sit-down with Ridley Scott. Claimed his mother was a studio head. Little juicer didn't realize I'd read his file. His parents own a day spa in Phoenix." I smiled and seized the pipe, inhaling the loamy smoke, proud of Video and Film Production's superior research and recon skills. In my four summers at SURPASS, I'd never worked with a faculty this talented, this committed to learning imperatives, this willing to oversee conflict resolutions and this devoted to illicit consumption. A superior crew of educators, we were all known by what we taught. They called me Gender Studies.

The drug sting and anticipated expulsions were unusual

for SURPASS but necessary for us to maintain command over our unruly charges. As faculty, we were advised by the administration to mostly turn a blind eye to controlled substances and promiscuity. SURPASS was, after all, an accelerated Precollege Edutainment Program dedicated to introducing adolescents to the challenges and choices of adulthood. Parents sporked over twelve thousand dollars (plus supplementary charges for snacks and excursions) for their teenaged wastelands to enjoy six weeks of college-level seminars, world-class international social networking, superior managed fun, and almost limitless freedom. This was high-concept experimental pedagogy. We weren't running a summer camp.

The job paid well, but the pressures of being on call and in charge of over two hundred overprivileged evildoers with superior test scores and inferior self-control often necessitated external motivation. Earlier in the day, Brad King—Philosophy and Ethics—had warned us that our own supply of marijuana, which Philosophy and Ethics himself had secured from Uptown Homeless Pete, was dwindling into seeds and stones. "If we want to blaze tonight, we'll need a human sacrifice. Take out those hippie midgets hopped up on growth hormone. Pot will stunt them silly."

Every July SURPASS rented out the entire New England campus of this impressive top ten liberal arts college. The school's octagon tower housed our classrooms and overlooked the muddy construction site of a new war memorial. A Famous Alum had recently donated the marble and bronze in honor of his firstborn who'd had his legs, arms, and torso blown off in Fallujah during a breakfast run. While delivering bagels to a hungry colonel, the Famous Son drove a bulletproofless jeep into a hailstorm of rocket fire. The unfinished monument resembled a giant poppy flower with a series of sundials and obelisks resting on an elevated starburst. As he smoked, Alex Pratt—Revolution and Anarchy—saluted our fallen heroes.

We took turns inhaling deeply. Philosophy and Ethics waxed on about the strong mossy overtones and caramel top notes of what he identified as Nicaraguan Zero-Zero Coastal Herb. "We might have to switch our supply chain from Uptown to Downtown Pete." We groused and whined about our evening dorm duty, quieting as we heard the Director scale the rickety wrought-iron fire escape. As he landed on the trembling tar paper roof, he announced, "The Andro Boys aren't going home."

"But we have evidence." Video and Film Production held up the baggie of pot. "One of my students took a Super-8 of the bust."

"I watched the rough footage. Nice close-ups." The Director raised a silver flask and tipped it back to his lips. He blotted the sides of his mouth and said, "The ringleader's stepmother is a major campaign contributor. Our power to expel has been suspended."

SURPASS began as the brainchild and cash cow of Gerry Progress, a local state assemblyman who was currently gearing up for a run at the governor's mansion. Bosswise, Progress prided himself on his hands-off administrative approach. At the beginning of every session, Progress gave the same speech to the faculty before escaping to his family's Nantucket compound. Progress liked to emphasize SURPASS's commitment to innovation: "You are here as progressive educators, subversive role models. I want you to tear down the boundaries between students and teachers. Just don't fuck any of the kids, okay?"

Business and Economics unbuttoned the bulky pocket of his cargo shorts, pulled out his own metal-and-leather flask, took a tug, and said, "I understand the numbers game during an election year, but word has already spread that these kids are going home. If we grant them a mulligan, how will the rest of the camp react?"

"This isn't a camp. It's an accelerated Precollege Edutainment Program." I unscrewed the top of my coffee thermos and took a belt of tequila. "We need to have a community meeting. We must address our concerns and allow the Andro Boys the opportunity to apologize. If we spin it like we're benevolent dictators, the cherubs won't realize we've been castrated."

"Gender Studies has a point." The Director briefly massaged my shoulders before pulling his bony fingers away.

Though we'd flirted these past four summers, the Director and I had only recently begun sneaking and sexing around. His overcompensating masculinity—his love of rugby, his constant desire to go bouldering, his fascination with Steve McQueen—made me suspicious of his sexuality, but he trimmed my split ends and did my laundry, so his possible love of cock failed to hinder our romance. Teaching Second Wave Feminism, Queer Theory, and the Performative Nature of Gender made me more open to the fluidity of human sexuality.

Revolution and Anarchy suggested we lodge a formal complaint against Progress's fund-raising practices and donate a percentage of our salaries to the Socialist party's gubernatorial candidate. No one ever paid attention to Revolution and Anarchy.

The Director asked us to retire to our dorms and put the children to bed. We retreated down the fire escape, our glassy eyes vibrant as stars.

When the Director came to my suite that night, he looked ashen and contrite. He played with the brushes on my bureau, fixed his wavy brown hair in my mirror, then said, "Progress insisted I fire Regina."

"Video and Film Production?" I asked.

"She's packing her cameras as we speak."

According to the Director, it wasn't enough for the Andro Boys to stay. "The parents wanted blood. They threatened a civil defamation suit."

"But the boys were buying weed—a lot of weed. In the real world they'd go to jail."

"Only poor people get paddy wagoned for cannabis." The Director took a Mason Pearson brush from my bureau and began grooming my long auburn hair.

"If they can fire one of us, they can fire all of us." I worried about faculty morale, worried about losing my own job. I needed this summer gig so I could afford not to work in the fall. I still had to finish my dissertation: "Chicks with Dicks: A Study of the Influence of Transvestites on American Culture." I'd completed the chapters on J. Edgar Hoover, RuPaul, and Janet Reno, but the book was still missing something. I needed to draft and revise a longer section on the phenomenon of gender swapping that seemed to exist historically within nearly every indigenous population. If there weren't enough men or women within a tribe, young children were often chosen and raised as the opposite sex. Native Americans called them berdaches, South Pacific Islanders referred to them as may mays, the good people of Papua New Guinea labeled them landies, the Egyptians had a special half-bird, half-camel hieroglyph, while the Aztecs built impressive ziggurats to honor their jaguar-skinned cross-dressers. Gender swapping had the ability to heal these often warring cultures, to bring relief and even love.

"Our best bet is to let the kids run wild. We can't restrain their nouveau riche entitlement." The Director began pinning up my hair into a tight French chignon. "You know, with your bone structure, you really could have modeled."

"Could have?" I asked.

"You still could. I mean—"

Before he had a chance to finish his statement, I unpinned my hair and pointed to the door. "It's been a long day," I said.

"No cuddles?" the Director asked.

I rolled my eyes and went to sleep.

At breakfast the next morning, Business and Economics kept repeating the phrase, "Nutella blow job." He'd been doing the rounds in the boys' dormitory when he heard giggling in the multipurpose room. "I walked in on five naked girls giving Frenchy McFrench-A-Lot and Chi-rish some oral tradition."

"The international students always score the most tail." Linda Adler—International Studies—folded a large piece of waffle into her small mouth, chewing as she spoke. "What did you do?"

"Followed standard protocols. Told the maidens to get dressed and return to their rooms. Threw throw pillows over the offending penises. Frenchy's on his way back to Versailles. Chi-rish is either exiled to Beijing or heading off to his summer home in Dublin."

"What's Nutella?" Philosophy and Ethics asked.

"It's a delicious chocolate hazelnut spread," I said. "Sort of like a classy peanut butter." I asked if the girls were also going to be removed from the program.

"Probably," Business and Economics answered. "We're not kicking them out for the sex, just for breaking curfew. This should make up for the Andro Boys."

During that morning's Gender Studies seminar, I attempted to lead the class in an analysis of Monique Wittig's abhorrence of the feminine pronoun. My students, all of whom were female, only wanted to discuss the recent slate of scandals.

"Is it true that Business and Economics was running a prostitution ring?" Sally Mantooth chewed her hair as she spoke.

Joy Walker nodded, shaking her double chin. "I heard one of the girls has syphilis."

Sally agreed. "I know for a fact that two of the girls have breast implants. I'm not naming names, but all of the ladies have eating disorders and the bulimic ones spent the night purging Nutella."

"What's Nutella?" Syreeta Pritchett turned her doe eyes at me.

I smiled and said, "I think this is what dumb people call a teachable moment." I hopped up onto the desk and sat cross-legged. "Why do you imagine it is that women always say disparaging things about other women? Are we our own worst enemies?"

"Look," Sally said, "sluts give all of us a bad name."

Vera Fuller, one of the few scholarship students, raised her hand. "If all language is patriarchal, then aren't all women at the mercy of our failed linguistic system?"

I nodded and asked my students if they could think of other negative terms describing females. The girls had fun shouting out words as I wrote the list on the board: whore, bitch, crazy bitch, gold digger, skank, ice princess, trim, tramp, twat, bimbo, hooker, prostitute, snatch, dyke, diesel dyke, lesbo, lipstick lesbian, rug muncher, spinster, stripper, Barbie, loose, virgin, Lolita, dragon lady, frigid, cocktease, superfreak, nasty girl, the other woman, chicken head, cougar, cum bucket, seductress, boob job, black widow, wench, slit, gash, hole, Hillary Clinton, Martha Stewart, Jennifer Aniston, stepmonster, JAP, jezebel, bridezilla, diva, old maid, prima donna, geisha, witch, wench, succubus, shrew, Pollyanna, brat, bubblehead, ho, muff, mommy dearest, dominatrix, dumb blonde, bambi, bunny, beaver, doll, ballbuster, nutcracker, thunder thighs, harpy, man-eater.

I added "trollop" and said, "We're forgetting the most important one."

My students looked at one another then shouted out in unison, "Cunt."

I stood back from the board admiring our litany. "Now," I said, "let's brainstorm a list of negative words for men."

"Bastard," Raquel, a svelte Long Islander coughed out.

"Well," I said, "isn't that word really still pejorative against the mother. I mean, you only have a bastard child if the father doesn't marry the mother."

"What about pussy?" Vera asked.

"You're still just really making fun of women," I argued.

Syreeta whispered, "Cock and prick."

I pointed out that both terms were still a celebration of the phallus.

Sally Mantooth said, "I think the worst thing you can call a guy is"—she lowered her voice—"a fag."

"Right," I said. "The worst thing you can do is question his masculinity."

"But most words for male slut are like totally cool and funny." Raquel rattled off her own list: "gigolo, player, pimp, Don Juan, man whore, Casanova."

"Excellent point, Raquel." I liked my students best when they held forth. "You ladies are totally becoming third-wave feminists."

Sally said, "I'm not a feminist, but I think if we appropriate the language, if we call one another bitches and hos, it's like the words lose their power."

"Well," I said, "we seem to have come full circle."

"We have some questions for you." Vera looked around the room as her classmates nodded for her to continue. "Why weren't the Andro Boys kicked out? And what happened to their pot?"

I assured Vera that the boys were contrite and that the controlled substances were safely controlled. "We always contact the proper authorities when disposing of any illicit materials." As I lied, I realized that I hadn't taken a shower that morning. I could still smell the sticky icky smoke in my hair.

Sally said, "I heard the Revolution and Anarchy class is organizing some sort of civil liberties protest. Maybe we should plan a protest too."

"What would you like to demonstrate against?" I asked.

"You're the teacher," Sally said. "Why don't you think of something for us to be angry about?"

After class, I went to the Director's office to apologize for being a bitch and to search the infirmary cabinet for stray Percocets. The Director asked if I wouldn't mind serving on a "mild suicide watch."

"One of the Nutella Girls is threatening to cut herself. We need to take precautions."

"Does her file confirm she's at risk?" Though I took every warning seriously, a number of our students were quick to blackmail.

"Red flags everywhere. History of self-mutilation, shoplifting, pyromania. She's a classic after-school special. Poor kid was a hysterical mess this morning during Revolution and Anarchy. I haven't been able to reach her parents. The other girls seem fine. I guess oral sex has really lost its stigma."

"You've got to admire their creativity," I said. "When I was their age, I had no strategy for transforming a blow job into a yummy snack treat."

"Where do you come out on the five-to-two girl/boy ratio?"

I gazed down into the Director's soft blue eyes. Though he wore his hair tall to compensate, the Director was a good three inches shorter than me. I said, "I guess I'm conflicted. As a feminist, I resent having the patriarchy literally shoved down the not-so-innocent throats of five of our students. The Marxist in me admires the division of labor while my horny teenager side thinks Frenchy McFrench-A-Lot is a real hottie. I'm sorry to see him go."

"It looks like he's staying."

It turned out that Frenchy, Chi-rish, and all the girls would remain in the program, while Business and Economics had already taken the turnpike home. The Director explained that the girls felt violated—Business and Economics had walked in on an intimate act.

"He followed protocol." I shook my head.

"Ethics and Philosophy has also been escorted from the premises. He made a joke during his morning class. 'Nutella: a hundred uses. Now, a hundred and one.' Apparently someone in his class taped him on a cell phone, posted the clip online, and e-mailed the link to Gerry Progress. It's too bad because Ethics and Philosophy was supposed to MC tonight's talent show. Now I'll have to put on my tuxedo and act like I'm really in charge."

"The inmates," I said, "are running the goddamn asylum."

The Director stretched out his arms and placed his hands on my shoulders. "Where does all your beauty come from?" he asked. "Your mother's side or your father's?"

"Seriously," I shrugged off the Director's hands. "What crime do these criminals have to commit before we can kick one of them out?"

"Progress told me not to call him unless someone burns down the camp."

"It's not a camp," I protested. "It's an accelerated precollege Edutainment Program."

The Director asked me if I could teach Aristotle or if I knew anything about Aristotle Onassis. "We're going to need coverage on courses."

"I thought I was on a 'mild suicide watch.'"

"That's right. Take the keys to Ritalin and drive Blowjob to the mall. I'll give you the corporate credit card. Buy her anything she wants."

As I piloted our minivan, Blowjob twisted her blue and gold dreadlocks and informed me that she didn't want to visit the mall. "My stylist buys all of my ready-to-wear." Instead she wanted me to set up a meet-and-greet with Downtown Homeless Pete. "I hear he's selling these transcendent mushrooms. I need something to take the edge off. Something to palate-cleanse the bitterness of hazelnut."

I put Ritalin in reverse. Every year we christened our fleet of minivans. My first summer, we named the vehicles after Supreme Court justices. When I got into a minor fender bender on a field trip to an AIDS hospice, I had the pleasure of telling the Director, "Antonin Scalia got rear-ended."

This year's decision to nickname the vans after popular prescription drugs was probably a mistake. The kids loved taking Viagra to the sports fields and Vicodin to the amusement park, but they were less interested in riding in Prilosec or Boniva. Nobody liked Lipitor.

Ritalin was the fastest and sportiest van—red with black racing stripes. Blowjob sat up front in the passenger's seat and pressed her bare feet against the glove box. Her fingers and toes were painted to match her hair—turquoise with gold seahorses decaled on each nail.

"Did you know that male seahorses actually get pregnant?" I asked.

"Look, Gender Studies, are you going to cop for me or not?" Blowjob had cushiony lips and large veneered teeth.

"I really don't think I can buy you psychedelics." I sounded firm yet reasonable.

"Didn't the Director tell you that I'm at risk? I mean, I might throw myself from a moving vehicle." Blowjob bared her horsy teeth at me.

"Maybe you need to go home," I said.

Blowjob explained that she couldn't go home. She had no home. Her mother was in the process of getting hitched and moving to Abu Dhabi. "She's marrying an emir. My sexy presence might destabilize their dynasty."

When I asked about her father, she rolled her eyes. "Arms dealer. All I know is he's somewhere in the sub-Sahara pedaling Kalashnikovs and fucking Berbers."

Blowjob suffered from extreme parental alienation. Goldilocks with fake dreadlocks. I suspected that she was the Nutella ringleader, her promiscuity a result of having been abandoned by her father and rejected by her mother. I understood her pain only too well, but there was almost nothing I could do for her. With her voluminous mane of blue blond hair she resembled Hélène Cixous's metaphorical Medusa—a woman burdened by her own powerful sexuality. I needed to see Blowjob smile.

"Let's brainstorm something positive." I beamed. "We could go for ice cream or find a place that does those temporary henna tattoos or maybe you'd like to go see a summer blockbuster or take a walk around the lake."

"I'm lactose intolerant, henna tattoos are like total cultural tourism, I refuse to support Hollywood's exploitation of women, and if I even glimpse water I might be tempted to Virginia Woolf myself."

Blowjob was no dummy. She couldn't be purchased for a song or easily entertained. I noticed she had her tongue and eyebrow pierced. Each earlobe held two small gold hoops with plenty of skin left over. Body modification required a parental permission slip, but I figured her mom and dad weren't in any position to offer or deny approval. Blowjob wore tight plastic bangles on either wrist that probably hid a row of self-inflicted scars. If Blowjob really was a cutter, then maybe the answer to her pain was more pain.

"How about"—I looked over my shoulder and changed lanes—"we both go and get our ears pierced?"

Blowjob pulled at the stud embedded in her eyebrow. "That might work." She considered my proposal. "But not at the mall. We need to go to a legit piercing parlor. I know a head shop that uses aboriginal needles. It's downtown, right by the sushi bar. Afterward, we can get maki rolls and numb ourselves with hot sake."

I'd never noticed the head shop before. Blowjob and I edged past a Dumpster-lined alley and down two sets of stairs until we reached an unmarked door. Blowjob knocked three times. An older white-haired woman with a thick grayish beard answered, gave us the once-over, and escorted us inside.

Despite its subterranean location, the head shop was immaculate. Hand-blown glass bongs cast red and purple shadows on the white cinder-block walls. A row of cushioned examination tables sat sheathed in wax paper. The sharp sterile scent of rubbing alcohol hurt the air. In the corner, a young man tattooed his own wrist, the buzz of the needle stinging the metal fillings in my mouth.

"What would you like?" The Bearded Lady folded her arms.

I surprised myself by saying that I wanted my nose pierced. "Just a little silver stud."

The Bearded Lady nodded and turned to Blowjob. "And you?"

"I'm thinking about it." Blowjob eyed the tattoo artist. "My sister can go first."

My heart swelled a little to hear Blowjob call me sister. Sometimes, I imagined that I'd chosen to work with children because of my own lost and lonely childhood. A fatherless only child, I'd spent my summers toiling at one job or another desperate to please my suffering mother. To most people, I came off as tough, cold even. Only I knew the depths of my vulnerability. Happily, I played along with Blowjob's sister lie, asking my false sibling if she'd hold my hand during the piercing. Wax paper crinkled beneath me as I stretched out across the hospital bed. The Bearded Lady snapped on plastic gloves before prodding my nose.

"Which side?" she asked.

"The left, I guess."

"Good choice." Blowjob stared down into my face. "You know, with your cheekbones and skinny bod you could totally model. Maybe not like print or runway but like an artist's model."

The last thing I remembered before blacking out was the warm feeling of blood spreading over my left cheek. Perhaps I tried to sit up too soon, or maybe I was light-headed from not having had lunch. When I came to, I heard loud sirens and found the tattoo artist at my side holding a cold cloth to my forehead.

"Happens all the time," he said. "I'll get you some orange juice."

I took small sips and slowly sat up. The tattoo artist handed me a mirror and promised that the swelling would go down—eventually. "Could take a half hour or a week or three months." My face didn't need a nose stud. I knew instantly that I'd remove the piercing later that night, praying that the hole sealed itself. I heard more sirens. Their noise amplifying my own emergency. Looking around the room, I noticed that Blowjob was nowhere to be found. The tattoo artist must have seen the panic in my eyes.

"Don't worry," he said. "Your sister's in our private room getting her nipples pierced."

The hot sake relieved the throbbing pain in my left nostril. I checked out my stainless-steel reflection in Blowjob's plump metal teapot. My skin appeared red and blistery, clearly allergic to the silver ball impaling me. With seahorses dancing across her fingernails, Blowjob squeezed her right tit and moaned, "It felt amazing. I wish you'd let me get the other one done."

Despite my dizziness, I'd managed to interrupt nipplegate. Once I explained to the Bearded Lady that Blowjob was not only underaged but also not my relative, we were asked to pay for our jewelry and instructed never to return.

While I wrapped a piece of pink ginger around my tongue, Blowjob complained, "I'm all asymmetrical. Might as well kill myself. Can't I at least have some rice wine?"

I poured myself more sake, ignoring Blowjob's request. "You now have something to look forward to. You have the rest of your life to get your other ta-ta harpooned."

I insisted on walking off the effects of the sake before getting back into Ritalin. Blowjob and I window-shopped the tacky boutiques of Main Street. We ducked into the pharmacy and charged some antiseptic soap and hydrocortisone to the corporate card. On our way back to the van, we strolled by Downtown Homeless Pete. He waved his heroin arm at us, offered up some wholesale hashish, and inquired about the terrorism.

"What terrorism?" I asked.

"Up at the college. I heard the Octagon got blitzed."

We arrived on campus just as the firemen were rolling up their hoses. The Octagon had lost four of its sides. The charred interior of the building exposed like an open-faced doll's house. Blowjob and I raced up the hill. A police officer tried to hold us back but I flashed my faculty ID just in time for a stocky firewoman to request I remove Sally Mantooth and Chi-rish from the roof of her lime yellow fire truck. Sally and Chi-rish licked and suctioned each other's necks as the engine idled. The recent series of teacher firings left me vulnerable. Interfering with their passion might be grounds for my own dismissal. I glanced at Blowjob and asked if she wouldn't mind intervening.

"No problem," she said, climbing up onto the ladder.

The firewoman stood in front of the wounded war memorial, the bronze and marble littered with debris, the poppy flower missing its petals. I needed to know if there were any fatalities. The Director was nowhere to be seen. The firewoman examined a small metal box that looked like the detonator switch to some sort of bomb. As she turned the object over, I noticed a decal glinting on one side of the box. The afternoon sunlight caught the familiar shimmering silhouette of a golden seahorse.

The firewoman pointed to Blowjob, who was busy flashing her new piercing at Chi-rish. "We were missing one, but is she part of your camp?"

"It's not a camp," I said. "It's a juvenile detention center."

The firewoman squinted at me and I asked about the adults, hoping no one had been hurt.

Several faculty members awaited treatment at the hospital for smoke inhalation. The Director, who'd been in the building when the explosion occurred, was at the police station dictating his statement. Revolution and Anarchy had been arrested.

"Looks like you're in charge." The firewoman paused, stared, and asked, "Did you ever model high-class swimsuits?"

I assured her that I'd done nothing of the sort.

"We have an old Pirelli Calendar hanging up at the station. I could have sworn you were January." She pointed up at Sally, Chi-rish, and Blowjob who were smoking cigarettes on the roof of the fire truck. "Please, get those little pagans off my vehicle."

While I struggled over whether or not to drop a dime on Blowjob, I decided the best way to distract the students and keep them far from the scene of the crime was to wrangle all of them into the auditorium for that evening's talent show. Standing at the front of the stage, my infected nose stud itching like hell, I passed around a sign-up sheet, hopeful that the children would manage to entertain one another until some executive decision was reached. There was no way the program could continue. I just hoped I'd be paid for the full summer.

"Wait a minute." Blowjob grabbed the sign-up sheet away from Frenchy McFrench-A-Lot. "Shouldn't the police be waterboarding all of us? There's a terrorist in our midst and you want us to tap-dance?"

Though I had legitimate suspicions, I also had protective instincts—ones Freud would wrongly label "maternal." I wondered if Blowjob wanted to get caught. If she'd acted alone or if her terrorism had been sanctioned by Anarchy and Revolution. Maybe the entire class was to blame and maybe there had even been some sort of exchange: blowjobs for bombs. But what I couldn't understand was what it was exactly that these children were protesting. Perhaps their own privilege and freedom.

"I minored in arts therapy." I projected my voice over the low rumble of adolescent malaise. "Trust me, a little song and hip-hop can go a long way toward healing a trauma."

Chi-rish rushed the stage and chirped, "None of us has any talent."

Sally Mantooth called out to me, "Why don't you entertain us? You're the hired help."

At that moment I understood the impulse to hide a bomb in a building, knew the desire to hit Detonate. I was a chapter away from my PhD and being ordered to amuse an elite coven of ne'er-do-wells. This was familiar territory. I'd always been the hired help. When I modeled for Versace—under the stage name Anima Animus—Eileen Ford instructed me to study acting and find out if I could carry a tune. "You won't be young and pretty forever." Gianni (may he rest in peace) and Donatella (what the hell happened to her face?) never imagined that my starved fifteen-year-old frame might one day offer insights into the commodification of the female body, might reveal meaningful truths about the fashion industry's compulsion to outfit women in gowns that would best fit a narrow-waisted and hipless twelve-year-old boy. The strangest gender swap of all. Back then everyone adored Anima Animus because I gave good face. Now I was forever cursed to be half recognized, my beauty half praised. If my mother/business manager hadn't mismanaged my funds and bankrupted me, I might be the wealthy parent of one of these students, all of whom were busy chanting, "Entertain, entertain, entertain us."

I was the last adult standing. The father of them all. There was only one thing I knew how to do.

"Why don't you all go back to your rooms," I said. "Return with your best clothes and we'll put on a fashion show."

The students cheered. They agreed that while they lacked the necessary talent to compete artistically, they excelled at the business of sartorial consumption. Everyone but Blowjob raced from the auditorium, eager to get outfitted. Blowjob stayed back. Pulling on her dreads, she challenged, "That was a cheap move. I expected more from you."

"Fashion's a powerful motivator," I replied. "Especially in a time of crisis. Did you know that on the afternoon of September 11th, thirty-two women phoned Bergdorf Goodman in Manhattan and ordered the same Alexander McQueen striped batwing blouse?"

"Of course I know that." Blowjob smiled. "My mom had me speed-dial for her."

"I saw your seahorse on the mercury switch. Am I your alibi?"

Blowjob backed slowly up the stairs. "I assure you," she said, "I'm not Patty Hearst. I know nothing about Astrolite explosives or amonium nitrate or thermite bombs."

"What's your motivation?" I asked. "Is your father really an arms dealer? Is your young life really so bad?"

"My daddy always says that as a girl, I'm powerless to do wrong." Blowjob reached the landing and performed an elegant pirouette. "Don't worry. I'm a revolutionary, not a martyr."

"I wish you'd taken my class." I sighed and rubbed my face, twisting the metal scarab lodged in my nose. "You know I'll have to turn you in."

"I'm glad someone has the guts to." Blowjob blew me a kiss and said, "Just give me a head start. Twenty minutes to pack and order a cab before you contact the police."

I admired her blond snakes of hair, her beauty turning me to stone. "It's a pity," I said. "No one ever suspects a girl."

"But don't you realize"—Blowjob smiled—"that's our greatest weapon."

While I programmed the auditorium's sound system, adjusted the lighting, the Director returned and explained that he and I were the only remaining faculty.

"Gerry's hoping we can hold out for a day or two. He wants to minimize refunds." The Director touched my nose ring. "Is that shrapnel? Were you hit?"

The Director acknowledged that while Revolution and Anarchy neither built nor hid any explosives, he did assign *The Anarchist's Cookbook* to his students. "We're pretty sure one of the kids tried to blow up the place. Gerry convinced the college and the police not to press charges. The Octagon should have been condemned years ago."

I said, "I know who did it."

The Director nodded his head. "It's best if you keep that information classified. Knowing the truth might weigh on my conscience."

"Let me get this straight," I said. "These kids can terrorize the school and nothing happens to them?"

The Director ran his fingers through my split ends. "They're untouchable."

"Do me a favor," I asked.

"Anything," he said.

"Wear a dress for me."

When the students returned to the auditorium with their Thom Browne button-downs, their Zac Posen tube dresses, their bespoke suits, and Badgley Mischka ball gowns, I explained that we were going to do things a little differently. "This morning my class requested that I organize a protest. I've decided that in honor of gender inequality we're going to launch a Drag King and Queen show."

I pulled back the curtain to reveal the Director's devastating lack of décolletage, his calves taut in my green patent leather platforms, his round ass bulging the seams of my Hervé Léger bandage dress—contraband from my modeling days. The Director struck a pose, then ordered his charges to swap their clothes.

The children responded surprisingly well. They wanted to be told what to do. As Sly and the Family Stone celebrated the need for everyday people, Chi-rish strutted svelte and pretty in an off-the-shoulder Nicole Miller. The Andro Boys pranced androgynously across the stage in suede miniskirts and fishnet stockings. My Gender Studies babies made me proud in their Paul Smith jodhpurs, their Gucci tuxedos. While the music so on'ed and so on'ed and scooby dooby doob-ed, I listened for the echo of mortar fire, confident that Blowjob had more felonies to commit. More scars to self-inflict, more landmarks to tear down. It was a crime that she'd gone unnoticed for so long. Her gold and aqua matted hair, her piercings roared out for attention. She was on the lam and running not from the cops whom I hadn't called, or toward her parents who didn't care. Had she stayed she would have upstaged us all in a Comme des Garçons flak jacket and fatigues. Her body armored against future pains.

I looked pretty good in my wife beater and Prada fedora. Almost as stunning as my infamous cover pose for the 1997 Pirelli Calendar. In the photo, all the viewer sees are the muscles and curves of my naked back and ass. With my short cropped hair, I could be a girl or a boy. Either way, I'm devastating. When the summer finally ended, maybe I'd drop by the firehouse and autograph my month. The firemen and firewomen thrilled to see me in the flesh. Perhaps an arson or two had blazed a little longer all because some station chief was busy stroking himself/herself at the sight of my tan lines. Maybe my beauty had burned down a few buildings.

The Director and I laughed and applauded as our children promenaded up and down the aisles. Like proud parents, we watched our boy/girls and girl/boys marry themselves, catwalking into their futures, surpassing our every hope. Within hours their real parents would need to alter their vacation plans and travel here to fetch their privileged progeny. Though

I missed my colleagues, though I feared the loss of my summer stipend, though I wondered where Blowjob would seek shelter, despite all of my dread and misgivings, as I soaked up my front-row view of Frenchy McFrench-A-Lot striding along in a mermaid-hemmed Carolina Herrera, I never felt more powerful. Here was my final chapter.

ACKNOWLEDGMENTS

I would like to thank the editors of the journals and anthologies in which these stories first appeared, including Tamara Straus, Michelle Wildgen, Jennifer Meyers, Stacey Swann, Anthony Varallo, T. R. Hummer, Ron Spatz, David Daley, Ed Hirsch, Peter Stitt, Joanna Yas, John D'Agata, John Kulka, Natalie Danford, and Jeffrey Hess. Special thanks to Jane Smiley, Dave Eggers, and Mark Jude Poirier.

Much gratitude and adoration to Ethan Bassoff, Daniela Rapp, Sally Richardson, Dori Weintraub, George Witte, Sarah Jae-Jones, Cynthia Merman, and Bethany Reis.

For their time and care, I am grateful to Robert Boswell, Antonya Nelson, Steve Yarborough, Michael Collier, Percival Everett, Diane Johnson, Justin Cronin, Claudia Rankine, Roxana Robinson, Cornelia Nixon, James Alan McPherson, Marilynne Robinson, Ted Weesner, Andre Dubus III, Connie Brothers, Deb West, Frank Conroy, and Barry Hannah.

Many of these stories were written with support from the National Endowment for the Arts, Inprint, the University of Iowa Writers' Workshop, the Bread Loaf Writers' Conference, the Sewanee Writers' Conference, Rice University, and Agnes Scott College.

For their friendship and guidance I would like to thank Amy Margolis, Justin Quarry, Andrew Porter, Jonathan Blum, Holiday Reinhorn, Sabrina Orah Mark, Reginald McKnight, Laurie Watel, James Allen Hall, Jericho Brown, Toby Emert, Christine Cozzens, Charlotte Artese, Peggy Thompson, Willie Tolliver, Elizabeth Kiss, Carolyn Stefanco, Waqas Khwaja, Steve Guthrie, Rachel Trousdale, Michael Dumanis, Cate Marvin, Aaron Reynolds, Maribel Becker, Tanya Ceccarelli, Chris Borg, Victoria Allen, and Periel Aschenbrand.

Thank you again and always to my family. My deepest love to my sister, Amy; my brother, Jared; and to our parents, Joseph and Joanne, who taught us how to listen, when to interrupt, and where to begin our stories.